THE CURSE OF KALI

Historical Drama set in India

By

Audrey Blankenhagen

'GOD IS LOVE,
IS THIS THE FINAL MESSAGE OF INDIA'

E.M. Forster, 1924

ISBN: 1-4033-8037-6 (e-book)
ISBN: 1-4033-8038-4 (Paperback)
ISBN: 1-4033-8039-2 (Dustjacket)

This book is printed on acid free paper.

1stBooks - rev. 12/17/02

Note to Reader

Extracts from investigations, 1835
Major General Sir William Henry ('Thuggee') Sleeman

Sleeman: 'Are you afraid of the spirits you murder?'

Thuggee: 'Never, they cannot trouble us.'

Sleeman: 'And how do they not trouble you?'

Thuggee: 'Are not the people whom we kill,
                killed by the orders of KALI?'

THUGS - A murderous, fanatical, secret society, which existed since the fourteenth century and roamed the country pretending to befriend travellers and then robbing and strangling them with their so-called sacred 'rumels' (a scarf or cord) and secretly burying their bodies. They lived on the proceeds of their homicidal activities and were often protected by local rulers who shared their profits.

The **THUGS**, whose worship of the Goddess Kali was the basis for their ritual murders and primeval sexuality, had long evaded the law, because the loss of a traveller in India could be attributed to a wild animal or some other mishap. When British travellers went missing on journeys to the interior, however, the British started to investigate and the activities of this ancient secret society came to light. Lord Bentinck appointed a special Commissioner for the Suppression of Thuggee and Dacoity, William Sleeman, and his investigations and interrogations of informers revealed the full extent of the activities of the secret society of THUGS. Over 3,000 Thugs were convicted and the Sect was virtually wiped out.

This was one of the most difficult, but necessary operations undertaken by the EAST INDIA COMPANY and is considered, along with the abolition of slavery, child marriage, female infanticide and the practice of suttee, as one of the important humanitarian reforms of British rule.

Historical Note to Reader

The Honourable East India Company

'It is the strangest of all governments

but it is designed for the strangest of all empires.'

Macauley, 1833

On New Years Eve 1600, that most esteemed of English monarchs, Queen Elizabeth I, read the document prepared by her merchants and, with the flourish of her famous signature and the stamp of the Royal Seal, granted a Charter to the Honourable East India Company.

Did that intrepid monarch foresee the importance of what she was founding? Did the buccaneering Elizabethans envisage that their enterprise would one day, with an army more powerful than any in Europe (except, perhaps, the French) and a revenue greater than that of Great Britain, govern nearly one fifth of the world's population? Could they foresee that that same Company would influence more than 200 years of British and Indian history and found the greatest Empire the world has ever known?

Historians have much to say about the British in India, but it is an irrevocable fact that the story of the Honorable East India Company will forever be part of the history of both Great Britain and that vast and glorious sub-continent, the whole of which was once called 'INDIA'.

Prologue
Eighteenth Century India

The cave was dark except for a few flickering oil lights in tiny clay bowls surrounding the base of the idol. The figure of a man lay prostrate at the foot of the Goddess, his fingers clutching at her feet, the knuckles tensed, his dark naked body covered in sweat even though the temperature in the cave was very low.

He raised his head to listen. Scuttling noises - bats or rats - these were not his concern, only the stealthy shadows of vengeance which he knew must come. His eyes looked up at the Goddess, her blackness towered above him, her bulging eyes glared down on him, her terrible fanged mouth with its lolling tongue poised to drink his blood. He cried out for mercy, but he knew 'The Destroyer' would not hear.

They came at last. A silk scarf snaked around his neck and his head was drawn back by 'The Arm Holder'. The rumel tightened and as the last breath was squeezed from his body, he looked into the face of 'The Strangler' and saw the face of his son.

KALI WAS AVENGED!!

Chapter 1
India-1851

Gavin studied the woman who lay asleep: her blue-black hair spread on the pillow, her long lashes framing dark eyes, now closed in slumber, her naked form exquisite in its beauty.

She was his wife, Maria, their marriage only a few weeks old, but he did not really know her.

Last night when he came to her bed, she had rejected him, pleading her usual headache, so he had returned to his own room, angry and frustrated.

It must have been some hours later, when he awoke from a heavy sleep to find Maria straddling his body. By the pale morning light streaming through the open window, he observed that she was stark naked, her pupils pinpoints in her dark eyes, her black hair wild about her shoulders and her fingers flexed like claws, as she reached down and scratched at his bare chest, forming tiny rivulets of blood. He stared at her in bewilderment. She laughed huskily and speaking in the native language of the bazaars, invited him to make love to her, to take her as as he would a prostitute.

'These women are my friends,' she giggled. 'They have shown me how to pleasure a man. Don't be coy, my husband, take me as you would one of them.'

She slid down his body to lick his genitals, her eyes watching him like a cat studying its prey, her mouth continuing to caress him until, despite himself, he was aroused. Maria cackled in triumph and straddling him once again impaled herself on him shouting, 'Now, now!' They coupled frenetically, almost in hatred, until Gavin opened his eyes and saw his wife's face, distorted and ugly, her teeth bared in feral ecstasy, her eyes growing wider and wider, as she howled her fulfillment.

Horrified, Gavin pulled free, although his erection was still alive and standing up, walked towards the window, his stomach churning. He had been repulsed by this sudden, incredible personality change in Maria, but when he turned to question her, she was watching him with cold, dark eyes, her red lips curled in a sneer. Even as he stared, she spread her legs wide, her fingers touching herself provocatively and with an obscene gesture, beckoned him to come to her again. Gavin winced, a feeling of sadness and dismay overwhelming him, as he turned away from this harlot, who bore no resemblance to the gentle, reserved woman he had married.

England 1854

It was a beautiful autumn day when Sir Terence French informed Helen of the family's wish that she should marry his son Gavin. They had just buried her own father, Doctor Arthur Forsythe, and all the mourners had left the Grange, except Sir Terence.

Helen sat in the bay window seat, the skirt of her black taffeta dress spread gracefully around her, accentuating her tiny waist. The sun's rays on her dark auburn hair made it shimmer like burnished copper. She was so still, her emerald eyes downcast, when she heard her uncle speak again.

'I know the death of your father is very distressing for you, my dear, but it was not unexpected; Arthur has been suffering for many years from this debilitating disease, which both you and I know robbed him of the quality of life and his will to live. I hope you do not think it indelicate of me to raise this matter so soon.'

Helen looked up and stared, almost unseeingly, at the aspects of the comfortable drawing room in which they were sitting and that still retained touches of her mother's taste; an elegant room, richly carpeted, with gleaming rosewood and mahogany furniture, silver-framed portraits and cameos, comfortable armchairs and a roaring fire in the grate of the white, marble Adam fireplace, above which hung a beautiful, gilt-framed Venetian mirror.

3

Audrey Blankenhagen

She had heard her uncle's proposition with incredulity. Did he really wish her to marry Gavin, the secret love of her life since childhood? Her heart was fluttering so rapidly that she felt it would jump out of her chest and she pressed her hand to her breast to still its beating.

'What do you say, Helen?' insisted her uncle. 'I know you and Gavin were friends when you were children. It is not as if he is a stranger.'

'Uncle', whispered Helen, trying to compose her emotions. 'I was but a child when I first met Gavin and over the years, before he went to India, we saw each other on a mere two or three occasions. Besides, his wife has been dead for only two years. Does he really wish to marry again so soon?'

'He knows he must produce an heir. There is no one in India among the European women that he wishes to make his wife and, frankly, I do not believe he is making much effort in that direction. You know, of course, about the conditions of the family inheritance. It is all explained in this letter from your father.'

Helen started in surprise. 'So my father knew about your plans for our marriage. Why did he not discuss this with me?'

'We decided, mutually, to await Gavin's reply before approaching you. Your father was well aware of my wish to unite our families once again in marriage. You have always been like a daughter to me, dear niece, and I promised your father...'

4

'What did Gavin say, precisely, to your astonishing proposal?' interrupted Helen impatiently.

Sir Terence smiled and produced a letter from his pocket in Gavin's handwriting. He read the words, "If I must marry again, Father, well why not to my little, auburn haired cousin, Helen. She will do just as well as any other woman."

'Not a very romantic acceptance, Uncle, which is hardly surprising I must admit,' remarked Helen caustically. 'Let me think about your proposal for a few days. You know I have commitments with David and Harriet Burton at the Missionary Clinic and there is also father's practice and, of course, Rosita to consider.'

'Your father and I discussed that too, Helen. I will give the Burtons an undertaking to pay the salary of another doctor to take your place and ask David Burton to take on your father's practice. It will augment his meagre salary from the Mission. And as for Rosita, I am confident she will wish to accompany you to India. You are her life!'

Sir Terence paused, his brow puckering slightly, 'Ah yes, Helen - David Burton - your father told me about his proposal of marriage to you. You have not accepted, have you? He is a charming man, a bit too serious in my view, but hardly the right husband for you.'

Helen laughed at her uncle's proprietary remark. 'No, I have not accepted David's proposal of marriage. I am very fond of both David and his sister, Harriet, but I had no intention of marrying anyone just yet. I will, however, consider your proposal, Uncle Terence. Give me two days, at least.'

How could she tell her uncle that she had already made up her mind to accept this strange, arranged marriage. To be the wife of Gavin French, whom she had loved secretly from the tender age of seven, was more than she had ever hoped. But she must behave with decorum and pretend that the proposal needed some thought.

When Sir Terence left, Helen rushed to find Rosita. She knew that at this time of day the Spanish woman would be sitting by the kitchen range with her sewing. 'Darling Rosita, I wonder what she will say,' muttered Helen to herself, as she made her way to the large farmhouse kitchen.

Rosita Llewellyn had been companion and nursemaid to her since her own mother's death when she was only three years old. Rosita had come to Cornwall some forty years ago from Spain, following her English soldier husband who had been fighting with Wellington's army on the Peninsular. After his death, she had found work with the doctor's family as housekeeper and nursemaid to their young child.

She looked up as Helen stood in the doorway, with flushed cheeks and shining eyes, displaying all the excitement of a little child bursting to reveal some exciting piece of news.

'So you have accepted, *queridisima*,' said Rosita in her inimitable Spanish accent, which she had never lost despite her years in England.

'Your dreams have come true, at last, and your handsome Prince will wed my Sleeping Beauty.'

She opened her arms as Helen rushed to her and knelt down in front of her chair and as she had done so often in her life, the young woman buried her head in Rosita's ample lap, both of them laughing and crying together.

Suddenly Rosita's words penetrated Helen's thoughts and she looked up, tears still glistening in her lovely eyes.

'So you too knew, Rosita, about this plan to marry me off to Gavin French. Why was I the last one to be told and, for your information, I have not yet accepted. Gavin is not exactly the ardent suitor. He is merely doing his duty by marrying me. Not a very romantic proposal.'

Rosita seemed suddenly anxious, 'Do not let your stubborn pride, Helen, stand in the way of something I know your heart has wanted all your life. Gavin will fall madly in love with you, whatever he feels now. How can anyone fail to love you, my beautiful child.'

'I will only accept,' teased Helen, 'if you will promise to come with me to India. I could not envisage life without you now, my darling Rosita. Will you brave that long sea journey and all those strange people to be with your Helen?'

Audrey Blankenhagen

'Well, I have no intention of letting you go to any foreign country without me by your side, so tell your uncle you will marry Gavin.'

••••••

Rosita had always known about Helen's love for Gavin French. There was nothing about the girl that she did not know. Since Helen's mother's death, Rosita and Helen had forged a strong bond. Her father, Arthur, had been devastated by his wife's untimely demise and welcomed Rosita's love and care for his motherless, little girl.

The Spanish woman remembered clearly the day when seven-year-old Helen had been brought back to the Grange by the teenage boy, Gavin. The child, who had been playing in the woods with her friends, was missing and Arthur Forsythe and Rosita were at their wits end until the message arrived from Charnwood Hall that Helen was safe.

Later, when she was safely tucked into her warm bed, Helen told Rosita about her escapade and could not disguise the effect her handsome cousin had had on her. Rosita recalled their conversation.

'I was tied to a tree by my friends who wanted to play our favourite game of Settlers and Red Indians. I was the youngest, so they decided I should be the "Settler" captured by the Indians.' Rosita knew this game, which the children played: it had evolved from the tales of sailors and adventurers returning from the Americas in the late eighteenth century.

8

'What happened then, *querida mia*,' asked Rosita as her beloved child started to look alarmed again recalling her terrifying ordeal.

'My friends danced around me with whoops and cries and then they disappeared, saying they were going to have a "pow wow" but they forgot about me. As it grew dark and started to rain and no one answered my calls, I became afraid, Rosita, because my friends had told me that the forest is inhabited by trolls and witches, who come out at night to devour little children who had strayed from their beds.'

'Oh, my poor little child,' said Rosita, stroking the auburn curls as Helen's green eyes filled with tears. 'I will make sure that those nasty children are well chastised by their parents for their unkindness to you.'

'It does not matter now, Rosita. My handsome cousin, Gavin, rescued me,' and Rosita saw Helen smiling, obviously remembering her dashing cousin.

••••••

Helen remembered, as if it was only yesterday, how afraid she had been when she heard a horse's hooves and the sobs died in her throat because she was certain this was the devil riding to a witches' coven. She was terrified and shut her eyes tightly, so that she could not see or, she hoped, be seen.

'Well what have we here?' the devil asked, for his horse had stopped near her tree and he was untying her bonds. Helen opened her eyes and saw a young, handsome, dark-haired prince bending over her, laughter in his brown eyes, as with gentle fingers he lifted her wet, dangling curls off her face.

'Why, if it isn't my cousin, Helen. Don't cry, little sweetheart, you are safe now and I'll take you home, but first we must go by way of Charnwood Hall to dry you off. It is our cook Martha's baking day so there will be delicious pasties and cakes for supper. Here, wear my jacket, you are shivering, poor child.'

Gavin had lifted Helen onto his horse, one arm holding her tight around her waist, his warm bantering voice making her feel as happy as she had been miserable a little while ago. Gavin French, her cousin from the big house: she had seen him on one or two occasions at family gatherings in the Hall and had thought how handsome he was. After that day she knew he was as kind as he was handsome and the little seven-year-old girl had fallen hopelessly in love.

Helen met him once more, when she was fifteen years old. Gavin had completed his final year at Addiscombe College near Croydon, the prestigious military academy of the East India Company and had been nominated by the directors for a commission in a cavalry unit. He came to the Grange to bid farewell to them before his departure for India with his unit.

On that occasion, Helen served the tea and cakes and as she shyly passed a cup to Gavin, she looked up to see, once again, that bantering look in his dark brown eyes.

'So, little cousin Helen, you have grown taller since we last met and I swear you are fast becoming a beautiful young lady. I guarantee you will be breaking many hearts before long. I hope your present beau is not one of those ungallant friends who tied you to that tree long ago', teased Gavin, with a wink in the direction of Helen's father and Rosita.

Helen replied, 'I have no beau, Gavin. I do not intend to get married until I am much, much older. You see, I want to study medicine, if Father will agree.'

Gavin left for India a few days later and the family heard no more from him directly, except that he had eventually married. His career in the East India Company was meteoric, first as a cavalry commander and ultimately as Resident at the Court of a Nawab, the Moslem ruler of a state in the foothills of the Himalayas. Coinciding with this appointment, Gavin had been honoured with a knighthood in his own right. Then the news came that his wife had died from smallpox and Helen chided herself for her uncharitable relief that Gavin was single again - little consolation, she thought, when ten thousand miles separated her from her charming cousin.

Not that Gavin was really a blood relative. His father, the squire of Charnwood Hall, Sir Terence French, was an old friend of Helen's father, Dr.

Audrey Blankenhagen

Arthur Forsythe, and by his first marriage to Arthur's only sister, had become his brother-in-law. Her aunt had died several years ago and Sir Terence had married again. Gavin was the son of this second marriage.

Helen, herself, had firmly quelled that romantic dream of her adolescence and plunged herself into her medical studies. Her success in achieving her medical degree was in no small way due to her determination to fight the nineteenth century male prejudice against women studying medicine. Unfortunately, when she graduated with honours, no hospital was prepared to give her a place on their medical staff, so all her clinical experience was gained in her father's surgery and, ultimately, in the Missionary Clinic run by David and Harriet Burton.

'The poor have no prejudice against a woman doctor diagnosing their illnesses or performing operations on their emaciated bodies,' Helen told her father and he knew that their confidence in his daughter was amply rewarded: Helen was a first-rate surgeon and physician.

******

Now as she opened his last letter to her, Helen felt sure her father would approve if she shared these final words with Rosita. She unfolded the letter and read,

'My darling Helen,

I knew this day would come and I welcome the release from my suffering and hope to be united soon with your beloved mother. My only

12

regret is that I must leave you, my dearest child, but my dear friend Sir Terence, has promised to take my place as your guardian.'

The letter went on to emphasise her father's wish to see Helen settled. His practice gave him a comfortable living, but he was not a rich man and wanted more for his daughter. Sir Terence French's desire to unite their families once again in marriage through Helen and Gavin was a wonderful solution to secure her future.

'There is another reason', her father explained, 'and that is the strange legacy of Sir William French, an ancestor of Sir Terence who, like many adventurers to the East, had made his fortune in India in the early 18th century.

'On his return to England, Sir William's substantial wealth purchased Charnwood Hall and its vast country estates and provided a rich inheritance for his heirs, but he left an unusual stipulation in his Will.'

'How strange,' Helen commented, interrupting the reading of her father's letter to look questioningly at Rosita. 'Did you know anything about this ancestor of Gavin, Rosita?'

'No, *querida*, but read on, I am sure your father will explain,' said Rosita gently.

Helen continued reading her father's words, 'There was, however, a rumour that most of Sir William's wealth had been accumulated during his work with the Thuggee & Dacoity Department[1] and the black marble statue of the Goddess Kali, now in the family vault at Charnwood Hall, which had once been encrusted with fabulous gems, seems to hold the key to his strange behest.

'I understand from your Uncle, Helen, that Sir William, before his death, set up a Trust for the family and heirs of Chandra Lal, a Thuggee leader who had been apprehended by the British for his foul deeds. On the day before his execution, Chandra Lal had escaped and it was rumoured that it was this man who gave the statue to Sir William French in exchange for his life. Chandra Lal had not survived too long after his escape, but as he had been found murdered by the ritualistic Thugee manner of strangulation, Sir William's involvement could not be proved. It was obvious, however, that something weighed heavily on the conscience of Gavin's ancestor, who had set up this strange bequest and, furthermore, stipulated in his Will that his fortune would revert to the heirs of Chandra Lal in the event of his own dynasty ceasing to exist.'

Helen paused, wondering for a moment about this strange ancestor of Gavin, then continued reading her father's words.

---

[1] Thugs - a murderous organization existing since the 14th century who under the guise of their worship of the Goddess Kali, robbed and murdered travellers by strangulation and secretly buried their bodies. Sir William Sleeman virtually wiped out the Cult between 1831 and 1837. For purposes of this novel, the Thuggee & Dacoity Department had been formed in the 18th Century.

'The Trust is administered by a legal firm in India, who refuses to divulge the names of Chandra Lal's heirs. However, whatever the history of the statue, the family believes that Its misappropriation has placed a curse on them. You see only one son had been born to every direct male heir and as a result, the French dynasty has become, to say the least, very tenuous.'

Helen could see now why Sir Terence was eager to find another wife for Gavin. His first marriage had been childless and Gavin's reluctance to marry again had forced his father to take a hand in his son's marital future.

'So you see, my dear child,' her father's letter ended, 'it is not only Sir Terence's wish but mine, too, that you should marry Gavin. I know you are fond of your cousin. He has a prestigious career in the East India Company and will be able to give you, materially, all that I could not. You will also be able to help the Indians, themselves, by your skill as a doctor, a career which I know you will wish to pursue.

'God Bless you, my child. I leave you now in the care of Sir Terence and our faithful Rosita.

'Your loving father,

Arthur J. Forsythe.'

How Helen had loved and respected her father. Everything she was she owed to him. Because of his love of horses, he had encouraged Helen to ride from an early age and she was a superb horsewoman. As if this was not enough, she had been trained by his friend, Count Kovrosky, an émigré from Poland, in the art of fencing and the use of firearms. Helen was always amused when she heard her father, usually a modest man, boast to anyone who praised his daughter's beauty, 'Despite my daughter's obvious femininity, Helen can outride, outgun and fence as well as any man and to boot she is a strong swimmer.'

She often wondered if her father's pride in her sporting achievements was a subconscious reflection of his hidden wish for a son.

Doctor Forsythe had not, however, neglected his daughter's education and by the time she was fifteen, Helen could speak French, Spanish and Portuguese fluently. Her interest in science and mathematics had encouraged Dr. Forsythe to foster her wish to study medicine. He was so proud of her achievements in this male-dominated profession.

So now if it was, fortuitously, her father's wish that she should marry Gavin French, then that was what she would do.

Chapter 2

It was six months later that Sir Terence arranged a passage for Helen and Rosita on the East Indiaman, the *Prince George*. The ship was one of the largest of the company's vessels, well armed and amongst the first all iron ships to be powered by steam.

Amongst the passengers were Brigadier General, Sir James and Lady Cameron, friends of Sir Terence, returning to India after a spell of leave in England. The couple had promised to watch over his niece and her companion and deliver them safely to Gavin. Helen understood that besides the crew, there were the usual company of marines and a platoon of a Highland Regiment (some of whom were accompanied by their wives).

'This platoon of the Seventy-Eighth Highlanders,' said Uncle Terence, 'is part of the British military contingent serving Company interests on the borders of Mirapore and closely liaise with Gavin as the British Resident in Mirapore. The Nawab is a distant relative, I believe through his mother's line, of Bahadur Shah The Second, the Moghul Emperor in Delhi. The Brigadier General is the new military commander of the fort near Mirapore and he and his wife, you and Rosita, will be escorted to Mirapore by the platoon of Highlanders.'

All this Sir Terence explained to Helen as they stood at the rail of the *Prince George*. A sailor was ringing the hand bell and announcing through a

17

hand-held loudhailer the imminent departure of the ship. 'All visitors disembark, please. We set sail in ten minutes!'

It was now time to say goodbye to Uncle Terence and as he clasped his niece to him in a tearful farewell, Helen wondered if she would ever see him again: India was so far. She had come to love this dear uncle, not only because of his kindness to his orphaned niece, but because she could see so much of Gavin in his tall frame and warm brown eyes.

Helen and Rosita watched with tears filling their eyes as the tugs steered the *Prince George* out to sea and the tall figure of Sir Terence disappeared from her view as the dock and, eventually, the shoreline of their beloved England receded.

Helen took Rosita's arm, 'Let us find our cabin. I believe it is down this companionway.'

She turned and saw a blond, bearded giant of a man, dressed in Highland military uniform, standing at the head of the companionway to which they were making, almost as if he was waiting for them. As they approached, he came forward and bowing slightly to the two women, took Helen's hand and said in a soft Scot's burr, 'Lieutenant John MacGregor at your service, Miss Forsythe. Let me escort you and Mrs. Llewellyn to your cabin.'

His bright blue eyes openly reflected his admiration of Helen's beauty. Helen, dressed in a bottle green woollen cape trimmed with arctic fox fur to match the little fur hat perched on the top of her dark auburn curls was, indeed, a striking woman, the fur enhancing her creamy, magnolia skin and long-lashed, emerald eyes. Helen was well used to the admiration she saw in men's eyes whenever they first met her and although she was feminine enough to be thankful that she had not been born plain, she was always slightly embarrassed by their obvious attention.

Helen gently withdrew her hand, which the Scotsman seemed reluctant to release and replied, 'Thank you, Lieutenant MacGregor. I understand that you and your platoon will be escorting us to Mirapore.'

'That will indeed be my pleasure. This is your cabin, ladies, and along this companionway is the saloon for our passengers.' He opened the door to the cabin and Helen glimpsed a comfortable, largish room with polished mahogany furniture, chintz hangings and sparkling brass fittings.

'We will be dining with the captain to-night, at seven bells, as the navy would say, so I shall have the pleasure of your company again, ladies,' said John MacGregor, his blue eyes twinkling, as he once again took Helen's hand and raised it to his lips.

He departed with a swish of his kilt and Helen turned to see Rosita's amused smile. 'That giant is obviously smitten, my girl. For Gavin's sake, you will have to discourage him.'

Helen laughed, 'Rosita you are an incurable romantic. The man was just being polite. But tell me, did you not think, when you first saw him, that he

19

was out of his time. Instead of meeting him on the deck of a nineteenth century British merchant vessel, I could imagine him standing at the prow of a dragon ship, wearing the horned helmet of a Viking war lord. It must be his giant frame, that blond hair and beard and those intense blue eyes set in the high-cheekboned face of a Norse ancestor, which gave me that impression.'

Dinner for his special guests was in the captain's saloon that evening. The captain of the *Prince George* was seated at the head of the table. A short, sturdy man, with a complexion reddened by years of exposure to salt spray, Captain White had a jocular personality and as Helen was soon to discover, he was a first-rate seaman. His bright, brown eyes above a full, bushy, white beard surveyed his seated guests whom he addressed after Grace with the words, 'Welcome, ladies and gentlemen. I hope you will enjoy your voyage and this meal, which I always like to share with my special passengers before our supplies of fresh meat and vegetables are exhausted. Then we will be reduced to salt beef and sauerkraut until our next port of call.'

Helen found herself seated between the Brigadier General and Lady Cameron, whom she had met on a few occasions at Charnwood Hall before their departure for India.

Sir Cameron was a tall, gaunt-faced man with a leathery tanned skin from his years under the Indian sun. His wife, Lady Cameron, was nearly as tall as her husband and reminded Helen of a haughty, thoroughbred mare, particularly when she tossed her head to emphasise some specific point. Her strong face was matched by a tightly corseted figure, which she carried with a marked degree of elegance, but Helen knew that beneath that haughty exterior beat a heart which was full of compassion for the under-privileged.

On her visit to Charnwood Hall, Lady Cameron had spent a great deal of time at the Missionary Clinic administered by Helen and the Burtons. Agnes Cameron had displayed a keen, unfeigned interest in their work and had made a more than generous contribution to their funds.

Lady Cameron, somewhat to Helen's embarrassment, now referred to this work and addressing the ship's doctor, James Grant, said with a toss of her head, 'Did you know, James, that our young and beautiful Helen has a first-class medical degree? I have seen her operating with the skill of a more seasoned surgeon but with, perhaps, more gentleness and post-surgery compassion for her patient than a lot of you male doctors.'

Doctor Grant, a taciturn Welshman, who was seated opposite Lady Cameron, looked over his half-rimmed spectacles at Helen and after observing her for a disconcerting second, smiled enigmatically and said, 'I hope Dr. Forsythe, you will demonstrate some of that skill. I would always welcome another medic on board, particularly when we strike rough weather.'

Helen noted the word 'medic' and thought that here is another male skeptic of a woman's capability in the field of medicine. She was determined to avail herself of this opportunity, not only to practice her beloved medicine, but to prove that she was no slouch where her professional skills were concerned.

'Thank you for your kind invitation, Dr. Grant. I shall be along tomorrow to see what help I can give you,' replied Helen, deliberately adopting her softest, most feminine manner.

Helen caught the eye of the amused Scots officer, John MacGregor, sitting opposite, who winked at her and laughingly commented, 'The lass has brains as well as beauty, Dr. Grant. I wager you will now have more malingerers than ever before, when the ship's unofficial telegraph announces the appointment of your lovely colleague.'

His comments were studiously ignored by the good doctor who, addressing himself to Helen, proceeded to quiz her about her degree, her medical experience and her reasons for choosing medicine as her profession.

The next morning Helen reported to the ship's hospital. This consisted of a ward with three beds, an operating theatre, a sluice room and a surgery. The first patient was a gaunt marine, named Roger Quinn,

'What do you think is wrong here, Dr. Forsythe?' said Dr. Grant indicating, with an arrogant waive of his hand, the patient lying on the examination couch. 'Mr. Quinn is complaining of tiredness, a feeling of chilliness and a loss of appetite.'

Helen examined the patient and noticed his painful reaction when she pressed his liver. His temperature was high, his skin yellow and the sample of his urine reddish in colour.

'Is this your first trip to the East, Mr. Quinn?' asked Helen gently.

'No, miss, I have served for several years in China but was sent home because I contracted malaria. I have been taking quinine.'

'Was your medication supervised by a physician?' asked Helen.

'No, miss, doctors cost money and I needed to buy the quinine.'

Helen was certain the patient was suffering from blackwater fever, a complication of the malaria he had contracted in the Far East, which seemed to have been treated rather haphazardly.

She turned to Dr. Grant, who had been watching her carefully and said, 'I believe we have a case of blackwater fever here, a complication of the malaria and the unsupervised use of quinine.'

'My prognosis, exactly, Dr. Forsythe. How do you recommend we proceed?'

'I would like Mr. Quinn hospitalized and kept lying down and he should have plenty of fluids with glucose and an alkaline mixture to alkalise his urine. We need to examine a blood sample before giving him any more quinine. Frankly, I believe he should return to Europe when he has

23

recovered,' replied Helen confidently, glad that she had specialised in tropical diseases.

Her next test was a young blonde woman, the wife of one of the Highland soldiers. She had already been examined by Dr. Grant, who turning to Helen said, less arrogantly, 'Well, Doctor, what is your diagnosis of this young woman's condition? She is bringing up clear, tasteless fluid each morning and tells me that she is not menstruating.'

The young woman looked quite nervous and Helen smiled at her and asked her to lie down on the examination bench. 'What is your name, dear?' said Helen as she opened the woman's blouse to examine her breasts.

'Mary Brown, miss, and this sort of vomiting started before the voyage.'

Helen observed the swollen blue veined breasts, the prominent nipples and the dark areola around them with slightly raised, pimply skin.

'Are you inclined to urinate frequently?' she asked.

'Yes, Doctor, up to three months ago, but not so much now.'

Helen was quite convinced that Mary was in the fourth month of pregnancy and was well aware of her condition, but had deliberately kept the knowledge to herself in case the Company refused to send her abroad with her husband.

'Well Mary, you are pregnant. Is this your first child?' said Helen, observing the young woman's heightened colour and sudden nervousness, which confirmed her suspicion that Mary was already well aware of her condition.

Dr. Grant interrupted and looking severely over his half-rimmed spectacles at the nervous Mary, said, 'If I had known, young woman, you would not have been allowed to embark on this voyage in your condition.'

'I think that would have been unfair, Dr. Grant,' said Helen. 'Pregnancy is not a sickness and Mary seems a strong and sensible woman who would wish to be with her husband when the child is born. If you do not mind, I shall personally supervise her health during this voyage.'

'As you like, Doctor. I shall have my hands full with more serious ailments during our passage,' said Dr. James Grant grudgingly.

With the permission of the captain, Helen arranged for the Irish chef to prepare a special nourishing diet for the young mother, who was instructed to take light exercise each day in the fresh air, if weather conditions permitted.

The next day Helen arrived at the hospital area to find an irate Dr. Grant trying to cope with a queue of young men.

'Good morning, Dr. Forsythe: please deal with these patients and refer to me any whom you think might need surgery. I shall be in the theatre,' muttered Dr. James, making no effort to hide his resentment and firm belief that the over-crowded surgery was entirely Helen's fault.

The queue of waiting patients was soon whittled down to only four men by Helen's piercing questions - one with a cut leg that needed a few stitches, a sailor who had a small splinter in his eye and a bad case of constipation, which Helen treated, much to the man's embarrassment, with a soapy enema.

The fourth patient, who had waited to the last, was Mary Brown's husband eager to express his gratitude to Helen on behalf of his young wife.

'My wife and I are both grateful to you, Doctor, for offering to look after Mary during her pregnancy. I feel less guilty now for allowing her to accompany me to India,' said the young, carrot-haired Scotsman.

At the end of the surgery, Dr Grant seemed friendlier and although he did not admit as much, Helen felt that she had satisfied his curiosity concerning her proficiency as a doctor.

The voyage settled into a routine. The ship steamed up the coast of Africa, stopping briefly at a few ports to take on fresh supplies and water and then rounded the Cape of Good Hope into the Indian Ocean.

Helen had read books about this vast black continent, so much of which was still unexplored. Her glimpses of the flora and fauna of the coastal regions and the people of every shade of colour, from pale brown to ebony black, filled her with amazement. As each day passed she realised that her life was changing and that England, that little island off Europe, which she called her country, was indeed a very minuscule part of this globe and would be even further away when she reached the sub-continent of India.

Everyone was relieved that the notorious weather around the Cape had not lived up to its reputation when suddenly, just off Madagascar, they were hit by a fierce storm.

Helen in the ship's hospital, was well aware of the increasing ferocity of the gale, as the ship bucked and reared in the troughs and crests of the raging sea, like a wild stallion endeavouring to shake off its tenacious rider. Although it was afternoon, the leaden skies darkened the small sick bay, waves beat against the glass of the portholes and the ship reared up to mount an enormous swell, pausing for a brief moment before her bows crashed down and down into a deep watery valley and then drunkenly rolled up again.

Dr. Grant said he would stay in the sick bay in case he was needed, but Helen's thoughts were of Rosita, who hated storms even on terra firma. She would be terrified on her own in their cabin, listening to the storm's mounting intensity. She had no alternative but to venture up on the top deck to reach the companionway leading to the passengers' cabins.

Helen struggled up the hospital companionway like a drunk, fighting to retain her balance and the sight that met her eyes on the open deck was even more terrifying. The black, rain sodden skies were forked by lightning, the wind howled, the ship creaked and groaned, her decks awash with the constant pounding of hungry seas, which swept away anything that was not fastened down.

Helen clung like a limpet to whatever solid object she could find, but the heaving deck, the furious wind lashing her body and her sodden, heavy skirt impeded all her endeavours to reach the door aft leading to the passengers' quarters. Battered and bruised and constantly brought to her knees by the savage ebb and flow of angry waves, Helen feared she would never reach her goal.

On the poop deck, the helmsman was lashed to his wheel and someone, noticing the woman struggling on the open deck, shouted something, which Helen could not hear above the howling of the gale.

A flash of lightning illuminated the darkness for a moment and Helen saw, to her horror, a gigantic, white-crested wall of water approaching the ship. Above the roar she heard the helmsman shout, *'Hard to Port'!* This was the end: that mountainous swell would surely overpower her and sweep her overboard. Suddenly an iron arm gripped her and a rope was fastening her to a stanchion. Her last sight before the seas rose over their heads, was John MacGregor's bearded face leaning over her and shouting, 'Breathe in Helen, here she comes!'

Helen was enveloped by the green wet leaves of that ancient English forest of her childhood and Gavin was holding her tightly against the terrors of the night. Then when she looked up again, it was not Gavin, but an anxious Rosita and a worried John MacGregor leaning over her in the safety of her cabin.

She smiled weakly and heard Rosita say, 'Fetch her some brandy if you please, Lieutenant. I must get her out of these wet clothes and into a warm bed before she catches her death from the cold.'

The Scotsman soon reappeared with a flask and a pannikin, which he placed against her lips. 'Drink this, lassie, it is not brandy, but the best Scotch whisky that will warm you inside and out.'

Then, on Rosita's instructions he lifted Helen, now in a dry night shift, into the high sided berth and gently covered her with a blanket.

'I believe I have to thank you for saving my life, John,' murmured Helen, recalling his gallant rescue and then smiling wearily, closed her eyes, the fiery spirit already warming her battered body and making her long for sleep.

She felt him bend down and kiss her forehead and whisper, 'Och, I would have given my life for you, sweet lassie,' and Helen felt strangely comforted and safe as she drifted into sleep.

When she awoke, the storm had passed and sunlight was streaming through the portholes.

Against Rosita's admonitions Helen dressed, breakfasted lightly and made her way to the sick bay. Dr. Grant seemed pleased to see her, not because there were many patients, but he appeared genuinely concerned for her welfare after her horrendous ordeal the day before.

29

'Welcome, Doctor, I hope you have not rushed back to work too soon. As I have been told, you have had a near fatal experience which would quail even the stoutest heart. We have been very lucky this time; not too many patients, despite the storm: a few cuts and bruises and a dislocated wrist. Could have been much worse, eh?'

The voyage continued without too much further drama except for the appearance in the Arabian Sea of several Arab dhows, obviously slave ships, their dreadful cargo evident from the stench which wafted towards the *Prince George* on the Trade Winds. John MacGregor told Helen, as they watched the dhows change course rapidly, 'The British Navy patrol these waters to prevent these slave traders from carrying out their pernicious trade and no doubt the Arab captains thought our merchant ship was a Royal Navy vessel.'

A more felicitous event was the birth of Mary Brown's child, which Helen delivered before the end of the voyage. A beautiful baby girl, with Mary's blue eyes and her husband's reddish hair, was born to the happy couple who named the little girl 'Helen' in honour of their doctor. The Regiment's Presbyterian minister baptised the baby and Captain White threw a little christening party at which even the serious Doctor Grant smiled his approval of the couple's happiness. Lieutenant John MacGregor was the godfather and the young couple asked Helen to be the godmother, a fact which the smitten Scot took to be a good omen for his and Helen's future.

Helen spent a lot of time in the company of John MacGregor since that fateful storm. She was grateful to him for saving her life and half remembered his words and her feeling of security as he bent over her cabin berth. John was attracted to her, she had no doubt, but the depth of his love was only revealed to her on their last night on board the *Prince George*. They had just dined for the last time with Captain White and were standing by the ship's rails watching a school of dolphins playfully swimming alongside the ship, with elegant dives and arced jumps over the water.

It was a beautiful evening, the sea calm, the setting sun shimmering on the waves and the thought that their journey would soon be over, drew the friends closer together.

Helen looked up at the tall Scot, smiling into his somewhat unfamiliar face, for he had shaved off his full beard that morning and looked even handsomer, but much younger. He took her hand and raised it to his lips. He watched her with his bright blue eyes, for a moment, a quizzical smile on his full, well-formed mouth. 'Helen Forsythe, do you know how much I love you? How can you marry another man when you ken you hold my heart in the hollow of this little hand?'

On an impulse, Helen reached up and kissed her gallant rescuer on his cheek, an impulse which she immediately regretted because as she began to draw back, the giant caught her up in his arms and bending her head backwards, kissed her passionately on her lips, murmuring, 'Oh, my lovely lass, please consent to be my wife. I will love you as you have never been loved before.'

His full lips, so sweet and close to hers, threw Helen's emotions into confusion and for a brief moment she wanted to stay in the sanctuary of this man's arms as she had on the day of the storm.

Then his words, his proposal of marriage, registered and Helen drew back. John MacGregor loved her with a fierce tenderness and devotion and she must now reject that love.

'I am honoured, John, that you should want me to be your wife, but you know that can never be. I am betrothed to another man,' said Helen as gently as she could.

'A man, Helen, whom you hardly know. You have told me, yourself, that you two last met when you were a teenager and what if he has changed; what if he is no longer the man of your childish dreams? Even if time has not altered him physically, then India, certainly, will have had a profound effect on his character,' argued John.

'Please, John, don't ask me to give up my dream. You will always be most dear to me and I hope that if not love, then friendship can be our bond.'

John MacGregor closed his eyes for a moment and when he opened them, Helen saw his pain, but with a smile twisting his lips, he withdrew his arms and stepped back saying,'Then, fair Helen, I shall have to be content with that, but remember my heart will always be yours if you need me.'

True to his word, John MacGregor never mentioned the word 'love' again, but Helen knew that in this giant Scot, she had found the staunchest friend.

****

The next day the *Prince George* sailed into the lovely, deep-water, island-studded harbour of Bombay. Helen recalled its strange history. This city in 1661 had formed part of the dowry of the Portuguese Princess, Catherine of Braganza, on her marriage to Charles II. From a small fishing village and a chequered history as a base for pirates, Bombay had grown into a prosperous commercial centre for the Honourable East India Company, which had leased it from the British Crown in 1668 for ten pounds per annum. Their grand, neo-Gothic buildings erected along the harbour front, testified to the commercial success of the Company's Nabobs.

Helen leaned on the ship's rail as the vessel docked and she saw another world - India. People of all shades of colour from the fair-skinned Indo-Arayans to the dark-skinned Dravidians thronged the port and an ambience, which she came to recognise as essentially that of India, pervaded her senses - the squawk of crows (mingled at this port with the cries of gulls) the smell of spicy cooking, of burning dung cakes used for fuel

Audrey Blankenhagen

and the unpleasant odours of human excrement and rotting garbage, their odiferous presence conspicuous to the eye by swarms of hovering flies.

She listened to the cacophony of dialects - overseers instructing their teams in the unloading of the ship, vendors raucously advertising their wares, itinerant beggars pleading for alms, half-naked little boys getting in everyone's way, shouting at and shooing away stray cows and pariah dogs, which seemed to roam at will amidst the human throng.

A fair-skinned Parsi came on board with John MacGregor to direct the passengers to the waiting horse drawn carriages, which transported them to the railway station and here Helen caught her first sight of the Indian *'choo choo gari',* a teak-carriaged train which ran along a rapidly expanding rail track.

The station master told them with pride, 'This is the first section of railway to be constructed between Bombay and Calcutta.'

The carriages were not as luxurious as the cabins on the *Prince George*, but they were comfortable enough and Helen and the other passengers had the opportunity to study the unfolding Central Indian panorama as the train snaked its way through the grand scenery of gorges, flat-topped mountainous regions, forests and wide rivers.

At last the train arrived in Calcutta and at the southern end of the City, 'Fort William'.

John MacGregor told Helen, 'After the disastrous occupation of the citadel in 1756 by Nawab Siraj-ad-Daula, the defensive capabilities of the new Fort William have been greatly improved.'

Their guide, an officer from the fort, showed the travellers a plaque which commemorated the hapless British victims of the 'Black Hole', the tragedy that occurred at eight o'clock on the night of June Twentieth, 1756, after the capture of the fort by the Nawab of Bengal.

'Out of one hundred and forty-five men and one Eurasian woman, Mary Carey, crammed into a room no more than eighteen foot long by fourteen foot wide with two small barred windows, only twenty-three people survived, including Mary Carey,' said their guide. 'The written record left by John Holwell, a senior East India Company official, told of the appalling conditions in which the British were incarcerated in the heat of June with no water. He wrote of the overpowering stench of urine, vomit, excrement, corpses and sweat and when at last, after ten appalling hours, he persuaded the guards to let them out, the press of bodies was so great that it took the guards twenty minutes to open the doors.'

The officer concluded this gory story and Helen sensed his next words were to reassure the new British arrivals. 'That was, of course, ladies and gentlemen, almost a century ago and the company and its armies are now firmly in control.'

Before leaving Fort William, the travellers enjoyed the spectacle of the festival of Durga Puja. Their Indian guide explained, 'This festival is based on the saga Ramayana which recalls the victory of the God Rama over the evil demon, Ravana. In this fight, Rama was aided by the Goddess Durga, another name for the black goddess, Kali.'

That goddess again, reflected Helen, as she saw the people dancing and singing in the streets enjoying this joyous Hindu festival. Large effigies of the demon Ravana stuffed with fireworks were exploded all over the city and Helen thought how far removed all this was from the tragedy of the Black Hole.

At last they continued their long journey, this time (as a rail link had not yet been constructed) along the river Ganges by wooden, gaily-painted barges towed by a steamboat. The journey was slow because the vessels were being dragged upstream against the natural flow of the river.

'Look, Helen,' said Lady Agnes as they stood on deck, 'those dangerous looking reptiles basking on the banks are the river crocodiles. The snub-nosed, flesh eating ones are called *"muggers"* and the long nosed ones are fish eaters and are called *"garrials"*. They are very useful for disposing of the half-charred remains of Hindu corpses, which float down the river from Benares.'

Helen shivered with distaste as a sleepy crocodile opened its reptilian eyes and slid down the river bank. Had it spotted a corpse amidst all the flotsam and jetsam of the muddy waters of Mother Ganga?

The barges passed little Indian villages and British 'stations', small enclaves of British residents. At the latter, when they tied up for the night, the residents came out to greet them with servants carrying trays laden with food and drink. Helen was touched by the hearty welcomes they received from these fellow countrymen, some of whom had been away from 'Home' for many years and seemed so eager to hear all the latest news from that little island ten thousand miles away.

In the sacred Hindu City of Benares, John MacGregor escorted Helen and Lady Cameron to the Burning *Ghats*, stone steps leading from the river to the embankment, its hallowed waters sanctifying both the living and the dead. Throngs of pilgrims bathed in the muddy waters, whilst nearby blazed the burning pyres of their dead. Helen and Agnes witnessed one such ceremony, when a dutiful son walked around the body of his deceased parent three times before holding the burning torch to the mouth of the corpse to signify the passing of its soul. Finally he set the pyre alight and sat quietly watching the cremation.

'This is one of the reasons a son is so special in a Hindu family,' said Lady Agnes.

Audrey Blankenhagen

Agnes pointed to another pyre where a woman sat some distance away from the preparations for cremation, 'You see that grief-stricken woman, Helen, dressed in a white sari, the Indian colour of mourning. She is probably the widow of the deceased and in the past, she would have been obliged to immolate herself on her husband's funeral pyre in the act of *Suttee,* thus avoiding the stigma of widowhood. Now, thank goodness, this brutal practice is forbidden by the British.'

From Allahabad, another sacred city at the confluence of the two holy rivers, the Ganges and the Jumna, the party left the river boats to travel by the Grand Trunk Road to the State of Mirapore in the foothills of the Himalayas.

Their caravan consisted now of horse-drawn carriages for the women and bullock carts for the luggage, all escorted by the Highland platoon and a brigade of Sikh troops and their British officer, who had joined them from the military cantonment in Allahabad.

Helen observed that these tall, bearded and turbaned warriors looked proud and strangely at home in the uniform of the East India Company's army.

Helen and Rosita shared a horse-drawn carriage with Lady Cameron who was a mine of information about the history of this great arterial highway and the cities through which it passed.

'You know, my dear', said Lady Cameron, tossing her head in her own inimitable 'horsy' manner, 'this great highway is as ancient as India, itself, and has for centuries been used by conquering armies, merchants and pilgrims, not to forget the great religious teachers, such as Lord Buddha. The East India Company has, of course, realised the strategic importance of this Imperial Road, as it was known in Moghul times. It runs for fifteen hundred miles from Calcutta to Peshawar, within a few miles of the Khyber Pass and the British reconstructed Grand Trunk Road is now a permanent highway and an acknowledged engineering achievement, unsurpassed by any other highway in the world.'

'Is that why there are so many British cantonments along the way?' asked Helen, who had not failed to notice the strong British presence along the Grand Trunk Road and their depots protected by armed guards.

'Yes', replied Agnes Cameron, 'they are called *Bardasht-khanah* and have replaced the old caravanserais (rest houses) built by the Moghuls, many of which were very beautiful, but have now fallen into disrepair.'

Helen was fascinated throughout the journey - the golden temples and stately mosques; the beautiful architectural monuments of Moghul power - particularly that symbol to everlasting love, the 'Taj Mahal'; the sites of famous battlefields of India's past and her great, wide rivers.

But even more intriguing to Helen were the people - the faces of India: the women knee deep in the waters of paddy fields; the herdsman and his small boy sitting under a banyan tree; women in brilliant saris, carrying huge loads on their heads; the beggars and the man with the dancing bear; the water seller with his silver cups and a leather water bag; the farmer wearing an outsize turban sitting on his horse drawn cart, his thin frame matching the equally emaciated pony in the shafts.

Even after this comparatively short space of time, Helen realised that India was a country whose people were as diverse as those in the countries of Europe, but with even greater variations of caste, creeds and ethnic backgrounds, all living together under the skies of this vast sub-continent.

After several days journey and night stops at the *Dak* houses with their potted palms, servants and as Agnes commented, 'the best chicken curry you will taste in India,' they left the Grand Trunk Road and followed the course of the River Ganges into the foothills of the Himalayas. There in the distance, the stupendous backdrop of the world's highest mountains stretched, range upon range, towards the heavens.

The paths were now too steep to allow the lumbering carriages and bullock carts to proceed any further and the baggage was carried up the steep tracks on the backs of sturdy hill men, taking the weight of their burdens by a tumpline around their foreheads. The British women were transported in open palanquins *(dandies)* each one attached to poles carried on the the shoulders of four men.

Helen, observing the precarious movements of the *dandies,* as the men moved their load from one shoulder to the other and glancing down at the precipitous depths below, decided to complete this part of the journey on horseback.

'Horses can shy, Helen, and the dangers can be just as ominous. As far as I know, these men have never tipped a passenger over the mountain sides from their *dandy,*' said John MacGregor, when Helen requested a horse.

One of the tall, bearded Sikh soldiers brought her a sturdy, little, hill pony and Helen whipped off her cumbersome riding skirt and mounted the pony with practised agility, her long legs showing to perfection in her tight riding hose and knee-high leather boots.

John's astonished admiration was only too apparent and Helen smiled, 'You see, John, riding astride I have a firmer seat, so you have nothing to fear and this little fellow is as sure footed as a mountain goat,' said Helen, leaning forward to tweak the pony's ear.

'You never fail to surprise me, Helen Forsythe,' grinned the tall Scot 'But, of course, I am delighted to have your charming company for a while longer, before I am obliged to hand you over to Gavin. How I envy that man.'

At last they reached the summit of the mountain and there below them was the beautiful valley of Mirapore. Helen exclaimed with delight at the panorama below. Pine and cedar clad forested hills enclosed the lush green

41

floor of the valley, which was traversed by a meandering river whose source, she was told, was in the glaciers of the mighty Himalayas, their snow-capped peaks rising majestically in the distance.

'You will love this valley, Helen,' called out Lady Cameron, whose *dandy* had come alongside the riders. 'The climate is alpine. Look, there are clumps of autumn heathers and in May these hills are covered with blue Himalayan poppies and giant, scarlet rhododendrons. This fertile region is famous for its fruit, especially apples and pears and as you can see, the orchards below are already being harvested.

'There at the head of the valley is the walled city of Mirapore, where your fiancé awaits you.'

Helen realised that she would soon meet Gavin again and she took this opportunity to ask Lady Cameron about him.

'I have not seen Gavin since I was a girl of fifteen. Do you know him well, Agnes?' enquired Helen shyly.

'Oh yes, we all have a great admiration for Sir Gavin French and the company values his skill as the Resident to guide and advise the Nawab. He is, I would say, a man above men. Handsome, yes, but with a charisma that sets him apart from the usual run. You will find that every woman is fascinated by him, even the purdah women in the harem of the Nawab.'

'But how do they know the Resident; do they not have to observe strict purdah?' enquired Helen, surprised that even these women had been able to assess the charms of her fiancé.

'Well, as to that, I believe with pierced screens separating them, he has frequent audiences with the Dowager Begum, who is very much interested in the affairs of Mirapore. On these occasions she is, of course, veiled as are the harem women who attend her, but they are notorious gossips and their servants have reported to our servants their views on your handsome fiancé.'

'Then I have a great deal to live up to,' laughed Helen

You, my dear, will bowl all of them over, just as Gavin has done, for you are, I believe, just the right wife for him - beautiful and intelligent, but with an independent spirit. Don't ever lose that,' said Agnes, tossing her head to emphasis her words.

The travellers made their way carefully down the steep mountainside to the valley below and just before the city gates, Sir James Cameron rode up to bid farewell to Helen.

'Well, Helen, this is where we must say *"au revoir"*. Unfortunately we won't be able to accompany you any further, as protocol demands that British troops need the Nawab's permission to enter the city, *en masse*. He is very prickly on the question of his suzerainty and if it was not for the diplomatic skills of Gavin, Mohammed Hassan Khan, could be a great deal of trouble to us.'

In reply to Helen's anticipated question, the Fort Commander replied, 'Gavin has, of course, obtained permission for you and a small escort to enter the city, so Lieutenant MacGregor and a handful of his Highlanders will escort you and Mrs. Llewellyn all the way to the Residency.'

So their little company broke up. Helen was sorry to bid farewell to them, especially Lady Cameron, who had become a good friend on their long journey from England. She stood up in her stirrups to wave until they were out of sight.

Then Helen and Rosita, escorted by John MacGregor and a few Highland soldiers, made their way to the gates of the city of Mirapore.

Chapter 3

A crenellated wall encircled the city with its four gates firmly shut and no evidence to indicate that they were expected.

Suddenly, when they were within a few yards of the walls, the huge south gate creaked open to allow a troop of fierce-looking cavalry to ride out. They were tall men dressed in long, red, gold-embroidered tunics, wearing blue fez-like caps and carrying lethal curved swords at their sides.

'The Rohillas,' explained John MacGregor, 'the Afghan cavalry of the Nawab; ferocious-looking lot, are they not, but good fighting soldiers. We have some of them in the Company's Army.'

The leader of the troop, with the features of a bird of prey, cantered up to John MacGregor, who addressed him in Urdu. John had taught Helen some of this language on their long sea voyage and she understood that he was requesting permission to enter the city as escort to the bride of the Resident Sahib. The man replied, pointing to the troop of Highlanders and shaking his head vigorously, 'There is no need for all these British soldiers: we, the Nawab's cavalry, will form the escort.' After a heated discussion, John MacGregor wheeled his horse's head around impatiently and rode back to his waiting party.

'It seems there is an objection to the presence of even our small party of British troops in the city. These Rohillas have been told to admit only one

45

British officer and the two ladies and their baggage. Damn impertinence and a deliberate misunderstanding of the Resident's request, I am sure, but unfortunately Gavin is away at present and I will have to comply to avoid further delay. You lads ride on. Follow the city walls to the North Gate, where I will meet you after making sure that the ladies are safely within the boundaries of the Residency.'

The gates opened and there before them was the city of Mirapore with its white painted buildings, beautiful gardens and an artificial lake in the centre of which, on its own island, stood the most magnificent building Helen had ever seen.

'That is the palace of Nawab Mohammed Hassan Khan; lovely isn't it?' said John MacGregor in response to Helen's gasp of admiration.

The palace was built in pink sandstone and white marble with intricately pierced marble screens, courts, fountains and exquisite gardens. Magnificent domes and minarets crowned its roof, Its pearl-pink beauty magnified by the clear blue sky and the shimmering waters of the lake.

'Indeed, an architectural jewel,' said Helen in awed admiration. 'Where is the Residency, John?'

'At the end of this road which skirts the lake,' answered the Scotsman. 'In fact, in the north of the City. The Residency is, of course, built on land bought from the Nawab by the Dutch, who were the first European Power to acquire a trading concession from his ancestors in the early seventeenth century. It, too, is a handsome building, more European than Indian in architecture.'

John MacGregor pointed with his riding whip to one of the high peaks towering above the city, on which stood the British fort. Its granite walls hewn out of the rocky massif, the fort dominated the valley below. On its keep fluttered the banner of the East India Company and the Union flag demonstrating, all too clearly, the real military masters of the State.

'There is the fort, which is about six miles, as the crow flies, from the northern gate of the city. It was built by the Mogul Emperor, the Great Akbar, at the beginning of the seventeenth century and commands the entrance to the Pass which leads into this valley.'

As they approached the Residency, large iron gates bearing the East India Company's crest - the Royal Arms and the flag of St. George - were opened to them by red-coated British sentries and they proceeded up a long, semi-circular gravel drive bordered by rhododendrons, oleanders, hibiscus and other exotic bushes, many of which were not familiar to Helen. The house was set in an enormous garden with manicured lawns and well-tended flower beds. A raised verandah running right round the front of the building was approached by a short flight of stone steps.

Before they had time to dismount, they were surrounded by dozens of servants dressed in white tunics and pantaloons, their red pugrees and cummerbunds bearing the crest of the East India Company. At the top of the steps stood a tiny woman wearing a bright red sari, which was a perfect foil for her jet black hair and large, slightly protruding, amber eyes.

The woman bowed over arched hands in the graceful Indian greeting, *namaste,* and turning to Helen said, 'Welcome to Mirapore, madam. I am Isabel de Silva, the housekeeper. Gavin *Sahib* is away until to-morrow on business with the Nawab and he has asked me to ensure that you are made comfortable.'

She led the way into the large vestibule, its panelled oak walls hung with the heads of hunting trophies and portraits of the white hunters. A servant stood with a tray of iced drinks under one of these portraits, which Helen learned, subsequently, was of the Dutchman who had erected this building.

Isabel de Silva looked inquiringly in the direction of John MacGregor and said, 'Will the Lieutenant *Sahib* be staying the night? If so, I will prepare another guest room.'

'Thank you, but no, I must start on my return journey before nightfall. My platoon is waiting for me at the North Gate.' Taking a glass from the tray, John MacGregor quenched his thirst and then turning to Helen, took her hand and kissed it lingeringly.

'*Au revoir*, beautiful lady. I shall see you on your wedding day, but remember if you change your mind...' John did not finish his sentence, but his look of longing into Helen's eyes, left her in no doubt that he wished he was the prospective bridegroom.

Then he kissed Rosita's hand and turning once more to sketch a half salute to Helen, ran down the steps to mount his horse.

Helen walked out on the verandah to watch the horse and rider disappear down the long drive, and wondered at her sudden feeling of loss. She knew she would miss the giant Scotsman's companionship and gallantry and the bond of friendship forged on that long, never to be forgotten voyage.

Helen looked around her new home and was surprised at its size and elegance. It had old timbered ceilings and polished wood flooring, covered by rich carpets, beautiful curving staircases leading to the upper floors and, as she eventually discovered, spacious reception rooms including a ballroom, a dining room and study on the ground floor and several bedrooms and bathrooms on the second and third floors.

After dinner, she and Isabel walked around the garden on one side of which stood a small bungalow that Isabel told her was the guest house where Gavin would reside until after their marriage at the end of the week.

The servants had their own quarters set well back to the rear of the grounds, extending to five acres, including a stable block and paddocks. At the far end, against the forested hillside, stood a strange, but beautiful, little, domed building, resembling a miniature Moghul palace.

Helen was surprised at the incongruity of such a building amidst the European architecture of the Residency until Isabel explained,'This building

49

is the tomb of a dancing girl with whom the heir of the first Khan fell in love. Legend has it that his wife had her murdered before she could bear the prince any sons.'

That night, after Rosita had brushed her hair one hundred times, a task she seldom missed, and then retired to her own suite of rooms, Helen sat for a while in the window seat of her bedroom, beautifully furnished in rose pink and grey, looking out at the Indian night. The sweet scent of jasmine and other exotic perfumes wafted towards her and looking up at the moonlit sky, she wondered why the stars seemed bigger and brighter than they had ever looked in the skies over Sussex. To-morrow Gavin would be home and Helen felt that strange excitement again that even the thought of this man aroused in her.

Before she went to bed, she took a lighted candle lamp and walked into the adjoining room. It was a man's room, with a narrow bed, a large carved wardrobe and a sandalwood chest. A roll-topped desk and shelves full of books completed the masculine furnishings. Helen opened the wardrobe and touched the clothes hanging there, wondering about the man who wore them. A dark green dressing gown lay across a chair, as if the owner had only just discarded it. Helen bent down and buried her face in its folds: it smelt faintly of sandalwood and tobacco. She chided herself for her foolishness and returned quickly to her own room.

She climbed into the large four poster bed, which, instead of heavy European hangings, had light nets all around, hanging from a central point in the ceiling, to ward off the ubiquitous mosquitoes. Its four feet rested in brass bowls of water to deter snakes, she had been told by Isabel.

Sleep soon overcame the young woman. She must have slept for some hours, but suddenly she awoke with a start of uneasiness. Someone was in her room. A figure was standing at the door leading to Gavin's dressing room. Had he returned last night?

'Who is that? Gavin is that you?' she heard herself asking softly. Then the figure vanished and Helen climbed out of the high bed and padded across the Persian rugs in her bare feet. She stood for a moment with her hand on the handle of the communicating door, then plucking up courage, opened it wide. The room was dark but appeared empty. Helen returned to her room to fetch the candle lamp on her bedside table, then slipped back into Gavin's room and searched it thoroughly by the candle's light. No one was there. Had she been dreaming?

Nevertheless, she decided to turn the key on her side of the communicating door before walking over to her bedroom window. Nothing moved in the garden below, but in the distance came a faint sound of chanting. It seemed to come from the little mausoleum, the dancing girl's tomb, and through the pierced marble screens of the edifice, Helen noticed a faint glow of light. Could someone be in there? She must enquire of the *chowkidar* in the morning. Then shaking off a feeling of unease, she went back to her still warm bed.

The next morning at breakfast, Helen decided to ignore the night's strange event. If she mentioned it, Rosita would only insist on sharing her room and, more importantly, Isabel de Silva would think she was a fussy little goose. Why, she mused, should she worry about the girl's opinion; she was, after all, an employee.

However, something about Isabel de Silva made Helen uneasy. Not that she was anything but polite, but she had a manner of approaching silently, which had on at least two occasions startled Helen when she turned around and saw her standing quietly behind her. She reminded Helen of a black cat with her almost furtive movements and strange amber eyes, which seemed to follow Helen everywhere.

'Stuff and nonsense, Helen Forsythe, you are being illogical,' Helen chided herself aloud. Isabel was half Indian. She had told her last night that her birthplace was Goa, a Portuguese colony in Southern India, and that her father had married an Indian woman; so it was natural that she would be different to an European and was, understandably, curious about her new mistress.

It was late afternoon and Helen decided to pick some blooms for the tall Benares brass vase in the Hall. There seemed to be a dearth of fresh flowers in the house, despite the well-stocked garden.

Suddenly she heard the clatter of horses' hooves on the gravel drive. As the riders came nearer, she realised that one of them was Gavin. Quickly, Helen stepped behind a thick bush. She wanted to observe Gavin before he saw her. Why, she did this, she could not say, but suddenly she felt nervous to meet him again after so many years.

A groom ran up to take the horses as the riders dismounted. The other rider, a short, stocky, oriental looking man was obviously Ram Das, whom Isabel had told her was Gavin's Nepalese soldier/servant. Ram Das untied the saddle bags and carried them into the house, whilst his master spoke to the groom.

Helen observed Gavin avidly. He was taller than she remembered, well over six feet. His boyish frame had developed into a man's lean, muscular physique with broad shoulders, slim hips and long legs, the muscles of his thighs accentuated by his tight riding breeches. He was wearing a linen shirt, the ruffled front open at the neck and as he turned to stroke the chestnut gelding before relinquishing the reins to the groom, Helen observed that his tanned skin was almost as brown as the Indian's. Gavin removed his pith helmet and wiped the sweat from his forehead with the back of his hand and Helen saw that his thick, dark brown hair, which he had worn almost shoulder length as a teenager, had been cut short to frame his head in unruly curls. She suddenly thought of the head of Michelangelo's David, the impressive sculpture she had so admired when she visited

Florence with her father years ago. Gavin French was, indeed, handsomer than ever and Helen felt that disturbing attraction once again, which only he could arouse in her.

A servant came down the short flight of steps leading to the verandah and Helen heard him inform Gavin in his pidgin English that the *memsahibs* had arrived from England. Gavin nodded and bounded up the steps. Was he in a hurry to meet her, she wondered, and what would he think of her after all these years?

Helen waited a few minutes to regain her composure and then followed her future husband up the steps, across the verandah and into the entrance hall.

Isabel de Silva was standing near him with a tray of glasses and a jug of iced *nimbu pani* and as he reached to take a glass, Gavin looked up and caught sight of Helen framed in the doorway. She was was quite unaware of the attractive picture she made in her apple green, sprigged muslin dress, the sunlight behind her making it almost transparent, despite her petticoats, and revealing her lovely, long legs. She saw astonishment in Gavin's eyes and then joy as he came towards her. He transferred the trug of flowers impatiently from her hands to the floor and lifting her off her feet, embraced her with such enthusiasm that she thought her ribs would be crushed. Then he put her down and held her at arm's length while he examined her from head to foot, his obvious admiration bringing the colour swiftly to Helen's cheeks as she heard him whisper, 'Is this beautiful young lady my little Helen Forsythe?'

Seeing her confusion, Gavin laughed mischievously and untying the emerald green ribbon fastening her chip straw bonnet under her chin, removed the hat. He stood back to admire her shining, dark auburn ringlets and with one finger tracing the tiny line of freckles across her nose, said teasingly, 'And you still have those charming freckles which are so attractive but which, I recall, you disliked intensely. I had forgotten, too, how green your eyes are, little sweetheart.'

Those last two words, spoken as only Gavin could speak them, brought back memories of their first meeting in those ancient English woods and Helen recalled how deeply she had fallen in love with this man, who was still able to tease her and make her lose her composure.

Isabel's voice broke the spell, 'Gavin, would you like this drink now?'

Helen was surprised at this sudden interruption and the almost familiar tone in which the housekeeper addressed Gavin. He, however, was still holding Helen's hands and gazing at her in amazement. He muttered brusquely, 'We'll have the drinks on the verandah. There is so much I want to talk to you about, Helen.'

Taking her by the arm, Gavin guided Helen to a cane armchair. He lifted a glass from the tray that Isabel had placed on a small wicker table, leaned his tall frame against the verandah railing, and drank the cool, citrus drink whilst steadily gazing at Helen over the rim of the glass with his dark, long-lashed eyes.

'My father told me you had grown into a beautiful, young woman and he certainly did not exaggerate. He also told me that you have a medical degree. Brains as well as beauty,' he quipped in the identical words that John MacGregor had used to rile Doctor James Grant, the ship's doctor.

Then, suddenly serious, Gavin asked, 'How is my father? I was so sorry to hear of your own loss. Uncle Arthur was like a second father to me and I regret that I will never see him again.'

'Death was a happy release for him, Gavin. He had been suffering for many years, but he always followed your career with such great interest. As for Uncle Terence, he has been so kind to me since my father's death. He, too, is getting older, but apart from slight arthritis in his hands, he is a very fit man. I have a letter from him for you.'

They talked on about England, about Charnwood Hall and its faithful staff. Helen told Gavin that Martha was still baking her delicious cakes and pasties and had instructed her to ensure that Gavin was eating well and sensibly in 'that foreign land'. Then Rosita joined them and Gavin hugged her and teased her about her striking Spanish looks.

"Rosita, you are as beautiful as ever and still my favourite Spanish lady. I will have to introduce you to Don Hernandaz, the Spanish Consul, and his family.'

A servant announced that dinner would be served in half an hour and Gavin excused himself to Helen and Rosita.

'I must have a bath and change after that dusty ride. There is still so much I want to know about you, Helen, and Rosita can tell me how many broken-hearted admirers you have left behind in England. I have met one of them this morning at the British fort, Lieutenant John MacGregor, a giant Scot who sings your praises and admonishes me for being betrothed to the only woman for whom he would willingly surrender his bachelor status. Now, the reason for that remark is something I am very curious to learn, little sweetheart.'

Gavin leaned down over Helen's chair and taking her chin in his hand, tipped up her face to within a few inches of his own, his dark eyes glinting with a quizzical, teasing expression. Helen felt her cheeks flush again and was more than a little irritated when Gavin noticed and chuckling wickedly, kissed her lightly on the mouth before he stood up and left the verandah.

Helen's annoyance, obvious in the way she bit her lip, was not lost upon Rosita who questioned her, 'What is the matter, *querida*?'

'He still thinks I am that little girl he rescued from the forest. Doesn't he realise that I am now a grown woman?' replied Helen.

Rosita smiled at the young woman's petulance. 'I think, *querida mia*, that he is well on the way to discovering that you are just that - a woman, a beautiful woman, but one who has a quick temper and a will of her own!'

Before dinner, Helen changed into a lilac muslin dress and tied her auburn ringlets off the nape of her neck with a matching lilac ribbon. She looked at herself briefly in the tall, gilt-bordered cheval mirror and was a little disconcerted to see that the dress and hairstyle made her look even younger than her twenty-four years - Gavin would surely continue to regard her as a little girl. A dinner gong was ringing downstairs and Helen wished there could have been more time to dress her hair into a more sophisticated chignon, which was the style she had adopted in medical school to emphasise her maturity and professionalism.

Gavin was already in the dining room talking to Rosita. Isabel joined them from the pantry with a tray of madeira-filled glasses and Helen noticed that she, too, had changed into a brilliant purple sari. She wore a garish display of gold jewellery around her neck and arms, the heavily engraved gold appearing too cumbersome for her tiny, slender frame.

Dinner was a lively affair with Gavin alternating his questions about England with his banter about Helen's beaux, particularly John MacGregor.

Rosita interrupted, 'You know, of course, Gavin, that if it had not been for that giant Scot, Helen would be at the bottom of the Indian Ocean.'

'What's that, Rosita?' asked Gavin, leaning towards the Spanish woman, his brown eyes serious for once, and despite Helen's dismissive interjection of the unimportance of the episode on the *Prince George,* he insisted on hearing every detail of that near tragic incident.

Rosita proceeded to outline the stormy event, embellishing every detail in her naturally loquacious Spanish manner, of Helen's danger on the storm-tossed decks of the *Prince* George and the Scotsman's courage in risking his own life to rescue her.

'So I have John MacGregor to thank for saving my fiancée's life,' said Gavin when Rosita at last came to the end of her account. 'Well, I'll certainly do that to-morrow at the Nawab's dinner party. Mohammed Khan is giving us a reception in your honour tomorrow night, Helen, and you will meet all his family and some of Mirapore's important citizens. It will be a formal occasion, but Isabel will tell you what is required by way of dress. She was Maria's lady's maid.'

Gavin's reference to his first wife and his assumption that Helen would need Isabel's guidance on how to dress, irritated Helen somewhat and she replied brusquely, 'I believe I will not let you down in the dress department, Gavin. I have brought a trunk full of formal clothes in the latest fashions from Europe. Rosita has always been my dresser and dressmaker and I see no reason to burden Isabel.'

Gavin, like most men thought Helen, seemed unaware how tactless his simple remark had been and replied, 'You could never let me down, little sweetheart. I am sure you will look delightful in whatever you wear. Let's have coffee on the verandah. I want to show you the lovely Himalayan sunsets. You know we do not have the long European twilights, but come, let me show you.'

Putting his arm around Helen's waist, Gavin guided her to the verandah balustrade. As they leaned against the rail together, he pointed out that the sky in the east was already dark purple with a faint, pink glow still in the west. The smell of jasmine and frangipani scented the air, cooled by a gentle breeze. Dark, wooded foothills were silhouetted against the horizon and beyond were the everlasting snows of the high ranges, their white caps blushing with the rosy glow of the dying sun and as they watched, the moon, like a giant yellow globe, rose above the peaks. Helen exclaimed at the beauty of the scene. 'What a moon! She seems bigger and brighter in her Indian skies.'

'You will soon fall in love with this country, Helen. It is fascinating and one can forget even the heat and the flies on an evening like this. There is so much I want to show you, little sweetheart,' said Gavin softly, looking down at her with tenderness in his eyes and Helen aware of his nearness, felt a weakness and a longing that surprised and disturbed her. She knew she wanted to be alone with him, to feel his man's mouth hard on hers and his hands caressing her body, but they were not alone and Helen felt herself resenting the presence of the others. Helen was used to being in control of her emotions and Gavin's proximity was unsettling, to say the least.

She moved away from him and said, 'Our coffee is getting cold. When does the Nawab expect us? Tell me something about him and his family, Gavin.'

'I have ordered our carriage for six o'clock to-morrow evening. This banquet is a twofold celebration - to welcome you and to celebrate the end of Ramadan, the Moslem month of fasting.

'As for the Nawab, now what can I tell you? His ancestor, an Afghan mercenary, came to India with the armies of the first Moghul Badshah, Babar. He helped Babar defeat the Moslem ruler of Agra, a fabulously rich city at the time and for his loyalty was appointed diwan, that is to say, revenue collector of this province. Eventually the Nawab's forebear became the subhadar - or as we say in English - governor of the state, with complete control over its tax collection and administration.

'You see,' chuckled Gavin, 'How this family have always been careful to choose the winning side and after the death of Aurungzib, who I would say, was the last truly great Moghul Emperor, the Nawab's great grandfather sought the protection of the British against the warring factions of the fragmenting Moghul Empire.

'Needless to say, part of my job here as Resident, is to maintain the company's influence in this province, which is of immense strategic importance, particularly against the aspirations of Russia to establish a foothold in India.'

61

'What about the Nawab's family?' asked Helen.

'There are two sons, Prince Hassan, the Heir Apparent and Prince Ali. Hassan's mother is dead, but he has the support of the old Begum, the Nawab's mother. Ali's mother, the Nawab's second wife, is French and very ambitious for her son and there are rumours that she would not hesitate to implicate the French in the succession; something, you can imagine, the company is determined to prevent at all costs.

'On the advice of the previous Resident, Prince Ali was educated in England and, according to the irascible Dowager Begum, has forgotten his Indian roots. Unfortunately, our playboy Prince prefers the company of beautiful European women, so watch out Helen,' teased Gavin. 'He is determined to resist all the Nawab's efforts to arrange an Indian bride for him.'

'What a fascinating dynasty, Gavin; all the intrigue of our own Plantagenets and Tudors,' said Helen, her eyes bright with enthusiasm.

Then, as a teasing afterthought, she rose from her chair and curtsied to Gavin, saying, 'I salute you, Sir Gavin French, the King Maker!'

Gavin roared with laughter and rising from his chair, picked Helen up and swung her around. Then putting her down, but still holding her with one arm, he lifted her face towards his with his hand and kissed her soundly on the lips. 'A little more respect for your future husband, little sweetheart. Remember you will soon promise to love, honour and obey this King Maker.'

'Then I will say, goodnight, Sir. I shall need all my rest to prepare myself for my future bondage!' retorted Helen, twisting herself out of Gavin's arms and smiling at him provocatively over her shoulder as she ran up the stairs.

••••••

When Rosita joined Helen later in her bedroom, Helen was half undressed and was sitting dreamily before her dressing table, staring at her reflection in its mirror. Rosita smiled and taking the silver-backed hairbrush from her, began to brush the beautiful, auburn hair saying, 'Still dreaming, querida mia. What do you think of your handsome Gavin?'

'He is dangerously attractive, Rosita, and I will have to be careful not to become his slave in body and soul. Do you think he will learn to love me as much as I have always loved him?' mused the young woman.

Rosita only smiled, remembering Gavin's look of frustration when Helen tore herself out of his arms a few minutes ago and his enigmatic remark to her, 'You have nurtured a dangerous, green-eyed siren, Rosita. I can quite see how our young Scot, John MacGregor, is so entranced by her.'

Gavin French was a man, Rosita knew instinctively, who would love with fierce passion and jealous possessiveness and would brook no rivals. His love, when it was given, would be all consuming, different to the gentle, patient love of Dr. David Burton or even the unshakable ardour of the Scot, John MacGregor.

Audrey Blankenhagen

The Southern Spanish woman prided herself on her ability to look behind the public masks that people displayed to the world. After all, Moorish and perhaps even gypsy blood ran in her veins, making her something of a psychic. Was Gavin French the right man for her Helen? Rosita had always believed that each human being has a soulmate with whom a union in this life would bring inexplicable bliss to the fortunate couple. But such a love, because of its intensity, could be destructive if things went wrong and Rosita suddenly feared for her lovely girl who had to walk this rocky road of marriage with such a man as Gavin French.

She stopped her brushing and kissed Helen gently on the top of her head, 'Now, querida mia, I think it is time we both went to sleep. You have a long day ahead of you to-morrow and must look your best to meet the Nawab and his guests.'

Chapter 4

Gavin had already left the house for the Palace when Helen came down for breakfast. She breakfasted lightly and then made her way to the strange *chaatri* of the former Khan's mistress. The door to the little monument was padlocked and Helen asked one of the *malis* working nearby where she could find the key.

'De Silva *memsahib* has the only key, madam. If you like, I will go and ask her for it.'

But the problem was solved when Isabel, herself, appeared suddenly from the direction of the house.

'Ah, Isabel, I believe you have the key to this monument. I would like to take a look inside if you will open the door,' said Helen, noticing with surprise the housekeeper's hesitation.

'It is empty, madam. No one ever enters except to sweep it occasionally. There is no need, as it is only a bare chamber containing the marble tomb of the dancing girl.'

'I would, nevertheless, like to look inside and ensure that it is being cleaned and maintained. I shall remove my shoes before entering, which I believe is the prerequisite for visiting Muslim holy places; so fetch the key please, Isabel,' said Helen, amazed that the woman was so reluctant to let her have access and wondering yet again about the strange glow and chanting she had heard on her first night in the Residency.

Isabel was soon back with the key and the obviously well-oiled door opened to reveal an octagonal room in the centre of which stood a marble tomb inscribed in Persian script. There was a stone bench at one end, presumably where the prince had sat to contemplate his love's resting place. Helen detected a faint smell of joss sticks and noticed fresh flower petals strewn near the bench.

'How strange!' exclaimed Isabel looking at the petals. 'Someone has obviously placed flowers here recently. No doubt the Nawab's family have a duplicate key, as I have not been asked to open the door.'

Helen was forced to accept this explanation, although she was uneasy at the glibness of the reply. She must ask Gavin if the Nawab's family had a key to the monument. In view of that Ruler's recent refusal for her British escort to enter the City, she wondered if the British soil of the Residency was subject to equivalent constraints on the Nawab's people.

Helen moved on to the stables where the groom was attending to Gavin's chestnut gelding. A pretty, grey mare was munching hay in one of the adjoining boxes. Helen exclaimed, 'Oh you little beauty!' and holding the back of her hand against the horse's nostrils, allowed the little animal to sniff her gently.

'That is Sultana, the horse that belonged to the first *memsahib*,' said the syce, coming towards Helen.

'Who exercises her now?' asked Helen, her expert eye detecting that the little mare was a bit plump and obviously not as fit as she should be.

'The *sahib* takes her out occasionally on a lead rein when he exercises Sultan. The other *memsahib* did not like riding very much and was a bit nervous of Sultana's high spirits. Would you like to try her?' enquired the syce, clearly trying to judge Helen's reaction.

'Yes, of course, but please don't saddle her up until I return. I would like to do that myself,' said Helen, returning to the house to change into her riding habit, once again eschewing the usual heavy riding skirt for a divided doeskin garment (copied from women's riding fashion in the former American colonies) and knee-high leather boots. This was the way she liked to dress when she rode out alone except, of course, on formal occasions when ladies were expected to ride the more elegant side saddle.

The syce had already led Sultana out of the stable and Helen went up to the little horse, blew down her nose and whispered in her ear, 'Don't be afraid, my beauty, we are going to be good friends.'

She ran her hand along the horse's back and down its hocks and then picked up each hoof to examine the shoes. Taking the saddle cloth and saddle from the groom, Helen confidently tacked up Sultana, all the while talking to her. She secured the bridle, tightened the girth and pulled the

67

stirrup irons down before mounting lightly. Then she sat quietly in the saddle for a moment, before applying slight pressure with both her legs. Sultana stepped forward immediately and Helen, keeping gentle contact with the horse's mouth, guided her to the paddock. Here she asked the horse to trot, squeezing gently with both calves and after a while rising to the rhythm of Sultana's movements. The horse soon realised that these hands holding her reins would not pull on her mouth and the little mare relaxed and whinnied with the joy of being outdoors. Helen had no trouble in urging her into a light canter, sitting firmly in the saddle and moving supplely with the horse's rhythm, then shortening her reins and leaning forward slightly, she extended the pace to a gallop.

When she returned to the stable, the *syce* who had watched this display of horsemanship with amazement said, '*Memsahib*, I believe Sultana has found the right rider at last.'

'Thank you, *syce*, I will ride her every day and if time does not permit, I will show you how to exercise her on a lunge line. Let me dry her off now and then give her some warm bran, fresh hay and a thick warm bed for the night.'

Helen left the stable feeling that Sultana and she were well on the way to becoming firm friends and would share many hours of good riding.

Rosita was waiting anxiously for Helen in the hall and reminded her that it was time to wash and dress her hair for the evening. Helen had chosen her gown carefully. A heavy, emerald green satin ruched overskirt parted to display a slim cream satin and lace underskirt shimmering with tiny seed pearls. The fabric of the underskirt was repeated in the front of her low-cut boned bodice, which was laced at the back and revealed her lovely, creamy shoulders and arms. Rosita had dressed Helen's hair in the formal Grecian style and her only jewellery was a string of tiny seed pearls plaited gracefully through her thick auburn curls. Little cream satin slippers, gloves and a quilted taffeta cape in the same emerald green completed her beautiful outfit.

Gavin was waiting for her in the hall, examining a velvet case lying on the hall table. He was wearing the formal dress uniform of the Resident - cream pantaloons and a dark red jacket interfaced with navy blue facings and silver lace, beautifully tailored across his broad shoulders. Helen's heart fluttered at the sight of his handsome profile. He looked up at the sound of the switch of her skirts and came forward to the bottom of the staircase, the admiration and wonder in his eyes confirming Rosita's comment that Helen had never looked more beautiful. He was smiling that gay, yet audacious smile she was beginning to know so well and stretched out his hand to guide her down the last few stairs.

'Ah, the beautiful Helen - the face that launched a thousand ships. I hope there is no young Paris to kidnap you to-night,' quipped Gavin.

'If King Menaleous had been as handsome as Sir Gavin French in that splendid uniform, Helen would not have been tempted by Paris,' replied Helen, her green eyes sparkling with amusement.

Gavin smiled at the reference to his uniform and said by way of explanation, 'The Company expects their civil administration to don formal attire on these occasions so as not to be eclipsed by the elegant uniforms of the Army, or the ostentatious dress of the Indian princes.'

He picked up the oblong velvet case from the table, which he now unlocked and removed a sparkling three-tiered necklace of emeralds set in delicate filigree gold, each gem as perfect as its companions.

'To my beautiful Helen, an engagement gift. Will you wear it to-night, little sweetheart?' asked Gavin as he led Helen to the large oval mirror in the hall and fastened his gift around the young woman's slender neck, his fingers lingering on her soft skin. Helen stroked the beautiful jewellery lightly and turning suddenly to the man who stood so close behind her, flung her arms about his neck in childish joy and kissed him exclaiming, 'Oh, Gavin, I have never seen anything so beautiful! How can I thank you for this lovely gift?'

'Another kiss would be adequate for now,' whispered Gavin, his dark eyes glinting with some hidden emotion, as he crushed Helen to him and claimed his kiss.

Gavin moved away from Helen and taking the taffeta cloak from Rosita, who was standing nearby smiling at their loving tableau, wrapped it around the young woman's shoulders saying in a voice still gruff from emotion, 'Come, my little sweetheart, we are the Nawab's guests of honour and must not be late.'

Then turning to the Spanish woman, he said, 'Don't wait up for us, Rosita, we may be quite late to-night.'

Helen sitting in the darkness of the phaeton, felt a glow of happiness. She was soon to marry this man, seated so close beside her, who had always been in her heart. She stole a glance at his handsome profile and was surprised to see that he was looking at her and even in the darkness of the coach, she saw the gleam of his white teeth as his well-formed lips parted in a smile. He reached for her gloved hand and turning it upwards, kissed the palm, saying, 'Are you looking forward to this evening, little sweetheart? You will be surprised at the opulence of the Nawab's court and I will be the envy of every man there with such a beautiful woman on my arm.'

Then abruptly changing the subject, he said, 'The *syce* tells me that you have been riding Sultana to-day. What do you think of her?'

'She is a lovely little mare, and from her beautiful head and conformation, she appears to have quite a lot of Arab blood. Am I right?'

'Yes, quite right. How did you learn so much about horses; the syce was quite impressed?' asked Gavin.

'Count Kovrosky - you remember him, Gavin, the Polish émigré who was a friend of both our fathers - he taught me not only to ride, but more importantly the art of handling and caring for a horse and that was not all I owe to his expertise. He also taught me the skills of fencing and use of firearms.'

Helen heard Gavin chuckle and knew that he was going to tease her again, 'Helen Forsythe, you never fail to surprise me. Am I marrying a little Amazon? Ah, here we are.'

The carriage turned into the causeway linking the palace to the city. On either side and along the whole length of this raised pathway were flaming torches lighting the way to the fairy tale palace and setting the waters of the lake on reflected fire.

So that his guests would not need to step on the grass, the Nawab had laid dark red carpets leading right up the marble steps into the magnificent Audience Hall.

The opulence, which Gavin had mentioned, was all too evident in this vast rectangular room - marble floors covered with Persian carpets, rich tapestries adorning the walls and crystal oil lamps set in burnished gold holders suspended from the high vaulted ceiling. Beautiful arches formed little alcoves, along two sides of the room, each alcove furnished with gold

72

cushioned divans and low, black marble-topped tables. The marble above the arches was pierced like lace and set with semi-precious stones traced with gold.

At each of the far corners of this vast hall stood a pair of magnificent elephant tusks formed into an arch and mounted on brass stands. From the centre of each arch was suspended a brass vessel burning aromatic oils, perfuming the air with exotic scents.

By the entrance to the hall stood a diminutive man with a birdlike face, wearing a dark blue, embroidered tunic and white pantaloons, his head swamped by an enormous blue *pugree*. Gavin introduced him to Helen as the Prime Minister of the Court, Abdul Asaf Khan, who greeted Gavin and Helen with the ritual *namaste*, his dark, bright eyes taking in every detail of the handsome couple.

His voice, surprisingly loud for such a small man, announced, 'Your Highness, your honoured guests, The British Resident, Sir Gavin French and his betrothed lady, Miss Helen Forsythe.'

Helen, her hand resting lightly on Gavin's arm, walked to the foot of the dais on which the Nawab sat cross-legged on the cushions of a magnificent golden throne. Mohammed Hassan Khan was a corpulent man, dressed in a jewel-encrusted, gold tunic and tapered gold pantaloons. He wore a gold *pugree* in the middle of which sparkled a ruby the size of a goose egg, The

Nawab was beardless, but sported large whiskers pointing downwards in the Moghul fashion.

On his right, behind the throne, stood the Heir Apparent, Prince Hassan, a younger version of his father, but already well on the way to equalling the paternal girth. On the Nawab's left stood Prince Ali, tall and slim, his golden skin and pale eyes testifying to his half French descent. Prince Ali would, Helen thought, have been extremely handsome if it were not for his rather hooked nose, but this served, somehow, to make him more impressive than the Heir Apparent. Both sons were dressed in blue, bejewelled tunics, although the Heir Apparent wore a heavy gold chain about his neck.

At the foot of the dais, Helen curtsied and Gavin bowed as the Ruler of Mirapore came down the steps of the dais to greet his guests of honour.

'Welcome to Mirapore and I congratulate you, Sir Gavin, on the beautiful lady you have chosen to be your wife.' Then taking Helen's hand, he introduced her to his sons. The Heir Apparent was content to shake her hand in the English fashion, but Prince Ali kissed it, his bold eyes raking her from head to toe, 'Are there many women, Sir Gavin, in your country with hair the colour of autumn leaves, eyes as green as emeralds and skin like magnolia petals?'

'My fiancée owes her beautiful colouring to her Scottish descent, a country which has many redheaded women and men,' replied Gavin, his eyes not reflecting the smile on his lips, as he led Helen away from the dais to join Sir James and Lady Cameron.

Agnes Cameron was dressed in elegant black lace, her hair topped by black feathers which made her look even taller. She tossed these in her habitual horsy manner as she embraced Helen warmly and said, 'How I have missed you, my dear, but Mirapore agrees with you; you look ravishing.'

Then turning to Gavin she said, 'When all the hubbub of your wedding is over, you must bring Helen to the fort, Gavin. She should meet our little British community.'

Assuring Agnes that he would certainly do so, Gavin excused himself and took Helen over to another couple—a tall, dark, elegant man, dressed in a well-cut dinner suit with a French order on the lapels of his black tail coat and an attractive, brown haired, golden skinned woman whose extremely low décolletage left very little to the imagination.

'Helen, let me introduce you to the Comte and Comtesse de Colbert, of the French Consulate in Mirapore,' said Gavin, who seemed amused by the flashing eyes of the Comtesse, smiling flirtatiously at him over her fan.

'Ah, at last we meet your beautiful fiancée and the rumours I have heard of her loveliness are no exaggeration. Gavin, you have exquisite taste; your betrothed is the most beautiful woman I have ever seen,' gushed the attractive Comtesse, smiling charmingly at Helen.

Despite her obvious attraction to Gavin, Helen warmed to this woman whose charm and gaiety were so infectious. She heard herself replying in French,"Thank you Comtesse; such a compliment from so lovely a lady as you, yourself, is very flattering indeed.'

'Ah, how charming you are and what perfect French you speak, my dear; but you must call me Blanche as I hope you will allow me to call you Helen. I feel we are going to be such good friends,' said the irrepressible Comtesse.

Then taking Helen's arm, she said, 'Let us leave our men to discuss affairs of state, Helen. You must introduce me to that handsome, Nordic-looking Scotsman who has hardly taken his eyes off you since your dramatic entrance. I have a great regard for the Scots, who have been so involved in my own country's history.'

Helen found herself propelled firmly by the Countess in the direction of John MacGregor, who was examining one of the tapestries at the far corner of the hall.

The giant Scotsman turned as Helen and the Countess approached and the tenderness in his eyes as he looked at Helen was all too obvious.

'John, let me introduce you to the Comtesse de Colbert. She is a great admirer of the Scots and Scotland.'

'My pleasure,' said John MacGregor, bowing low over the Comtesse's gloved hand, which he raised to his lips. 'Scotland and France are, indeed, old allies.'

'Have you known our charming Helen for a long time?' asked Blanche. 'Perhaps as children in your beautiful country, because am I not correct in thinking that Forsythe is a Scottish name?'

'Yes,' said Helen, 'I have my Scottish ancestry from my father - my mother was, however, an Englishwoman. John and I met only a few months ago; we were fellow passengers on the long sea voyage from England and he, at great risk to his own life, saved me from being swept overboard during a ferocious storm off Madagascar.'

A deep voice behind Helen interjected, 'For which I have yet to thank him.' Gavin, who had come up behind Helen placed one arm possessively around her waist and drew her so close to him that she could feel the buttons of his jacket through the material of her dress.

John did not miss this almost proprietary gesture of Gavin's, but replied calmly, 'No thanks required, Gavin. Och, I would...' For a breath stopping moment Helen thought John would repeat the words he had whispered on the night of the storm *'Och, I would have given my life for you, sweet lassie.'* But after a brief pause the Scotsman said, 'I would gladly do so again, if the opportunity arose.'

Helen noticed Blanche de Colbert's brown eyes darting from the tall Scotsman to the equally tall Englishman, her quizzical, yet amused look scrutinising the reaction of both men. Gavin, perhaps sensing her interest, smiled at her in his impudent, mischievous manner and said, 'For that I am doubly in my Scottish friend's debt. Do you not agree, Comtesse?

'Now if you will both excuse us, I must introduce Helen to the Spanish Consul and his family, who have just arrived and to the Nawab's Arab physician, who is anxious to meet her.'

With that, he steered Helen away and when she turned to look over her shoulder at John and Blanche, Gavin murmured whilst looking straight ahead, 'Don't worry about your friend, John MacGregor; our charming Creole will keep him amused.'

So, thought Helen, that was where the golden skin of Blanche de Colbert came. She was a Creole and she remembered that other famous Creole who had enslaved the heart of the Emperor Napoleon in the last century.

The Spanish Consul, Don Hernandez and his wife, were delightful and their dark-haired daughter, Pura, was obviously flustered in Gavin's presence, stealing sly glances at him through thick black eyelashes and blushing as he bent over her hand in greeting. Both women were dressed in the Spanish fashion of black lace over coloured underskirts and wore lace mantillas.

Helen spoke in Spanish which seemed to put these fellow countrymen of her beloved Rosita at ease.

The tall Arab physician, Mahmoud Bin Said, was even more interesting. He wore the traditional Arab caftan and his dark intelligent eyes above his pointed grey beard, seemed to hold all the knowledge of the world in their depths.

'I have so much to discuss with you, Dr. Forsythe, for we are both disciples of Hippocrates,' said the Court Physician, the only person in the assembly who had given Helen her professional title.

'Unfortunately, I shall have to postpone that pleasure until after dinner, for here comes Abdul Asaf Khan to invite us to take our seats,' said the Court Physician as he offered his arm to the young Spanish Pura, to escort her behind her parents into the large dining room leading off the reception chamber.

This room, Helen noticed, which was referred to as the 'English Room', would not have been out of place in the setting of an English stately home. In fact, it was not unlike the banqueting room at Charnwood Hall. A thick, wine coloured Turkish carpet covered the marble floor and set off, perfectly, the oyster pink silk upholstery of the Chippendale chairs arranged around a highly polished mahogany dining table. From the ceiling hung crystal chandeliers and the centrepiece of the table was a magnificent vase of Dresden china in the shape of a swan which was filled with exotic blooms.

The walls were covered in oyster pink silk and hung with gilt framed paintings of English hunting scenes and landscapes. A large, bow-fronted, mahogany sideboard stood against one wall and an elegant Adam fireplace completed the English decor of the room.

The meal was, however, entirely Indian served, nevertheless, on a fine English porcelain dinner service. Moghul dishes: flaming lamb kebabs; chicken pilau rice garnished with plump raisins, roasted almonds and edible silver paper; roasted goose; succulent fish in delicious sauces and a variety of vegetable dishes, each spiced to enhance the flavour of the particular vegetable which was its main ingredient: all expertly served by white coated servants. Cut glass goblets of pomegranate juice replaced the European wines, the Nawab being a strictly teetotal Muslim. After the dessert of halvas and kulfis, large golden platters of fruits and nuts were placed before the guests and at the end of the meal, the servants brought little golden bowls of rose scented water and damask linen napkins for the guests to wash and dry their fingers.

Gavin guided Helen through the menu and the exotic names of the delicious dishes. Helen was glad that silver cutlery was available for the Europeans, although she was intrigued by the dexterity of the Indians who ate with their fingers, picking up the food delicately and transferring it to their mouths without any spillage.

The meal over, the guests were asked to retire to the adjoining room, once again Moghul in its decor and they sat on low, cushioned divans placed around the room to be entertained by dancing girls and Indian musicians.

Then it was all over and time for the guests to depart as the Chief Minister organised their carriages.

Helen, sitting once again close to Gavin in the dark interior of the carriage, felt the proximity of his disturbing masculinity and shivered at the awareness of her own sensuality.

Gavin feeling her shiver said, 'Are you cold, sweetheart? Come, let me keep you warm,' and putting his arm around Helen's waist under her cape drew her to his side adding even more to her confusion as she caught the faint, evocative scent of his cologne. She was glad of the darkness of the coach to hide her emotions.

'Did you enjoy the evening, lovely lady?' said her unwitting tormentor.

'Oh yes, Gavin, it was wonderful - so exotically different to anything I have ever experienced. It was lovely, too, to meet my friends from the fort again.'

'Especially, your handsome Scot,' chuckled Gavin, tightening his clasp on her waist.

'I have asked him to be my Best Man. I hope you do not mind,' continued Gavin.

Helen surprised, replied, 'How kind of you. Did he accept?'

'Yes, with the enigmatic remark that if he could not be the bridegroom, then he must be content to be the Best Man,' said Gavin cupping Helen's chin in one hand and turning her to face him, and by the faint light of the coach lamps, she saw his quizzical smile. Then he brought his mouth down onto hers in a lingering kiss, which he ended, reluctantly, when the driver of their carriage was challenged by the sentries at the Residency gates.

The house was quiet when Gavin took Helen's hand and led her into the library where a roaring fire was still burning because the late autumn evenings in the Himalayan foothills were quite cool. A carafe of wine with glasses and a cold collation were set on a table in front of the fireplace and Gavin filled two glasses, one of which he handed to Helen.

'Would you like something to eat, darling?' asked Gavin, an unmistakable caress in his voice and his dark eyes as he came towards Helen.

'No thank you, I have eaten enough already,' smiled Helen, her green eyes looking up at him as he took the glass from her hand and enveloped her in his arms.

'Oh, Helen, I have wanted to do this all evening.'

Held so close in his arms and swept along by the storm of his passion as he rained kisses on her lips, the little hollow in her throat, and the gentle swell of her breasts above the low-cut dress, Helen, her senses reeling, entwined her arms about Gavin's neck. She felt his strong arms tremble as he held her even closer to him until the beating of both their hearts was as one. Gavin's mouth was on hers again, sensuously demanding and Helen's lips parted to answer his demand. His teeth nibbled softly at her quivering lips, his tongue traced the contours of her mouth and penetrated the sweet moistness within.

With his lips still on hers, Gavin's hand loosened the lacing of her bodice and slid her dress down her shoulders to reveal her beautiful, round, full breasts. Helen heard herself moan softly, as his hand cupped first one breast and then the other and he bent his head to kiss and lick their taut nipples. She wound her fingers through his dark hair and before he came back to reclaim her mouth, she whispered his name with all the pent up love she had felt for him over the years, 'Gavin, oh Gavin.'

Then, suddenly, he released her and held her at arms length, his frustration twisting his lips in a crooked smile, his face flushed with emotion, his dark eyes burning into hers.

'My darling, you are a green-eyed siren who would tempt the gods. Another minute and I would have taken you here, to-night, before our wedding ceremony,' said Gavin huskily.

Then adjusting her dress and putting her cape around her shoulders again, he guided her masterfully across the hall to the foot of the stairs, that buccaneer's smile playing once again about his lips.

'Now be a good girl and go to bed, before I change my mind and ravish you to-night. I promise I will not be so scrupulous on our wedding night, my lady,' and then with a courtly bow and an impudent grin, he returned to the library. As Helen mounted the stairs, she thought she heard another door open and close softly. Perhaps one of the servants was still awake, although it was very late.

Once in her room, Helen undressed in a dream, her emotions in turmoil. Gavin had kissed her, made love to her, not like a cousin but like a lover. Was this the threshold of love?

Helen blew out the candles and walked over to the window in her thin cotton shift. She opened it to let in the cool night air and saw the light burning in the little guest house. Gavin was in there! She touched her lips and her breasts, feeling once again his mouth caressing her. Her body was trembling, not entirely from the cool night. She reached for the catch to close the window, but hesitated when she saw the front door of the guest house open and a small woman in a sari come out to stand on the threshold, looking back to say something to someone in the room. The light behind her went out and the woman moved towards the main house, the bright moonlight making her red sari look almost black, her demeanour silent and furtive. Helen recognised Isabel de Silva.

Helen gasped and staggered backwards. She sat down heavily on the edge of the bed and hid her face in her hands. Isabel de Silva was Gavin's mistress! The thought swept over her, making her feel quite sick. A knot of pain clutched at her diaphragm and she found herself shivering uncontrollably. Subconsciously her medical training made her realise that she was suffering from shock and, automatically, she sought the warmth of the blankets on her bed. As her blood pressure returned to normal, Helen remembered the cause of her distress.

Now she clenched her fists in anger and beat them on the bedclothes. How dare he, this man whom she loved and placed so high on a pedestal. He had gone from her arms to the arms of his mistress - the Eurasian woman, who was his employee. And yet he had been swept by passion for her a short while ago in the library. Helen had no doubt that Gavin's ardour had not been feigned; she had seen his eyes swollen with passion, the flush on his cheekbones and felt his heart beating against hers. But, of course, he was a man with all that sex's weakness for a desirable woman. How many others had there been since his wife Maria's death, or had this Isabel de Silva been his mistress even while Maria was alive? So that was why he had been reluctant to remarry and when pressed by his father had consented to marriage with his little cousin hoping, no doubt, that she loved him and would be glad for any crumbs from his table! Well he was wrong. The little, lost child he found in the English woods was now a grown woman with her pride and independence of spirit.

All these thoughts raced through Helen's mind making rest impossible until as the first light of dawn lit her window, her exhausted brain and body succumbed to sleep.

Chapter 5

It was late morning when Helen at last awoke to see Rosita standing by her bed. 'Ah, my beauty is awake at last. How you have slept, *querida;* unusual for you. Gavin told me not to awake you but to serve you breakfast in bed.'

At the mention of Gavin's name, Helen shuddered and Rosita, thinking she was cold, placed a warm cashmere shawl around her shoulders.

'Gavin has already gone out. He said not to keep him waiting at the church tomorrow and he has left this letter and gift for you.'

Helen took the letter and gift and put them unopened inside the drawer of the bedside table. She poured herself some strong black coffee and watched Rosita fussing about the room, hanging up her beautiful dress from the night before and she remembered that she would not see Gavin again until the church ceremony. Agnes Cameron had insisted, before they left the Nawab's palace, that he should be their guest and she could still hear her words spoken in that rolling Scottish accent, 'Now Gavin, laddie, you must be our guest to-morrow night. It is unlucky to see the bride on her wedding morning and I am a great believer in not tempting Lady Luck.'

How could luck change anything now, Helen thought. She was to marry a man she did not really know. A numbness had possessed the young woman making her indifferent to everything about her.

She knew, of course, that the wedding ceremony was to be conducted in the chapel at the British fort and the guests would return to the Residency for the wedding breakfast. Sir James and Lady Cameron would call on the wedding morning to escort Helen from the Residency. Sir Terence had already asked them, before they sailed from England, to be Helen's proxy parents, a task which they had gladly accepted.

She could not alter events now, could not break her promise to Sir Terence, or flout her dead father's wishes. This was an arranged marriage and she had no right to expect a romantic union. Gavin had never said he loved her. She would have to go through to-day as if nothing had changed. Now she would need all her reserves of courage to hide her heartbreak.

She smiled at Rosita and asked her to bring out her riding clothes. 'I feel like a good gallop this morning to counteract the effects of all that rich food we were served at the Nawab's banquet.'

Sultana whinnied with delight as Helen gave the little mare her head and she took her rider away from the city onto the winding forested paths, almost as if she knew Helen wanted to escape. At last Helen pulled her up in a grove of tall pine trees in which she had noticed a little ornately-carved wooden temple. She dismounted and taking a picket peg from her saddle bag, tied Sultana's halter rope to it. Helen loosened the girth and unfastened the snaffle at the cheek piece so that the little grey could graze on the lush grass nearby and then she entered the temple, wondering if she should first ring the bell hanging above the door. A marigold-garlanded Hindu goddess, sitting in the lotus position, watched her impassively from a raised dais around which were offerings of rice and sweetmeats in banana leaves. Little oil-filled clay lamps lit the temple and scented joss sticks perfumed the air. Helen was alone in this pagan chapel and she fell to her knees and cried as if her heart would break.

Suddenly a hand touched her shoulder and she look up startled to see a wiry, old man wearing a saffron robe and a string of brown beads about his neck.

'What breaks the heart of the young and beautiful *memsahib*?' said the old *sunyassi* in perfect English.

Helen, surprised said, 'You speak English, sir.'

'Yes, I was sent to one of your hill schools when I was a boy and taught by the good Christian Brothers, although I, myself, am not a Christian. But why are you so sad? Is it a faithless lover, or perhaps the death of someone close to you which troubles your heart? If it is the first, then you must forget him and if the second, death is only a door to eternal life and you must not grieve so much for their passing.'

The *sunyassi* lifted Helen to her feet and the dark pools of his compassionate eyes seemed to hold the key to all human life.

He picked up her palm and turned it over and after a while said, 'You will find your *Nirvana* in this life even before you cross the *Kala Pani* to return to your own country, but you will need courage and determination, for I see a rocky road ahead.'

'So, I will return to England soon?' asked Helen, fascinated by the depth of meaning in the holy man's words.

'No, not soon, but it will happen. Our people long for *swaraj* and the British will not be able to deny them for long. But my people, too, will suffer greatly and some may long for the stability of the old days under the guidance of the British.'

The old man took his beads from around his neck and gave them to Helen.

'Please accept these holy beads, my child, as a talisman against the evil which will seek to destroy your family. You need not wear them but keep them with you always, especially when you are alone.'

Helen was touched by the little gift from one so poor and she undid her gold stock pin and gave it to the old man. '*Sadhu Ji,* please accept this from me; it is gold and may be of some use to you on your long journey.'

The old man looked at the shining pin in his hand and seemed to hesitate for a moment before placing it in his wooden bowl and covering it with a cloth.

'Unless it is stolen from me, my child, I shall not part with it in this life. Now let me escort you and your horse out of this forest. It is not good to travel alone. Dacoits and *badmashes* are no respecters of even an *Angressi*

Memsahib. But before we go, let me give you my *dharshan.'* The old man raised his hand and muttered a prayer.

He helped Helen to mount Sultana and then walking quite rapidly for his age alongside horse and rider, did not utter another word until the walls of the City of Mirapore came into sight.

'Farewell, my child; remember what I have said and do not judge your lover too harshly. If he is the man I believe he is, he will be worthy of your love no matter what he has done,' and Helen wondered if the old *sunyassi*, his eyes filled with merriment as he spoke these words, had guessed the cause of her grief and knew who she was.

Rosita and Isabel were waiting for her with some agitation. 'You have been gone so long and the caterers are here already with the wedding breakfast menus,' said Rosita, leading Helen by her arm into the study. A sharp-faced man rose from the chair and bowed to her.

'I am Monsieur Boucher of Boucher et Fils, Caterers. We have been recommended to your husband by the Comtesse de Colbert.'

'Ah yes,' said Helen, ashamed that she had forgotten this appointment and kept this poor man waiting. 'I was rather delayed on my morning ride but please accept my apologies for keeping you waiting. I hope you have had some refreshment.'

'Yes, thank you *mademoiselle*, your staff have been very attentive,' and Monsieur Boucher handed Helen a selection of printed menus. She chose

91

one which was not dissimilar to the food served for grand banquets at Charnwood Hall. Gavin had ordered the best wines and champagne and Helen asked the Frenchman to lay on a good supply of pomegranate juice for the Nawab. She reminded Isabel, who had now joined them, to ensure that the Residency's silver, plate and crystal were at their sparkling best.

There was not a great deal more for Helen to do except to inspect the banqueting room. Gavin had thought of everything, even to the ordering of fresh flowers for delivery on the wedding morning: it seemed that he had been planning this occasion for many weeks. She heard again the *Sunyassi's* words, *'If he is the man I believe he is, he will be worthy of your love no matter what he has done.'*

Rosita insisted that Helen retire early that night. 'To-morrow is a busy day for all of us but especially for you, *querida*. You will no longer be my little girl, but Lady Helen French. But I am happy for you because you are to marry the only man you have ever loved.'

Darling Rosita, Helen mused, when the Spanish woman had left her room. How could she guess that the man she admired had feet of clay? Then Helen remembered the letter and little box in her bedside table. She opened the box and found the most exquisite ring - two flawless diamonds cut in the shape of entwining hearts set on a circlet of gold. With trembling fingers, Helen opened the letter and read:

'My little sweetheart,

This ring is a symbol of my love for you. You hold my heart in your little hands. Treat it gently.

Until the moment I hold you in my arms again,

Your loving husband to be,

Gavin.'

Tears welled up in Helen's eyes as she saw the unmistakable, bold flourish of Gavin's signature. And the ring, it was exquisite and, she was sure, extremely costly.

'Oh, Gavin, my darling, how could you pretend you love me when another woman is in your heart,' whispered Helen, as she kissed Gavin's signature, unable to dispel his image from her mind and her heart. She saw again his teasing smile, felt the strength and sweetness of his lips and his sudden surge of passion as he held her last night in the library.

Then falling on her knees at her bedside, she prayed for strength to bear this unexpected cross. The letter and ring she placed carefully in the little safe behind a portrait of her parents and vowed that the ring would never grace her finger until ... until what? she wondered.

The sun was shining on Helen's wedding morning as Rosita helped her to dress. Helen looked in the mirror and the image reflected in it was of that of a lovely bride. Her gown of heavy oyster satin with its long train was cut skilfully by one of the top couturiers of London to emphasise her superb figure and lovely colouring. The low cut bodice was encrusted with seed pearls and Helen wore no jewellery except for a glittering diamond diadem to hold her veil in place. This jewelled circlet and the wedding dress had been presented to her as a wedding gift from Gavin's father, Sir Terence French, before she sailed from England.

The Brigadier and Lady Agnes arrived early. 'With the express intention of inspecting the wedding presents,' said Lady Agnes, as she was smartly saluted by a uniformed Ram Das discretely guarding the cornucopia of silver, gold and crystal displayed on a damask-covered table in the library. The centrepiece was a magnificent solid gold replica of the Nawab's palace standing on a crystal simulation of the lake. The present had been delivered the previous morning by the fierce Rohilla guards. To Helen, however, the most treasured wedding gift was a beautiful tapestry, worked by Rosita, depicting her favourite English landscape in all its autumnal glory.

Helen felt that events were overtaking her too swiftly. The carriage with its passengers - the bride, an emotional Rosita and her proxy parents, Lord and Lady Cameron - was climbing the steep track that wound around the mountain at the peak of which stood the British Fort. The enormous iron gates of the fort were raised at their approach and the horses trotted smartly to the door of the little chapel. An Honour Guard of the 78th Highlanders gave a cheer as they caught a glimpse of the beautiful bride of the Resident.

Their spontaneous acclaim had been heard in the chapel and everyone was looking around towards the entrance as Helen, on Sir James' arm, walked slowly up the aisle to the strain of Mendelssohn's *Wedding March*. She heard the gasps and whispered comments, 'Lovely, beautiful, exquisite!' from voices either side of the aisle but her eyes were fixed on the two men standing at the end of the chapel. John MacGregor, tall, blond and adoring and Gavin, even handsomer in his light grey wedding suit, watching the approach of his bride with pride and admiration. How could he look at her like that after what she had discovered, thought Helen, but immediately steadied herself by smiling at his Best Man.

As if in a dream she heard the chaplain intone the words of the marriage vows and heard herself agreeing to love, honour and obey and she looked deep into Gavin's eyes as he promised to put all others aside and cling to her until death. The love she saw in their dark depths seemed to mock the silent pain in her heart.

Then the minister pronounced them man and wife and her husband kissed her long and tenderly and whispered, 'I love you, little sweetheart.' They were words she had longed to hear since the boy, Gavin, had put his arm around that seven-year old girl and lifted her onto his horse: now what did they mean to the woman he had betrayed.

Helen felt throughout the reception - the wedding breakfast and the speeches - that it was not her, but someone else seated next to Gavin and she recalled the painted Goddess, Sati, in that little Hindu chapel in the forest and wondered if Helen Forsythe (*no, now she was Helen French*) had been turned to stone.

Finally, the last guest departed and Helen saw Gavin exchange some words with Rosita, who was about to follow her up the stairs to help her undress.

Helen removed the pins from her hair and brushed it into a shining cape around her shoulders. The fastenings of her dress were more difficult to manage on her own and she wondered why Rosita was taking so long. Suddenly the door to the bedroom opened and it was not Rosita, but Gavin who stood there. He had removed his coat, waistcoat and neck cloth and was wearing only his tight grey pantaloons and silk shirt open at the neck, more or less as she had seen him at their first meeting in Mirapore. He was holding a bottle of champagne and two glasses, which he placed on a little table as he came towards her.

'Are you waiting for Rosita, darling? I have sent her to bed so that I can perform her duty as lady's maid,' he smiled with that strange quality of teasing impudence she had come to know so well.

'Come, turn around, I will undo those fastenings for you. You'll see how adept I am at undressing a beautiful woman.'

Yes, thought Helen, a born seducer of women and as the dress fell from her shoulders and he undid her flowing petticoat to join the satin material about her feet, she stood before him naked, proud and as beautiful as Boticelli's Venus.

Gavin gasped at her loveliness as he drew her to him and crushed her in his strong arms. Then lifting her up as if she was a feather, he carried her over to the large bed and laid her down gently, still holding on to her as if he was afraid this fantastic woman would disappear. His dark head bent over her as he explored with lips and hands her beautiful body, his mouth encircling her full, firm breasts and taking the rosy nipples softly between his teeth, then his fingers followed by his lips, traced a path over her stomach and her pelvic bones until they stopped at the sweet triangle of her Venus mound, covered with soft auburn hair. He was moaning with longing, 'My beautiful wife, how I want you!' Helen gasped as his intrusive fingers and tongue sought out the sweet, moist secrets of her womanhood. Her breathing quickened as the delicious sensations Gavin was creating in her threatened to undo her self-control - she, a doctor familiar with male and female physiology, had never dreamed that desire could be so overwhelming and as she tossed wildly on the bed, her nerve endings on fire, she suddenly envisaged, in her mind's eye, the dark body of Isabel de Silva writhing under this connoisseur's caresses.

'No, No!' she heard herself scream and pushing her astonished husband away, sprang to her feet, shivering with frustration and anger.

97

'What is the matter, Helen?' implored Gavin, now on his feet too, his arms seeking her again as she moved away from him. 'Are you afraid, my darling? I promise I will be gentle, but you are so lovely and I wanted to bring you to ecstasy before I made you mine. Come let me show you how much I love you.'

But Helen beat her fists on his chest, trying desperately to escape his imprisoning arms and her own desire. 'Go away, please. Go away,' she whispered huskily, tears streaming down her cheeks.

Gavin released her and stepped back his arms falling to his sides and a look of bewilderment and then of anger darkening his face. 'Not you, too,' he murmured and moving away, walked stiffly towards the communicating door, only turning once to say, 'Don't worry, madam, I will not trouble you again. I have never taken a woman by force,' and then he added caustically, 'never had the need to. Goodnight, little virgin. Sleep well in your cold bed.'

Helen found herself shivering in the cool night air and snatched the embroidered silk night shift at the foot of the bed. It had been crushed by the weight of Gavin's body and she could smell the male scent of him on the silk, as if he was still there beside her. She climbed between the sheets but sleep did not come to still her chaotic emotions. Gavin, too, was restless; she could hear him pacing up and down in the adjoining room like a caged animal and then she heard the door to the landing open and shut and his footsteps running down the staircase.

Was he going to Isabel? But, of course, not; Helen remembered that Isabel had left after the wedding on a few days' leave to visit her brother in Lucknow.

Gavin had told Helen, shortly after she arrived from England, that Isabel had been Maria's lady's maid but that he had kept her on as the housekeeper after his wife's death, partly because that is what Maria had wished and partly because Isabel needed the money to support her feckless brother. Helen knew now that it was a ruse to keep Isabel by Gavin's side. Had she, by refusing her husband his marital rights, made Isabel even more indispensable to Gavin?

Helen did not wish to see anyone that morning after her wedding night and she crept downstairs before the household was awake to saddle up Sultana. The groom was just awaking to attend to the horses and his surprise to see his master's bride so early, was reflected in his all too obvious astonishment. Helen was, fortunately, unaware of his unspoken thoughts that no Indian bride would leave her wedding bed so early to ride a horse, but then these *Angressi* were all mad!

The ride was invigorating in the cool of the morning but did nothing to dispel Helen's image of the previous night. How easy it would have been to give in to her desire to hold Gavin close in her arms and return his ardour, kiss for kiss and touch for touch. That he was a master in lovemaking, Helen had no doubt. A man like him could enslave a woman and she even felt a little sorry for Isabel de Silva. The little dark, half-caste must have been overwhelmed by the attentions of the handsome British Resident.

Helen had heard that many British men had taken Indian wives and borne children of mixed blood in the early years of the Company. She recalled that a former Resident to the Court of Hyderabad, Lt. Col. James Kirkpatrick, had married a great niece of the Diwan and his close association with the Indians had deterred a pro French faction gaining influence over the British. Then there was the famous Colonel James Skinner who founded the distinguished cavalry regiment, 'Skinner's Horse'. He, too, was the son of a Scots captain serving the East India Company who had married a Rajput woman of noble family. Maria, Gavin's first wife, had Indian blood from her great grandmother.

Now, however, this practice was frowned on, not only by the Army, but also in the Civil Administration. Europeans, whose wives had not joined them in India, still took willing mistresses from among the native population. She could even see the attraction of these Eastern women to a Western male - they were so submissive and learned the arts of loving and serving a man even before they reached puberty.

Whatever Gavin had done in the past, he had no right to inflict his mistress on his wife and for that Helen could not forgive him.

The day was now reaching mid-morning and Helen decided she could not delay her return to the Residency.

A rider was coming up the track she was taking and as he came nearer, she recognised Gavin. He rode his horse across the narrow bridle path to block her escape and anticipating her urge to turn back, leaned forward and restrained Sultana's reigns causing the little animal to shy at these unexpectedly forceful hands.

'Don't pull at her reins; her mouth is so soft,' said Helen, irritably.

'Then sit still while we talk. What was all that about last night? I know you are not a prude or frigid. Is there someone else?' Gavin's dark eyes looked questioningly at her.

Helen smiled bitterly, 'How like a man to believe that a woman who resists his charms must be either a prude, frigid, or in love with someone else. You really have an enormous conceit.'

Gavin's face darkened and he clenched his fingers on his riding whip as if he would like to strike her with it.

'Tell me, Helen, why did you marry me?' he asked in a deceptively soft tone of voice.

'I know why you married me, Gavin. You needed an heir and I was to be that simpering little wife who would be your brood mare.'

This was too much for Gavin, who reached forward and grabbed her shoulders, nearly unseating her.

'You know that that is not the sole reason for our marriage. But tell me, why did you consent to be my wife and what a consummate actress you are

101

to have played so well the part of a loving, delightful fiancée? Answer me!' There was no mistaking the cold anger of the man whose face was so close to hers.

Helen looked deeply into his blazing eyes and after a moment said, 'Perhaps I, too, wanted something from you - a husband, a title and a fortune. Most girls of my age are already married, so your father's offer was very opportune. Don't worry, Sir Gavin, I intend to keep my part of the bargain and give you an heir when, and only when, I am ready.'

Gavin blanched under his tan; he looked as if she had hit him with a sledge hammer. He started to say something but stopped and releasing her reins, wheeled his horse around and galloped back the way he had come. Helen knew she had wounded him deeply and she was glad because of the pain he had caused her.

She wanted desperately to see the old *sunyassi* again to ask him what he had seen in her palm, perhaps even to hear him say that Gavin loved her. The temple was deserted except for a young woman performing some *puja* rite in front of the goddess. Helen remembered reading that this particular Hindu deity was a goddess of fertility.

The woman looked up as Helen came in. Her features were not Indian but more Mongolian, like the hill people of Nepal. Perhaps she was the wife of one of the Ghurka brigade stationed at the fort. Of the *sunyassi* there was no sight, so Helen, not wishing to disturb the rather nervous woman, smiled and left the temple.

Would Sati bless her with the heir she had promised Gavin? She laughed bitterly at her own thoughts and the ridiculous impasse of the situation she had created in her marriage.

Chapter 6

Helen went straight to her room when she returned, hoping she would not have to face Gavin again. As usual after her ride, she stripped down to her underclothes and poured some warm water from a china jug into a wash basin on the marble-topped washstand. She never failed to be surprised how this water was always in her room at the right temperature and exactly in time for her return from her morning ride, almost as if one of the many servants had nothing to do but watch and prepare for her mistress's return.

She was just about to soap a sponge when the door to Gavin's room opened and he stood there, smiling at her dismay and obvious embarrassment. He said impudently, 'Don't look so alarmed, Helen, we are married, but I have not come to force myself on you, simply to wish you adieu before my journey.'

'You are going away, Gavin?' Helen heard herself framing the unnecessary question, as she saw Gavin's eyes wander over her state of déshabillé. White cotton combinations, with broderie anglais frills tied below the knees with baby blue ribbons, were hardly the garment she would have chosen to face her disturbing husband.

He was still smiling as he came towards her and said, 'Yes, I am afraid so; a telegram arrived this morning from the Governor General bringing forward the date of his conference in Simla. I would have asked you to accompany me, but I fear you would not wish to burden yourself with your unwelcome husband.

'I just wanted to give you this invitation from the French Consul to a masked costume ball in a few weeks. I shall, of course, be back to escort you and I believe Rosita has some ideas for our costumes.'

Helen took the gold embossed invitation but noticed Gavin was opening another case containing two, pearl-handled pistols.

'I want you to carry one of these whenever you are out alone on your daily rides. I hope it won't be necessary to use them, but there are a few unsavoury characters wandering these hills. The holsters can be strapped to the front arch of your saddle, cavalry style. I have organised this with the syce.

'Come,' he continued, 'taking her arm and leading her to the open window. 'Show me how good a marksman you are. Aim for that tree.'

'I shall do better than that,' challenged Helen, checking and loading the pistol. 'See those three lemons on that branch? I shall hit the middle one.'

She forgot about her state of undress, not even noticing Gavin's appreciative smile as he stood behind her, arms crossed against his chest, and observed with narrowed eyes, the unconscious wriggle of her shapely derrière as she positioned her knee on the window seat and took aim. The designated lemon exploded and fell with her shot and Helen turned to Gavin with a triumphant smile on her lips.

'Bravo!' exclaimed Gavin, then taking the pistol from Helen's hand, he uncocked it and laid it back in the case.

'You amaze me, Madam French. Which of these women are you really? The intrepid Amazon who can shoot and ride as well as any man, the scientist, the foolish woman who fears she will be an old maid and travels half-way across the world to marry a man she does not love, or this green-eyed siren who can drive a man mad, if he lets her get under his skin? Pity I do not have the time at the moment to find out. But never fear, I shall be back and you have a lot of explaining to do, Lady French.'

His brows lifted sardonically and moving towards her, he cupped her throat in his hand and forced her mouth up to meet his in a bruising kiss. Then he was gone and Helen heard the clatter of horses' hooves in the forecourt below. She slipped on a lace negligee and stood by the window. Ram Das and a *chaprassi* with two pack mules were awaiting Gavin. He ran down the steps and mounted Sultan and then, as if he sensed she was standing at the bedroom window, looked up and gave her a half salute, his lips parting in that audacious, buccaneer's smile, before he spurred Sultan into a brisk canter.

Helen, watching the dust from the horses' flying hooves as the broad back of her husband disappeared from sight, felt her breath catch in her throat and she knew that whatever kind of man Gavin French was, she still loved him with every fibre of her being. Life without him now would be meaningless for her and and she fell to her knees and prayed for his safe return.

Rosita was bursting with eagerness about the masked ball. She had thought of a costume idea - Helen dressed as a flamenco dancer and Gavin as a matador. They would make a striking couple, she thought.

Helen not being inclined to suppress Rosita's excitement, was persuaded by her Spanish friend to take the Residency *phaeton* into the bazaars of Mirapore to find suitable material.

As they drove along, Helen was struck by the many faceted aspects of this city. The beautiful palace rising from the glistening lake, around the banks of which were gardens and marble pavilions. Then behind this gardened embankment stood the tree lined Mall serving the commercial centre of English banks, stores and, incongruously, an English tea shop run by two ladies from Devonshire. Higher up on the hillocks nestled pink and white bungalows, the summer residences of rich Indians and the English.

But it was not to any of these that the gleaming carriage, with dark red leather upholstery and the Company crest emblazoned on its sides, was bound. The road wound down, past the walls of the mosque built by the Nawab's grandfather, to the bazaar in the hollow of the valley, its narrow streets and wooden stalls spreading even beyond the city walls. Here all life seemed to be congregated and the scents of India assailed the nostrils - spices, frying sweetmeats, dung fires. The vendors squatted on the wooden

107

platforms of their stalls offering silks, cottons, coloured saris and jewellery to the passing crowds, whilst women from the fields outside the city spread their fruit and vegetables on sacking, noisily advertising their wares. Half naked children and pariah dogs ran after the *phaeton,* the former soliciting *bucksheesh* and when Helen reached into her purse to throw a few coins to them, her hand was held by Rosita.

'Not now, *querida*, when we are leaving, perhaps, otherwise we will be harassed every step of the way. Ah, here is the shop I was looking for.'

The carriage stopped in front of a larger and brighter shop with a fat *bunia* sitting cross-legged at the door, smoking a *beedi* through his clenched fists. When he saw the two women alight and recognised the Residency crest on their carriage, he came towards them bowing obsequiously and smiled, displaying his red, *pan* - stained teeth.

'How can I be of assistance to the *memsahibs*?'

'I would like to see some blue and dark blue silk satin, black woollen cloth, embroidery silks and gold buttons,' said Rosita, ready to bring all the bargaining power of her race to obtain the best price for these materials.

When at last she was satisfied with her purchases, Helen instructed the driver to return and stop at the Devon tea shop. The smoke from the dung fires, Rosita's haggling and this unfamiliar market had given her a craving for a cup of genuine English tea.

The little tea shop was already full with the wives of English soldiers, all seeking some familiarity in this foreign land. The proprietors, Misses Minto, had come out to India looking for husbands - two of the 'Fishing Fleet' as these hopeful ladies were uncharitably dubbed. The elder and prettier had married a British soldier who had been killed on the North West Frontier and she and her younger sister, reluctant to leave the luxury of British life on the sub-continent, had settled in Mirapore and opened their tea shop. The little shop was a slice of Devon set in the foothills of the Himalayas. It had low wooden beams, gleaming brassware and fresh flowers on the net - curtained window sills and blue checked table cloths. The proprietors served the most delicious cakes and pastries and an assortment of teas in fine English bone china crockery.

On their return to the Residency, a *chaprassi* from the palace was waiting patiently with an invitation from the Begum for Helen to attend her.

Helen wrote her formal acceptance to the invitation on Residency notepaper and handed the envelope to the servant.

The next day, the Residency *phaeton* conveyed Helen across the causeway to another part of the palace. Huge carved wooden doors set in high walls marked the entrance to the seraglio guarded by the fierce Rohilla guards. They examined the invitation handed to them by the driver and then opened the gate to admit the carriage. Beyond the walls was a beautiful garden with fountains, scented shrubs, flower beds and proud peacocks in full display strutting on the manicured lawns. At the end of the drive at the front door, stood the dignified Arab physician, Mahmoud Bin Said. He bowed and touched his breast, mouth and forehead in the formal Arab greeting saying, *'Alsalãm Alaikum'*, to which Helen replied, *'Alaikum Alsalãm*, Doctor.'

'Please follow me, Lady French. As you see, we are now in the harem, the domain of only women and eunuchs.' The Arab doctor laughed, at Helen's unspoken question, and explained that apart from the Royal family, he alone as the Court physician (although an 'entire' as he laughingly put it) was permitted into this cloistered seraglio with its scented gardens, inner courts, fountains and marble pavilions. At the entrance to a covered passageway leading to one of these inner courtyards stood a tall, hairless Ethiopian dressed in a rich gold silk tunic and baggy pants, with black kohl outlining his eyes and a curved dagger tucked into a jewelled belt. His voice when he spoke was high-pitched, although unlike most of the other eunuchs Helen had passed on her way though the harem, the Chief Eunuch was not corpulent.

Bowing low to the guests, this noble personage, who introduced himself simply as 'Ibrahim' said, 'Please come this way; Her Highness awaits you.'

They followed the eunuch across a paved courtyard with a fountain at its centre gushing rose-scented water from the mouth of a golden dolphin. Coloured fretwork lanterns were suspended from trees and pillars surrounding the walled garden, which at night, Helen guessed, would create a magical ambience. The soft music of a sitar emanated from the marble pavilion to which the eunuch was leading them. When he stepped aside at the open, carved sandalwood door, Helen saw a beautiful room - marble floors covered with rich Turkish carpets and red and gold cushions strewn against the walls. Seated on a gold upholstered divan raised on a platform, was a striking gray-haired women dressed in a white silk *kurtha* and pantaloons. Over her head she had draped a long, white silk scarf anchored with a diamond circlet and Helen guessed that this was the Queen Mother, the Begum Shalima. The Begum's beautiful unlined skin belied her age, only her blue veined, brown speckled hands identified her advancing years, but it was her eyes which held one's attention. The colour of agates, they gazed out on the world with the unseeing stare of the blind.

The musician of the sitar was an elfin-faced, raven-haired girl of about fifteen, sitting at the feet of the Begum. The young girl's beauty was a mirror image of the Begum as she must have looked in her youth and even before they were introduced, Helen guessed that this was Muna, the daughter of Prince Hassan and the great granddaughter of the Dowager Begum.

'Welcome, Lady French, it was good of you to visit me,' said the Begum in singsong English. A gilt, high-backed chair had been brought into the room by one of the servants. Princess Muna placed this opposite the enthroned Begum and with a smile indicated that Helen should be seated.

111

'As you will observe. I am almost blind but if you do not mind, Lady French, Princess Muna will describe you to me,' said the Begum.

Helen was embarrassed when she heard the young Princess extol her beauty, but seeing Muna's mischievous smile, guessed that she was often called upon to perform this unusual task.

'Then I am pleased, for Sir Gavin is an outstanding man and deserves a beautiful wife. Unlike so many of your countrymen, he is without prejudice and loves this country and its people. What are your impressions of India and Mirapore in particular, Lady French? I understand from my son, that you come from a place called Soosix in England.'

'Sussex, a county in the Southern part of the British Isles, Your Highness. As for my impressions of India, from what I have observed on my journey to Mirapore from Bombay, it is a fascinating country and one which I have been warned gets into the blood of every visitor. As for Mirapore, my first impression from the mountain ridge overlooking the valley was of a veritable garden of Eden,' replied Helen.

'You say India gets into the visitors' blood, Lady French: but the British are no longer just visitors - they are our virtual rulers. But will they ever really become Indian? I have heard that they live in their cantonments, their forts and their bungalows and carry on their English way of life as they would in your Soosix, segregated from the people of India.'

Helen was surprised at these almost critical words spoken in the Begum's soft, singsong voice as her blind eyes stared straight ahead and she felt compelled to answer, especially as she knew Gavin worked so hard for the good of the State to which he was appointed Resident.

'It is natural that foreign communities tend to cling together in a country which is not their own. In England we, too, have Jewish, Chinese and even Arab quarters in our cities. There are, however, many English, like the two ladies who run the tea shop in Mirapore, who have made India their home and have not returned to live in England and many of our famous soldiers have married Indian ladies.'

'What will the British do for India? We have had many conquerors, from the Harapans and Arayas to the Moghuls and each has put their stamp on this country,' continued the Begum.

'I believe you will find that unlike the great Moghuls, whose Courts were excessively opulent and who spent vast amounts on their armies and monuments, the British, although not entirely altruistic, will do a great deal more for the territories they administer. Give us time and you will see - already we have begun to build a railway system that will link all of India and there are universities and hospitals in the main cities. I am sure you will agree, your Highness, that our system of government has brought stability to a country formerly torn by the internecine struggles of warring rulers. But I hope you have not invited me to discuss politics, your Highness: I am the

113

Resident's wife, not the Resident,' replied Helen, politely, but firmly refusing to continue a conversation along these lines.

The Begum smiled and clapped her hands for a servant to bring refreshments, then she said, 'I see you are a woman of courage and integrity, Lady French. Your husband, Sir Gavin, is one of the few Englishman who understands India and his advice is invaluable to my son, the Nawab. Tell me, what should we do to help our own people?' enquired the Begum.

'It is not for me to advise your Highness, but when I was in England I found that clinics for the poor, who could not afford medical fees, was one way we could bring relief to the under-privileged.'

'Will you help us to set up such a clinic, Doctor French, especially for the peasant women and children? It is something my good Mahmoud Bin Said has always wished to establish,' said the Begum, turning her blind eyes in the direction of the Arab physician, who sat cross-legged and upright on a cushioned divan, observing with dignified silence the exchange between the two women.

'I will be honoured to be of assistance,' said Helen, wondering if the irascible old lady's request was a test of Helen's personal altruism.

'Good, then that is settled. Mahmoud Bin Said will contact you. Come, let me offer you some refreshment.'

Princess Muna handed Helen a silver cup of cold spiced milk and a little plate of sugary sweetmeats, smiling sweetly at the English woman. The conversation turned to Helen's life in England, the English Royal family and, finally, the movement for women's suffrage in that strange country across the seas.

Before she let Helen leave, Begum Shalima had one last request.

'Will you, Lady French, allow my granddaughter to assist in the clinic? She will need to be veiled, but it is my wish that she should learn her responsibilities as a princess and one day a prince's wife.'

Helen liked the little princess and was only too pleased to agree to this request, but she wondered what role the young woman would be allowed to play in any forthcoming marriage to a strict Muslim prince.

Before she left the palace, she handed a printed copy of Lord Lister's paper on antiseptic surgery to Mahmoud Bin Said, which had been sent to her from England by David Burton. The Arab doctor was very touched at Helen's thoughtfulness and when he escorted her to her carriage, he bowed and said, 'It will be a privilege to work with you, Doctor, and I hope there will be many opportunities for further discussions on subjects concerning our mutual interest. *Assalãm Alaikum* and may Allah go with you.'

The days before Gavin's return passed quickly and Helen had to admit to herself that she was longing to see him again. She accompanied the Arab physician on many occasions to inspect the warehouse behind the Mosque

115

that was to be converted into their Clinic for the Poor and together they drew up a list of all that was required to equip the little hospital.

Money was so readily available from the Nawab's coffers that Helen could not help but write to the Burtons, 'When I think of how we struggled to equip and maintain our little Mission Clinic, I feel somewhat embarrassed to write to you about my new venture. Suffice it to say that these people have a great need. Poverty on the Indian sub-continent is on a far greater scale than on our own little island and these people have to suffer the ravages of epidemics, floods, earthquakes and famines with little or no personal resources. What horrifies me, too, is the mutilation of some children in the poorest families to attract alms. This is something both my Arab colleague, Mahmoud Bin Said, and I are determined to stop, at least as far as Mirapore is concerned.'

Isabel de Silva returned from her holiday looking thinner and more troubled. Her brother had lost his job in Lucknow and was now seeking work in Mirapore. Helen remembered that Gavin had told her that Vincent de Silva was on no account to be admitted to the Residency. Maria, Gavin's first wife, had thought that he was light-fingered and had noticed several valuable ornaments missing after his calls on his sister. Helen felt no need, however, to remind Isabel of this ban for the moment, unless she had reason to believe it was being flouted at any time.

That night Helen awoke suddenly, hearing again the strange chanting she had heard on her first night in Mirapore. She got out of bed and leaned out of the open window. The garden was bathed in the bright moonlight of a full moon and once again the faint smell of incense drifted into Helen's room and she saw a glimmer of light through the pierced screen of the little tomb.

She quickly covered her nightdress with a travelling coat and tying a scarf around her hair crept down the stairs and out into the garden. As she made her way to the monument, she noticed that there was no sign of the *chowkidar* and made a mental note to question him in the morning. The aromatic smell of incense was stronger as she approached the monument and she reached out a hand to try the door.

Strong fingers gripped her wrist and Helen startled, turned to see Isabel standing beside her, but an Isabel so different in appearance to the little housekeeper. Her hair was tousled and wet and hung about her shoulders in black, snake-like strands; her diaphanous sari only just covered her naked body. But it was her eyes that were so disturbing - black pools with strange pinpoints of light - staring at Helen with undisguised malevolence. Helen gasped, suddenly afraid, 'Isabel, is that you, where did you come from?' and Helen noticed again the vicious strength of the claw-like hand which gripped her wrist.

The woman laughed a deep throaty chuckle and her red lips parted to reveal sharp pointed teeth. The clouds suddenly obscured the moon and in

117

the momentary darkness, the figure before Helen seemed to grow and grow and the throaty chuckle became a rasping cackle.

Then, just as suddenly, the cloudy veil over the moon was lifted and the woman before Helen was indeed only Isabel de Silva, who looked anxiously at Helen and whispered, 'I saw you come out of the house and I was worried that you might be sleep-walking, madam. Why are you trying to open the door of the *chaatri* at this time of night?'

'I thought I heard chanting coming from within and a gleam of light and I can still smell some sort of incense,' said Helen, watching the woman closely.

'The chanting you heard was probably made by pilgrims going to the tomb of Sita in the forest and also the smell of incense was from their lamps. As for the gleam of light, look through the window again, it is quite dark inside, but it may have been a reflection of the moonlight on the white marble,' explained Isabel, once again in her normal singsong voice. Helen wondered if she had indeed imagined the whole thing, but she went back to the house, closely followed by Isabel, with a feeling of disquiet that she had been in the presence of something really evil.

The next morning Helen decided not to mention the matter to Rosita, who was too busy with the preparations of their costumes for the masked ball that evening.

Rosita's skill as a needlewoman had produced a beautiful, Spanish flamenco gown in sky blue satin, cut low over the shoulders and close fitting to the hips, from which the skirt flared into rows of dark and light blue flounces, stopping just above the ankles. When Helen tried on the dress, Rosita produced her guitar and to the rhythm of the flamenco, had Helen whirling and snapping her heels with all the passion of the dance, which the Spanish woman had taught her beloved foster child years ago in England.

So absorbed was Helen in the intricacies of the dance, that she did not notice the door open and the tall figure of her husband enter the room, a burning glint in his dark eyes as he observed the beautiful dancer. Helen, oblivious to everything but the passion of the flamenco, twirled and moved seductively from her hips. She raised her lovely arms outlining the curve of her full breasts and stamped her feet to the beat of the castanets, her glorious hair flying about her shoulders as she moved her head from side to side. Then, unintentionally, the movements of the dance catapulted her into the body of the enraptured man who caught her in his arms, holding her fast in their circle.

'Gavin!' Helen exclaimed in surprise, momentarily unable to mask the joy in her voice and in her eyes.

He was laughing now, smiling at her confusion and saying, 'So, a lovely Spanish gypsy has invaded my home, Rosita. Where did she come from with all that fire and beauty? I thought I had married a reserved Englishwoman.'

'Don't tease me, Gavin,' chided Helen, extricating herself reluctantly from his encircling arms before he became aware of the rapid beating of her heart, which was only partly caused by the exertions of the dance. 'This is my costume for the masked ball and you should see how handsome your own is.'

'You must try it on after lunch, Gavin, I may have to make some adjustments,' said Rosita.

I'll certainly do that, Rosita, but first let me remove the grime of my journey with a hot bath and I promise to be your patient model immediately afterwards,' said Gavin following his blushing wife with his dark eyes as she left the room.

Lunch was a genial meal for Helen, seated opposite her husband, who seemed determined to put their differences behind him. He had bought presents for them all, a beautiful lapis lazuli necklace and earrings for Helen, thin gold bangles for Rosita and a box of aromatic oils for Isabel's massage therapy.

'Have you benefited from one of Isabel's massages yet, Helen? She is an expert masseuse, and will do your muscles a power of good, especially after a long ride,' said Gavin, as if to explain the gift he had bought for the Goanese woman.

'Isabel has offered her services, but I have not yet had the need,' replied Helen, unable to dismiss the disturbing picture of her handsome husband stripped naked for the subtle administration of Isabel de Silva's skills. She felt, once again that gnawing pain in her diaphragm which she had experienced that night when she had observed Isabel leaving the guest house and she remembered, with clarity, the horrible apparition of the night before. The room started to spin and Helen felt herself slumping sideways, but before she touched the floor she heard a chair being overturned violently and Gavin's strong arms encompass her.

'My God, darling, what is the matter; are you ill?' Gavin was asking anxiously and as he spoke, he picked her up and carried her to a chaise lounge near the window. Helen had not quite lost consciousness and through the mists of her dizziness, she heard him telling Isabel to send Ram Das immediately to the fort for the army doctor.

'No, no, please don't bother Doctor Graham, Gavin. I am a doctor, myself, and know that I am suffering only from slight vertigo. I know what has brought it on. Please let me go to my room. I'll be better soon,' argued Helen faintly.

'What is it? You are not the fainting type, Helen. You must be ill,' said an unconvinced Gavin.

'It is only a stomach upset from which I have been suffering lately. Perhaps something I have eaten,' said Helen quietly.

121

'She is doing too much, Gavin. Every day taking long rides and spending so much time at the Clinic, but she is too stubborn to listen to me,' complained a distraught Rosita trying to hide her concern under a barrage of complaints.

Gavin insisted on carrying Helen up the stairs to her bedroom and laid her gently on the bed. Then reluctantly, on Rosita's insistence, he left the room. Rosita drew the drapes to shut out the sunlight in the hope that the darkness would encourage Helen to sleep.

'You need rest, *querida mia*, especially if you are to be radiant for this evening's masked ball,' Rosita said anxiously, watching Helen's closed lids and wondering why her dear child had felt so faint. Her constitution had always been as strong as an ox and it was too early for her to be *enciente*.

Chapter 7

A desperate need to see her friend the Sunyassi again, drove Helen to leave the Residency before the household was awake. She saddled up Sultana and rode out to the little temple.

It was empty: there were only the flickering lights of the clay lamps and the Goddess garlanded with flowers sitting impassively on her dais. Helen was about to turn and leave the little temple, when a figure of a man emerged from behind the statue. She was startled at first until she recognised that he was dressed in European clothes. His well oiled, black hair was parted in the middle and he had a thin moustache above equally thin lips.

Further examination of his badly tailored linen suit and dusky complexion convinced her that the man was not European, but Eurasian.

'Good morning, Lady French,' said the man, bowing from the waist, 'At last we meet. I am Vincent de Silva, the brother of your housekeeper, Isabel. Are you interested in temples?'

Helen now noticed the resemblance to Isabel in the man's dark skin and features, but Vincent de Silva's eyes were light grey and close set and his thin-lipped mouth was curved in an insolent smile.

Before she had time to answer, he took her arm in a strong grip and propelled her towards the goddess's statue behind which there appeared to be another entrance to the temple. He was saying, 'You must let me show you the temple of the Goddess Kali, which is not far from here but in a cave behind the waterfall in the forest.'

Helen pulled back and said impatiently, 'No, I do not wish to visit any other temple today. I must return to the Residency now.'

The man's grip tightened even more on her arm as he leaned towards her, 'Kunkali insists that I bring you to visit her. Come, we must not disappoint this particular goddess - her wrath can be terrible.'

'How dare you try to force me, Mr. de Silva. Unhand me at once!' shouted Helen angrily, determined not to show any fear in the face of this repulsive man.

'You heard what the *memsahib* said,' a voice behind them spoke and Helen turned, relieved to see the wiry figure of her *Sunyassi* standing at the door of the temple, a stout *lathi* in his hand. Not taking his brilliant eyes off the Goan man, the *Sunyassi* pointed a bony finger at him and chanted some words in a dialect, which Helen did not recognise.

Vincent de Silva paled, immediately releasing Helen's arm and fell to his knees in front of the holy man, a look of abject terror on his face. 'Please do not curse me, holy man, I meant no harm to the *memsahib*, but only wanted to show her Kunkali's temple.'

Then he scuttled away by the exit behind the idol and Helen, relieved by his departure, rushed towards the *Sunyassi* and embraced him like a long lost friend. Almost at once she realised how presumptuous her over enthusiastic welcome must appear to this quiet, dignified man.

'Oh, forgive me, holy Sahib, for the liberty of embracing you, but I had come here for the sole purpose of seeing you and when that horrible man appeared and you came to my rescue, I admit it was as if an old friend had intervened.'

'I am glad you consider me an old friend, my child. I have thought a great deal about you since our last meeting and hoped to see you once more before I continue my journey to those snow-capped heights. There I hope to find *shruti,*' said the old man, smiling and pointing to the high peaks of the Himalayas, visible through the open door of the temple.

'But must you go on that long journey so soon and I am so afraid the cold of the mountains will be hazardous for you. Why not rest for a while before leaving Mirapore as my guest at the Residency,' pleaded Helen, not even stopping to think what Gavin would say when she introduced him to her *Sunyassi.*

'You are very kind and I thank you from the bottom of my heart, but I have already wasted a great deal of time and must be on my way. The cold will not harm me, child, and I will stay at a Buddhist monastery until I am well acclimatised, before venturing out for long periods of contemplation. Come, let me escort you back to the city.'

Once again the holy man walked alongside Helen, now mounted on Sultana.

'There is something which I do not understand, holy *Sahib*. Who is the Goddess 'Kunkali' and why is she so important to that Goanese man?' questioned Helen.

'Kunkali is another name for the Goddess Kali and means "Man Eater", because of her alleged ferocious lust for blood sacrifices. She is also known as Bhowani, Durga and to the Moslem sect of Thuggees, Fatima. The legend is that she is the consort of Lord Shiva, the Destroyer and Regenerator and she defeated the demon Raktavija and drank his blood, which gave her that black appearance. The ancient cult of Thuggees sacrificed to Kali with their murderous rumels and pickaxes, preying on travellers, but your own Major General Sleeman was responsible for hunting them down and destroying them,' explained the holy man.

'Do you believe in this deity, holy *Sahib*?' asked Helen.

'Not in the goddess, herself, but in the evil which is perpetrated in her name by superstitious men who believe they can evade their *Karma* by human sacrifice. It is not unlike the cult of devil worship in Christian countries.'

Helen was tempted to tell the *Sunyassi* about the alleged curse on Gavin's family, but her friend did not need to be troubled by these pedestrian matters when he had his own spiritual journey to make, a journey

126

she feared which would not be easy at his age. Tears glistened in the old man's eyes as he gave the Englishwoman his final blessing and Helen overcome with sadness, watched him disappear up the forest path with a feeling of deep loss - something pure and beautiful was walking out of her life.

The masked ball, and their preparations for it, were from another world to that of her *Sunyassi*, the Goddess Kali and Vincent de Silva. When she was dressed in her beautiful flamenco dress, she clasped the lapis lazuli necklace about her neck and fitted the earrings to her earlobes. Gavin could have chosen their colour and design precisely for this dress, which they matched so beautifully,

He was waiting in the study with Rosita when Helen came downstairs and when he saw her standing at the door, surveying his handsome figure in the striking costume of a Spanish bullfighter, he grinned like a sheepish, little boy dressed, unwillingly, in his Sunday best. Helen chuckled, remembering how his father, Sir Terence, had hated dressing up for their masked balls at Charnwood Hall and she suddenly had an urge to clasp Gavin to her and kiss his little boy expression, so different to his customary air of self confidence.

'So, Helen, I look as ridiculous as I feel,' said an embarrassed Gavin.

'But of course not, Gavin. The costume is splendid and makes you look handsomer than ever,' countered Helen quickly.

'Then what do you find so amusing, young lady?'

'Oh, Gavin, it is only because your expression reminded me of your father, who hated wearing fancy dress, unlike my own parent who loved the opportunity to dress up - the difference, I suppose, between the Anglo Saxon and Scottish temperaments.'

'Your husband is the handsomest *torrero* I have ever seen, Helen, and in that costume, with his dark hair and sunburned skin, Gavin could pass for one of my fellow countrymen,' said Rosita, somewhat crossly.

The costume was indeed splendid. Rosita had copied it from a painting of a famous Spanish matador, which hung on her sitting room wall - black velvet knee breeches, with gold and silver embroidered panels at the sides and a heavily embroidered, velvet shell jacket which fitted Gavin's broad shoulders perfectly. Even the pink hose, flat leather pumps and red cape were an exact replica of the bullfighter's costume in the portrait.

The drive, and the road in front of the French Consulate, were packed with carriages and the usual throng of onlookers crowded around the gates watching these strange Europeans arriving for their *tamasha*. Helen wondered what thoughts were passing behind their dark, phlegmatic faces. They and their forefathers had, of course, witnessed even more splendid displays organised for Moghul rulers and feudal princes, but this was different, because these people from across the seas were so dissimilar to

Indians. Is that what they were thinking, mused Helen, as the carriage door was opened and Gavin helped her out?

The French Consulate was smaller than the Residency, but it was beautifully appointed and the interior tastefully decorated according to French traditions.

Blanche and her husband were standing at the entrance to the large ballroom to greet their guests. The Comtesse was dressed in the Empire style favoured by the Empress, Josephine, and her husband, the Comte (too tall for Napoleon he told his guests) was dressed in the rich scarlet robes of Cardinal Richelieu, the eminent ecclesiast and virtual ruler of France in the reign of Louis XIII.

Their Scottish friends, too, were magnificently costumed: Agnes Cameron was dressed in the sixteenth century dress of Mary, Queen of Scots and her husband as the hapless Lord Darnley: John MacGregor had donned the wild, thirteenth century Highland dress of the brave Sir William Wallace, who defeated Edward I and, ultimately, was so cruelly executed by the vindictive 'Longshanks'.

The Spaniards, Don Hernandez and his family, were extremely effusive about Gavin and Helen's choice of Spanish costumes and seemed to take their choice of fancy dress as a personal compliment to Spain. They, themselves, wore the fifteenth century Spanish court dress of Isabella and Ferdinand of Spain and their daughter, Pura, the gown of the Infanta.

The costumes were all so marvellous and Helen could imagine the little Indian tailors, cutting and stitching till early dawn in their ill-lit shops, to produce these strange clothes, the like of which they had never seen except in the history books loaned to them by their European customers.

The music of a waltz was playing and Gavin whisked Helen into his arms, holding her closer than the dance dictated.

'You are looking so lovely to-night, Helen; a different hairstyle, I see,' he whispered in her ear.

'Thank you, Gavin. Rosita dressed it in the Spanish style so that I would look less like a gypsy and more like a Spanish lady,' she smiled, alluding to his remark when he had come upon her, so unexpectedly, dancing the flamenco.

Helen realised that Gavin had not failed to notice the glossy, heavy coil of hair braided at the nape of her neck in a Spanish style chignon, into which Rosita had entwined blue silk flowers.

'The style suits you,' said Gavin softly and Helen was aware of his eyes on her neck, her bare shoulders and the cleft between her breasts.' The blue of the dress makes your eyes look deeper and almost turquoise. Do you know you take my breath away?' he murmured and when the music stopped, he seemed reluctant to let her go.

Helen, too, could not fail to observe how Gavin stood out from all the men in the room with his dark good looks and striking costume and she found herself suddenly jealous of any attention he paid to other women, particularly the flirtatious Blanche. Even young Pura, shyly smiling and looking up at him with those limpid dark eyes, as he guided her in the steps of a dance, seemed to pose a threat and Helen felt suddenly she must get some fresh air, or scream.

Out on the balcony, the Indian night was cooler and Helen looked up to the dark skies and saw the same stars which twinkled in the firmament over England, but here they seemed brighter. Crickets chirped and bats swooped amongst the mango trees in the garden and high above the city stood the magnificent backdrop of the Himalayas whose everlasting snows had beckoned to her *Sunyassi* to find his *shruti.*

A figure detached itself from the far corner of the balcony and came towards her. It was Prince Ali who was representing the Nawab at the French Consul's banquet. Prince Ali was dressed in a sartorially cut English dinner suit, eschewing any fancy dress, although Helen supposed his European apparel was just as much 'costume' to this Moslem prince.

'Ah, the beautiful Lady French. You seemed so lost in thought, I did not want to disturb you,' said the prince and Helen wondered how long he had been observing her.

'Good evening, Your Highness, I trust you are enjoying the ball. I met your mother a few days ago at the invitation of Comtesse de Colbert when she was taking tea at the Consulate,' said Helen, offering this information for

131

no reason other than to hide her mounting embarrassment, because Prince Ali was now standing so close behind her with his hands resting on either side of her on the balcony balustrade.

'Yes, she told me and she is quite entranced by your beauty, as I am at this moment. English women have always fascinated me and if I was not a good Moslem, I would like to take a woman such as you for my wife. Do you think I could do that, Lady French; after all my mother is European?'

Helen laughed nervously. 'It is something for you and your family to decide, Prince Ali. Do not ask me such a question, please.' Helen tried to move away from the circle of the Prince's arms, but he had now dropped his hands from the balustrade and wound them around her waist, drawing her nearer to him until she could feel his hot breath, disagreeably well laced with alcohol, on the nape of her neck.

'Helen, this is my dance, I believe,' and once again her saviour, John MacGregor, had come to her rescue.

At the sound of his voice, the rather inebriated Prince dropped his arms and moved unsteadily away from Helen.

'Of course, John, I have not forgotten. Come, let us go in,' and Helen took the Scotman's arm with an air of relief.

'That drunken oaf will get his just deserts one of these days. It is only because I did not want to cause a diplomatic incident, that I did not punch him on his long nose. Just as well Gavin did not see his over familiarity with you,' muttered an angry John as they joined the dancers in the ballroom.

Helen looked up into the blue eyes of her Scottish friend and smiled affectionately and it was this look that Gavin saw as he looked around the room to seek her. The bright room, the music and wine and all the other guests seemed to vanish from his sight; all he saw was his lovely wife smiling gently into another man's eyes. A searing pain clutched Gavin's heart and he felt a raging jealousy, which he had never experienced before in his life.

He came towards them, his face grim and said hoarsely, 'It is time we went home, Helen. You will excuse us, John, my wife has not been well lately and has had enough excitement for one night.'

Then taking an astounded Helen's arm, Gavin propelled her towards their hosts and in a mood of forced control, he made the customary polite exchanges with the Comte and Comtesse, before bundling Helen away and into their carriage.

Coldly furious, he sat beside her, his fingers clenched into fists and his head turned away from her.

'What is the matter with you, Gavin? I am not ill at all and you were so impolite bundling me away from the ball like a naughty child, even before supper was served. What have I done?' said Helen, wondering if he had, in fact, seen the Prince's unwanted embrace on the balcony.

'Done, nothing yet, at least not with me, but as long as I am present you will refrain from flirting with your Scottish lover,' growled her husband.

'Flirting with John MacGregor? Are you mad? He had just rescued me from the embarrassing attentions of a drunken Prince Ali when I went out on the balcony for some fresh air. If you had not been so taken with all the other women, you would have noticed my plight,' Helen said angrily, not realising that she, too, was giving vent to her own jealousy.

'So you blame me for your flighty behaviour, Lady French. I have ample proof of your continued meetings with the Scotsman whilst I have been away and of his desire for you. What was it he said the day he delivered you to the Residency; let me think. Ah yes, "*Au revoir*, beautiful lady. I shall see you on your wedding day, but remember if you change your mind..."

'Who told you that?' said a furious Helen, surprised, and then she remembered the words John MacGregor had spoken to her on the day of her arrival in Mirapore. Only Rosita and Isabel de Silva had heard those words and Rosita would not have repeated them to Gavin.

'So you listen to servant's gossip, Sir Gavin French. Did this gossip also tell you that John MacGregor has escorted me to the fort on only a few occasions whilst you were away and those were at the request of Lady Agnes to meet the other British women? I usually ride alone!' emphasised a now seething Helen.

They had arrived at the Residency and Gavin followed Helen into the reception hall. She had just put one foot on the stairs to go up to her bedroom, when he caught her arm and turned her around to face him.

'You are angry with me, Helen,' Gavin said with some surprise.

'What do you expect, accusing me of flirting and worse, and making such a fool of us both in front of all those people!' Helen's eyes glared at her husband, leaving him in no doubt that he had over-played his role of aggrieved spouse.

Gavin's mood softened and his lips twisted into a fleeting smile, 'Please forgive me, Helen. I promise I will not embarrass you again.' Then drawing her into his arms, he kissed her gently on the top of her head and held her close for a moment before he turned on his heel and went out into the night.

Helen lay awake turning over the scene with Gavin and wondering where he had gone at this time of the night. He had displayed jealousy, which made her wonder if he loved her after all - but no, his masculine pride would insist on her fidelity, even though he, himself, was faithless. Then she heard him enter his room and his footsteps stop outside her door, but he didn't come in and she soon fell asleep dreaming that she was sitting on an Himalayan peak, calling to her *Sunyassi* to help her find her love.

Helen saw very little of Gavin during the following weeks. They met at dinner and he was polite but distant.

The Clinic for the Poor was now open and Helen and the Arab doctor were busy with their patients. Helen had taken it upon herself, with the aid of Princess Muna as translator, to instruct the women in hygiene and child care, especially the young mothers.

The little princess was a charming pupil and quick to learn the skills of nursing. She seemed to enjoy this break from the harem where her only companions were the corpulent eunuchs and spoilt harem women, with nothing to do all day but pamper themselves and gossip.

'Helen, can I ask you a favour?' said the princess at the end of one day when they were alone in the surgery.

'Yes, of course, how can I help?' enquired Helen.

'Oh, it is only that I would like to come riding with you some time. I am a good horsewoman, but am permitted to ride only in the grounds of the seraglio.'

'Well, if Begum Shalima has no objection, I would be glad of your company, but you must ask her first,' said Helen not wishing to break any rules of purdah.

The Begum agreed, provided that Helen always accompanied the princess, who must wear a veil and the women would have to be escorted by an armed Rohilla guard.

And so it was that Helen found herself riding occasionally with an excited Princess Muna and a fearsome Rohilla guard, the latter carrying a carbine and ammunition belt and the curved *talwar*.

It was only on their third ride that Helen noticed Princess Muna's interest in the guard. The man that usually accompanied them was young, handsome and obviously part Caucasian, because of his fair skin, grey eyes and light brown hair streaked with blond.

Helen noticed Princess Muna drop her veil deliberately when the guard assisted her to mount and although she recovered it immediately, it was long enough for the poor boy to catch a glimpse of those lovely eyes and elfin-faced beauty. The princess alternated between imperious haughtiness and womanly wiles towards the smitten guard and Helen, although amused by the girl's teenage antics, was slightly alarmed. A love affair between these two, even if it was conducted only by eye signals and smiles, could never be and Helen was forced to warn Princess Muna that she was not being fair to the young man, 'Perhaps, another guard should accompany us,' she warned.

'Oh no, please, Helen. He will be sent away if we complain. I promise not to tease him, but he is so handsome and there are no beautiful men in the seraglio,' little Muna pleaded and Helen did not have the heart to spoil the princess's harmless fun. Let her dream whilst she can, because soon she will be forced into a marriage not of her choosing.

Princess Muna was as good as her word, although Helen noticed how the young guard's fingers lingered on her little foot whenever he helped her mount and one day when the princess had organised a picnic for them by the lake, Muna thoughtfully chose some choice savouries and sweetmeats. These she arranged carefully on a silver plate and with a glass of *lassi,* handed them, personally, to the guard who sat some distance away from the two women.

She was rewarded with a flashing smile and a lingering look of love from the young man's grey eyes.

The next day the Nawab, Prince Hassan and Gavin paid a visit to the clinic. Helen was in the operating theatre performing a tonsillectomy on a young boy and it was left to the Arab physician to escort his visitors around.

'Where is my wife?' enquired Gavin.

'Ah, she is in surgery. I leave her to perform most of the surgical procedures as she is a first-class surgeon and more recently qualified than I am. Would you like to observe, Sir Gavin?' enquired Mahmoud Bin Said.

He led them to an annex separated from the operating theatre by a glass wall. Helen was bent over her patient, with Princess Muna and another Eurasian nurse assisting.

Gavin watched with admiration as his wife performed this delicate operation with deft fingers and a confidence worthy of a surgeon with many years' experience.

That night after dinner Gavin joined her on the verandah for coffee and lighting his cigar, he drew up a rattan chair near Helen and said, 'I visited your clinic today and saw you operating on a young boy. Your skill as a surgeon impressed me, Helen. I have never seen a woman surgeon in action before.'

'No, I expect you will not see too many of us around. There is a great deal of male opposition to women practising medicine in England, but here in India and amongst the poor at home, the sex of the medical practitioner is irrelevant.' replied Helen, rather brusquely, remembering the prejudice she had encountered in the past.

Gavin leaned forward and touched her knee. 'I hope I did not sound patronising, sweetheart. I have nothing but admiration for your skill and I know Mahmoud bin Said is deeply impressed. Tell me about your training and the work you did with the Burtons at the Missionary Clinic.'

Helen found herself relating all her experience at medical school and the difficulty she had as the only woman on the course and, subsequently, in finding a post as a surgeon in a hospital, despite her first-class medical degree.

'It was only my work in Father's practice and the Burton's Clinic that gave me the clinical experience I needed so desperately,' concluded Helen, suddenly realising that she had monopolised the conversation

'Oh, forgive me, Gavin, I am talking non-stop about myself. Tell me about your early years here in India and … and your marriage to Maria. She was very beautiful, I believe, but I do not see a portrait of her in the Residency. Please talk about her, if you wish, I will not mind. I can imagine her death was devastating to you so soon after your marriage,' whispered Helen, desperately wanting to know more about this woman, about whom no one spoke.

Gavin stood up and walked to the verandah balustrade and for some moments he said nothing, only stared out into the dark garden, drawing on his cigar. Helen wondered whether she had raised a subject that was still too raw for him to discuss.

Then he turned to face her and said quietly, 'Maria … her death was a tragedy waiting to happen, because she insisted on visiting the bazaars to paint Indian women. She was an artist, you know. As for a portrait of her, she did paint a self-portrait but it was never hung because … well, it was not suitable,' said Gavin enigmatically, making Helen even more curious about the lovely Maria, but she sensed that Gavin did not wish to pursue the conversation, because he turned once more to look out into the night.

A deep sadness clutched at Helen's heart, for Gavin, for the tragic Maria and for herself, who would always be second-best in his heart. She rose from her chair and walked to her husband's side and impulsively placed her hand on his bare, muscled forearm exposed by his rolled up shirt sleeve.

'I am so sorry, Gavin, if I have inadvertently upset you. I hoped that by talking about Maria, it might relieve your pain. Please forgive me,' said Helen her voice breaking.

Gavin turned again towards his wife and lifting her chin with one finger, noticed by the light of the oil lanterns, the tears shining in her lovely eyes, 'Are you crying for a woman you never knew, my darling? Of course, you have not upset me. Maria died as she had lived and we were relieved when death released her, because the smallpox would have left her disfigured with scars she could not have borne. But you, my love, have had a long day and I noticed dark circles under your eyes at dinner. Please take more care of yourself, little sweetheart.'

Then drawing her shawl more closely across her shoulders, he gently guided her into the hall.

'I have some reports to write in my study, but you must go to bed, Helen. I'll call Rosita to attend to you.'

'No, don't bother her, Gavin. I can manage and my Rosita, too, needs her sleep. Goodnight,' and Helen reached up and kissed Gavin gently on his lips. She heard his sharp intake of breath and knew, as she walked up the stairs, that he was watching her.

Did he, Helen wondered, think of his first wife, Maria, when he looked at her?

Chapter 8

Gavin was away again, this time in the Punjab. The Company used his diplomatic skills in more areas than Mirapore and he was often called away, sometimes at short notice.

Helen, determined to find out more about Gavin's first wife, rode over to the Fort to play bridge with Lady Agnes and some of the officers' wives. After tea, she drew Agnes Cameron aside and asked her if she had met Maria.

Looking at her curiously, Agnes replied, 'We met her parents, of course, when we first came out to India and James succeeded her father as Commander of this Fort. Maria was already married to Gavin, but we saw little of her. She preferred to keep very much to herself and then she contracted that terrible scourge of smallpox. It was all very sad and after her death, we took Gavin under our wing. We were so happy that he decided to marry again and when we met you, my dear, we knew he had made the right choice. There, I do prattle on, don't I?'

Helen rode back to Mirapore, escorted by some of the soldiers who were relieving the guard at the Residency.

A few days later on her return from the clinic, she met Blanche de Colbert in the European commercial centre of Mirapore. 'Ah, the beautiful

Lady French. When are you coming to see me again, Helen? I hear you are busy attending the sores of all those unfortunate natives.'

Helen laughed, knowing that Blanche de Colbert's indifference to the poor was feigned, because the beautiful Creole devoted a great deal of time to a Catholic orphanage on the outskirts of the city.

'Come and have tea with me, Blanche. We are near that delightful tea shop run by the English ladies and I would like to treat you to a real Devon cream tea', invited Helen.

In the cosy little tea shop, the flamboyant Countess quite overwhelmed the little Devon women, who outdid themselves with their delicious cream tea. The scones were freshly baked, the cucumber sandwiches the thinnest cut and the homemade cream cakes the very best. After her second cream cake, Blanche exclaimed, 'Ladies you are ruining my figure with your delicious pastries,' her charm making worthwhile all the culinary efforts of the Devon ladies.

During their conversation, Helen introduced the subject of Maria. Perhaps the Countess could tell her something more about Gavin's first wife.

'Did you know the first Lady French, Blanche? There is no portrait of her in the Residency and Gavin does not often speak of her. Was she very beautiful?'

143

'Beautiful yes, but Gavin never looked at her the way he looks at you, but why this interest in a dead woman, Helen?' quizzed Blanche.

'I am naturally interested because no one speaks of her. Did you know her well?' asked Helen.

I knew her, we all did, but well, *mais non.* She was not easy to know - very, how do you say in English 'secretif' and Sir Gavin, he was *charment* but I think not so in love with her as he is with you.'

'Oh Blanche, you are an incorrigible romantic,' teased Helen, relieved that to the onlooker, at least, Gavin seemed to love her.

A few days later, Helen asked Rosita to find out from Isabel if Maria's portrait was still stored in the Residency.

The little Goanese woman took them to an attic room which had been converted into a studio for Maria. The room was carpeted and a fireplace constructed to warm it in winter. It was clean and looked as if the occupant had only just left, because there was still the scent of oils permeating the room and all the paraphernalia of an artist carefully displayed on shelves. The pictures were housed in zinc lined chests to protect them from dampness and Isabel took each painting out of its covering and displayed it on an easel for Helen and Rosita to view.

There were six in all, five of them depicting nude Indian girls in erotic poses. The sixth was of Maria, herself, half undressed reclining sideways on a studio couch. At her head stood a naked Indian girl waving an enormous peacock feather fan and a second nude girl knelt at the foot of the couch, removing the rest of Maria's undergarments, the portrait already revealing one naked hip. The reclining figure was so beautiful - black, long, straight hair, white skin, small pert breasts and large, dark, elongated eyes in which the artist had caught an expression of sensual languor. Helen gasped. She knew now why the painting could not be hung on the Residency walls. It was far too hedonistic for Victorian society.

'Maria liked painting nudes,' said Isabel, as if trying to explain the eroticism of the oils.

'Did she never paint men and landscapes?' asked Rosita who sounded quite shocked.

'Yes, one painting of two lovers. Here it is,' said Isabel, almost triumphantly producing another picture.

This one, too, was extremely sensual - a naked man and woman entwined in each other's arms on a tiger skin rug. The woman was looking over the man's shoulder and Helen, astonished, recognised Isabel - and the man - although his back was to the artist, that well greased hair with a centre parting was unmistakable.

'Is that your brother with you, Isabel?' asked Helen, trying to disguise the disgust in her voice.

'Yes, the first Lady French wanted two models for the picture and prevailed upon us to pose for her,' answered Isabel quietly.

'Has my husband seen these paintings, Isabel?' asked Helen, wondering why Gavin still allowed them to be stored in the Residency.

'Yes, but only after Maria's death and he wanted them burnt, but they are all that is left of Maria. Please let me keep them. I will remove them from the Residency if you wish,' said a tearful Isabel who had obviously adored her former mistress.

Helen did not have the heart to refuse and was later soundly berated by Rosita, who felt that Gavin's wishes should have been carried out.

'They are well painted, but disgusting and I can understand Gavin not wanting them around. You should respect his wishes, Helen,' said a shocked Rosita, her strict Catholic upbringing unable to accept the hedonistic subjects.

'We must not forget that Maria had Indian blood, Rosita, and eroticism is part of their culture. You must recall those engravings we saw in that temple on our journey here,' Helen said, remembering Rosita's astonishment when they visited the temple near Benares whose walls were covered with carvings of the most carnal nature and even John MacGregor's Calvinist soul had been affronted.

Helen lay awake that night thinking about those sensuous paintings and the woman who had been the artist. What sort of person was Maria - beautiful and secretive, but obviously extremely lascivious? Was that the sort of woman Gavin wanted and is that why he turned to Isabel when Maria

146

died? Despite her own passionate nature, Helen had no experience of intimate love. Oh, she was a doctor and was aware of the mechanics of mating, but the veiled references to burning desire in her favourite Jane Austen novels, was all she knew. Even if she allowed Gavin to make love to her, would she be able to satisfy him?

Helen did not have too much time to dwell on her husband and his first wife: India kept intruding by its own varied culture.

It was the festival of Bakr-Id which reminded her of Islam's affinity to Christianity and Judaism. During this festival the Moslem servants sacrificed rams and goats to commemorate the Old Testament story of the Prophet Ibrahim (Abraham) offering to sacrifice his son as a burnt offering to God. Mirapore was mainly a Moslem state and there was much celebration of this Feast.

But how different Bakr-Id was to the poignant festival of Muhurram celebrated in the following month. On this occasion, Helen and the Arab doctor set up a first aid centre to deal with the wounds of the participants.

She had heard that this was a sad occasion for Shi'ite Muslims, who commemorated the martyrdom of Imam Hussain, the grandson of the Prophet Mohammed, but nothing prepared her for the fanatical grief which was demonstrated.

The procession started early in the morning and was proceeded by a long banner. Men of all ages and young boys, some of whom could not be more than eight years old, carried paper models of the tomb of Imam Hussain called *'tazias',* the little ones looking proud, but bewildered. They lifted their voices in constant chants of

'Ali, Hussain; Ali, Hussain', raising their fists to the sky and crashing them down brutally on their naked torsos and heads.

When the main procession had passed, Helen heard a faint tinkling sound and saw a group of men carrying little oval shaped blades attached by short chains to a wooden handle. The tinkling sound was made by these blades, which were being whirled around the heads of the self-flagellators and brought vigorously down on their bare backs, until the smell of blood and sweat mingled with the sobbing cries of 'Ali, Hussain'. Some of the men and boys collapsed and had to be drawn to the side of the road where their black veiled women, who were not allowed to join the procession, revived them with water: others were brought to the first-aid station.

Helen noticed that the display of self-torture increased when they saw the foreigner at the first-aid station, as if these sons of Islam took pride in demonstrating their heroic fervour to the Infidel.

Mahmoud Bin Said explained the history of Muhurram to Helen. 'The Prophet Mohammed', he told her, 'nominated his son-in-law, Ali, to succeed him on his death, but after his death, the Sunni sect of Muslims insisted on a succession outside the family. Ali was murdered and neither of his sons was allowed to succeed him. The first was poisoned and the other died on a desert battlefield. These are the deaths honoured by the Shia Muslims at Muhurram. They say 'Live like Ali, die like Hussain!'

'Which sect do you belong to, Doctor?' asked Helen, who could not imagine this quiet, dignified man displaying so much fanaticism.

'I am a Sunni Moslem but find the grief of the Shi'ites very touching. But we are all believers in One God - Allah is God and Mohammed is his Prophet,' said the wise Arab, once again reminding Helen of the affinity of Islam to Christianity and that other great religion, Judaism.

Gavin returned from the Punjab and Helen's heart sang when she saw him standing on the verandah watching her dismount from Sultana. He came towards her smiling that slow attractive smile that was so much part of his charm and taking her hands in his, greeted her, 'Hello, Helen, you look as if you have had a hard day.'

Helen, impulsively, reached up to kiss her husband and his dark eyes looked at her quizzically. 'Is it too much to hope that you missed me a little,' his tone, not quite as bantering, as his words would suggest.

'But, of course, how could I do otherwise,' replied Helen, not even trying to hide her joy at seeing him again.

She had removed her topee and Gavin reached up to touch a wayward auburn curl which had fallen over her forehead, his forefinger tracing the curve of her mouth and the contours of her face.

She left him to bath and change for dinner and when she reappeared, looking fresh and beautiful in a white muslin dress, with no other embellishment but a pink silk rose tucked into her deep décolletage, she had the satisfaction of seeing him pale and his fingers tighten on his wine glass. My handsome spouse is not entirely immune to me, thought Helen.

Despite his obvious attraction to her, Gavin stayed firmly on his side of the bedroom door and Helen's attitude towards her proud, stubborn husband varied between coquettishness and subtle resentment. He still showered her with expensive gifts of jewellery and had arranged a generous annuity for her beloved Rosita.

Helen knew how much Rosita admired Gavin and she wondered why her beloved companion had never mentioned their obvious estrangement. Helen had always taken her troubles to Rosita, but about her marriage she was secretive and she was glad that Rosita did not probe.

March heralded the Hindu festival of Holi and Gavin warned Helen and Rosita to keep well away from the boisterous crowds if they did not wish to be pelted with pink dye or powder. 'Foreigners are a specific target at this time,' he said. 'Mirapore is mainly Muslim, of course, but there is a substantial minority of Hindus amongst its citizens.'

Helen was riding back from the clinic through the European sector when a mob appeared from a side street near the Residency. They laughed and shouted to her, but they all knew and loved this English Doctor Memsahib,

THE CURSE OF KALI

who had treated many of their children and wives and they deliberately refrained from showering her immaculate clothes, or her horse, with colour.

She had nearly reached the gates of the Residency, when one of the British guards shouted and pointed his rifle at an urchin who was being urged by a man to squirt the English Memsahib with the pink dye. The urchin bolted in fright and Helen just caught a glimpse of the man who was encouraging the youngster. The thin face, close set, light eyes and well oiled, centre parted hair was unmistakably that of Vincent de Silva.

The soldier ran up to Helen and placed himself firmly between the crowds and her horse. 'Did you see that fellow urging the *chokra* to squirt you with their coloured water, Milady? Diabolical cheek, I'd say.'

'Thank you for spotting him, but I dare say to the Hindu it is only an outpouring of exuberance like our bun fights in school,' and Helen, nevertheless grateful to the Highlander for his concern, ordered the servants to take out a further tray of cakes and tea to the guards at the gates.

Spring had come early to the delightful valley of Mirapore and the pine and cedar-clad mountain sides were now painted with giant scarlet rhododendrons and carpets of spring flowers coloured the green pastures.

Agnes Cameron, who often accompanied Helen on her rides was nostalgic for Scotland. 'There is so much about the topography of Mirapore that reminds me of our Highlands, especially at this time of the year, Helen,' mused Agnes. 'But look at those rhododendrons, have you ever seen them grow to that size in Britain?'

'No, indeed not,' said Helen,' but then everything is much lusher in these foothills. When I first arrived, I was astonished at the size of the poinsettia bushes in the Residency and the hibiscus shrubs bearing huge exotic blooms of every colour.'

The two women were making their way back to the fort for lunch. Beyond the city, the valley narrowed and the river was no more than a fast flowing stream, swollen now by the melted snows of the high peaks.

Helen was the first to notice the two men in the distance and wondered why they were restraining a third. As they rode nearer, it became obvious that the third man was being strangled and Helen, without any thought for her own safety, urged Sultana into a gallop, and discharged her pistol into the air. She could hear Agnes Cameron's shouts of warning behind, as the older woman spurred her slower mount in an effort to catch up, 'Oh my God, be careful, Helen!'

The two stranglers looked up on hearing the gunshots. They released their victim and fled into the forested hillsides, not even stopping to rob their victim.

The man they had planned to murder had lost consciousness and was turning blue, his eyes protruding. Helen, assuring herself that his neck was not broken, quickly turned him on his stomach, positioning his face sideways and, sitting astride his lower body, began to resuscitate him with artificial respiration. Agnes had come up by this time and on Helen's instructions, placed a saddle bag under his lower chest to assist the respiration.

'He is coming around,' said an excited Agnes after Helen had worked on the victim for almost half an hour. The women turned him around on his back when his breathing was normal again. The man's eyes opened. He looked at Helen in amazement and muttered something in a language she did not understand, except the words, *"Alla-hu-Akbar."*

Then hearing the women speaking in English, he said in hoarse tones, 'You have saved my life, *memsahib*. When I opened my eyes, I thought I had died and gone to paradise and that you were a beautiful houri. Those *badmash,* have they fled?'

'Yes, but why were they trying to kill you? You don't seem to have anything of value on you,' enquired Agnes. The man was simply dressed in the clothes of the mountain tribes - baggy pants, a long shirt and a waistcoat.

'I believe they were Thugs, followers of the Hindu goddess, Kali. They slaughter for the fun of it, but thanks to your timely intervention, I will live to see my home again,' said Helen's patient, now sitting with his back leaning against a boulder and she remembered her *Sunyassi's* explanation of this worship of the Goddess Kali.

Helen observed the man closely, he was not unlike the Rohillas, but his nose was well shaped, not aquiline. He wore a well-trimmed beard and thin moustache and his clothes, although simple, were of good quality. He looked quite noble and she guessed he was an Afghan, perhaps a tribal chief. She tried to persuade him to accompany them to the British fort, at which suggestion he looked quite uncomfortable.

'I am on my way to Mirapore, so I must continue my journey. But before I go, please allow me to present you with this token of my debt,' and he took a heavy silver ring off his finger, with an engraving of a crescent moon, and gave it to Helen. 'I am a Khan, a man of some importance in my country and anyone on the borders of Afghanistan will recognise that engraving. If you ever need my assistance, *memsahib*, please let me know by sending that ring to me.'

He rewound his turban which had become undone in the recent scuffle with the Thugs and taking his leave of the two women, went on his way towards Mirapore.

Lady Agnes dined out often on this episode, embellishing the danger and Helen's courage, each time she told the story.

'I did not see what was happening at first and suddenly there was our Helen galloping towards the men and firing her pistol in the air. Her topee had come off and her auburn hair was streaming about her shoulders. The two Thugs took one look at this enraged Valkyrie and fled.

'Our handsome Afghan was so entranced with his rescuer when Helen's medical skill revived him. He even thought he had died and gone to heaven and that Helen was a beautiful houri.'

Helen was always embarrassed when her friend related this incident, especially when Gavin was present on one occasion. He laughed with the others, but the amusement did not reach his eyes and later, when they were alone, he almost ordered her to desist from riding alone.

'Gavin, I was not alone, Agnes was with me and I always carry one of the pistols you gave me.'

'Nevertheless, I would prefer you to take the groom or one of the soldiers with you, Helen. Please obey me in this matter, at least.'

Helen looked at the firm set of his jaw and the steel of his dark eyes and realised that this was one occasion on which she should not argue with her husband.

Chapter 9

The clinic was as busy as ever, women and children awaiting the doctors' attention.

Princess Muna was assisting her with a little boy. When only children and women were present, Muna threw off her veil and Helen looking up from examining the patient, was surprised to see tears in the lovely eyes of the princess.

When the last patient had left, Helen took Muna aside and asked, 'You seem sad to-day, Muna, what has upset you?'

'I have been informed by the Nawab that I am to marry a prince of the Royal family in Delhi, a man older than me by many years and, I understand from harem gossip, cruel to his wives and concubines,' replied Muna, bursting once more into tears.

Helen put an arm around the girl and producing a handkerchief wiped away her tears. 'Gossip is not always accurate, Princess, and I cannot believe that your father, or your great grandmother, would allow you to be married to such a man. Have you mentioned your fears to Begum Shalima?'

'All she says is that princesses must be prepared to marry for political reasons and my union with the family of the Moghul Emperor, Bahadur Shah the Second, is a great honour for our family. But that is not all; I love another man, a man who although poor, is handsome, kind and gentle.'

Helen's start of surprise at the princess's confession was followed by a sense of foreboding.

'Who is this man, Muna? You are never in the company of men, only eunuchs and guards.' Then suddenly recalling their riding companion, Helen exclaimed, 'Oh my God, you have not formed a romantic attachment to that young Rohilla guard who accompanies us on our rides? But how? You are so well guarded.'

Helen's sense of foreboding increased as she realised by Muna's downcast eyes that their rides were not the only times these two had met. Somehow the princess had found an opportunity to meet her young Afghan.

'Muna, how far has this love affair gone? You are, I hope, still a virgin? You know the penalty for adultery in your religion.' Helen remembered hearing how Moslem women were stoned to death and men executed when taken in the act of adultery; moral laws as old as Islam and Judaism.

'Oh, but of course, Helen, Abdul is a devout Muslim and loves me too much to sully me. Besides we have no real contact, except on our rides, when you are there to watch over me, but he sends me such adoring letters through a maidservant of mine, who would cut out her tongue rather than betray me,' whispered the tearful Muna.

'Muna, sweet princess, you must forget about Abdul. You and he could never have a future together, even if you were not betrothed to a Royal prince,' pleaded Helen, hating these customs that tore a young girl from a

157

loving environment to become the slave of some old man. Her heart heavy for the young princess, Helen sought out her husband after dinner that night.

'Gavin, what do you know about Princess Muna's betrothal to a Prince of Delhi? She is heart broken to be promised to a man who, she has heard, is a heartless and debauched playboy.'

'Bahadur Shah the Second, is a very old man, and under Lord Dalhousie's Doctrine of Lapse, will probably be the last Moghul to sit on the Throne of Delhi. Even now, he is a mere shadow of his great ancestors, his sovereignty under the protection of the Company. So none of his sons will be allowed to succeed him. But there are not too many Muslim princes of royal blood for the princess to marry and I know that the Court in Delhi is impoverished and would be glad of the Mirapore dowry,' said Gavin.

The matter of Princess Muna's betrothal had to take second place as Helen prepared for the last ball of the season before the arrival of summer. This ball, held as usual in the British Residency, was called the Hunt Ball because it preceded the Nawab's annual *Shikar* to which all the 'guns' of Mirapore were invited.

'Once again,' said Lady Agnes, 'Helen's organisation of such grand occasions as this ball has brought a touch of the elegance associated with our life at home - so essential in this far off land to remind us of our roots.' Lady Agnes's remark reminded Helen of the Begum Shalima's words about

British segregationism and she realised that she, too, was guilty of establishing a 'Little England' in India.

Helen, in a gown of black lace, cut low over her shoulders, wore Gavin's emeralds around her neck and when she was held in his arms during a waltz, he remarked, 'That is a beautiful gown, Helen, you look charming; your eyes are brighter than those emeralds, but I have never seen you wear that heart-shaped diamond ring, my gift to you on our wedding morning. Don't you like it?'

'It is exquisite, but the occasion to wear it has not yet arisen,' replied Helen, remembering her vow never to wear the ring until Gavin loved her and her alone.

Gavin was looking at her quizzically and Helen was glad when the music ended and she was able to escape his further probing.

The morning of the *Shikar* was a beautiful May day. The Nawab's guests set out from the palace on elephants, horses and carriages. Helen opted to ride Sultana: the swaying, ponderous elephants were slow and rather too reminiscent of a ship's movements on a choppy sea.

The Nawab's guests consisted of neighbouring princes and their retinues and the Europeans in Mirapore - the English, the French and the Spanish. Only Helen and Lady Agnes were considered 'good guns', the rest of the women coming along exclusively for the enjoyment of alfresco life, which was unlike any camping experience Helen had ever had.

The women were housed in the Nawab's comfortable hunting lodge embellished with all the luxuries of the Court, except for the bathrooms, which were in the Indian style. Remembering her experience from previous shikars and the discomfort of having to squat over a hole in the ground, Lady Agnes had brought along several commodes.

The men camped in tents, elegant affairs in themselves, furnished with carpets, divans, desks and sandalwood chests. A great deal of food, fruit juices and wine for his non-teetotal guests, was conveyed on camels' backs and beautiful silver tableware and crystal glasses graced the white damask tablecloths at mealtimes.

'Each year the Nawab awards a gift to the hunter with the most kills,' explained Gavin to Helen, 'but this year, his award will be presented to the owner of the gun which kills *"Sher Saitan"* the name given to a tiger, which is preying on the villages around the forest hunting site.'

'But is that so strange, tigers are predators, after all?' queried Helen.

'Yes', agreed Gavin, 'but the Nawab feeds his tigers in the hunting reserve to ensure their conservation and to provide his hunting guests annually with superb specimens. It is not often that a rogue animal preys on human settlements unless it is too old to hunt swifter prey, or has been wounded.'

A little hunting was done in the cool of the early morning, mainly from the backs of elephants. Helen and Lady Agnes climbed into the howdah, in this case a canvas box secured to the elephant's back, which enabled the *shikari* to stand upright. Helen was amused by the love songs whispered by the Mahout into the large ears of his beloved elephant, whilst that great beast plodded through the thick jungle undergrowth crushing the foliage and disturbing the chattering monkeys.

The afternoons were reserved for a light lunch and siesta. It was only at night that the hunters occupied their *machans* (wooden platforms built in the trees and camouflaged with brushwood) the tiger being a nocturnal predator. A rota was drawn up by the Nawab's chief huntsman for an early, middle and late night watch and everyone hoped that 'Sher Saitan', attracted by the live prey tethered in the forest clearing, would show himself on their particular watch.

However, each morning, the chief huntsman reported to the company that the elusive tiger had not yet taken the bait. Sher Saitan had been around for a great many shikars and was perhaps too wise to be disturbed from his lair by the beaters.

After an unusually sultry night for the time of year, Helen remembered the little waterfall near the hunting lodge and the delight it would give her to shower in its cool spray. Collecting her rifle, a towel and a change of underwear, she crept out of the lodge silently in the early morning so as not to disturb her sleeping companions. The sun was rising over the mountains, setting the snowy peaks and the clouds above them on golden fire. Helen was entranced, especially by the scenery around the waterfall - lush vegetation, moss covered rocks, rhododendron bushes with their enormous scarlet and pink flowers and darting in and out of the trees, exotically plumaged birds. The waterfall cascaded in cooling splendour, its three columns of water plunging into the river some sixty feet below.

Helen propped up her gun against a boulder and discarded her divided riding skirt and silk shirt. Suddenly she became aware of a slight movement near the ridge of the fall. Between the foliage she saw the unmistakable outline of a leopard watching her, its tail flicking like a cat's and Helen with racing heart, reached carefully for her rifle, hoping that a shot fired into the air would frighten the animal into flight. Helen raised the rifle and pressed the trigger, but nothing happened; she pressed again, still silence: then fear clutched her throat as she realised her gun had jammed. Abruptly a shot rang out and the leopard somersaulted and plunged into the river below. Helen screamed as the heavy body fell a few feet from her into the swirling water. Another shot was fired into the animal and Helen turned and saw Gavin striding towards her, his face ashen with concern.

'Helen, are you all right?' shouted her husband, grabbing her shoulder in a vice like grip. 'What the hell are you doing out here alone?' he shouted again, the concern in his eyes giving way to annoyance at her foolhardiness.

'I just wanted a bath in that cool waterfall. I have my gun and if it had not jammed...'

'So you wanted a bath and decided to leave the camp without a word to anyone. Don't you know, you little fool, that you are not in the woods of England hunting foxes or deer, but in the jungles of Asia where the fauna is red in tooth and claw. How could you be so stupid!' stormed Gavin still clutching her shoulder and now shaking it to relieve his own tension.

'Please let go of my shoulder, you are hurting me,' whispered Helen fighting back tears, but Gavin tightened his grip and spun her around to face the dead animal in the water.

'Hurting you, that is nothing to what that leopard would have done to you. Why, of all the women in the camp, it has to be my wife who decides to take an early morning swim alone. For an intelligent woman, Helen, you can be really stupid at times,' growled a still furious Gavin.

Helen, stung to anger and remembering Gavin's words about Maria's death, said very coldly, her eyes blazing with indignation, 'I am sorry you have been put to so much trouble, Gavin, but if you had lost a second wife, you could always tell the third that she brought it upon herself.'

Gavin was obviously not listening because suddenly he threw back his head and burst into laughter.

'And what is so amusing, sir?' asked an even more indignant Helen.

'You, my darling, standing there in your combinations and lace-up boots, looking like a defiant little urchin.'

'So now I look like a boy. What further insults do you wish to level at me, Gavin French!'

'Sweetheart, you could never look like a boy; even in a suit of armour, you would still be the most feminine creature I have ever seen.' As if for emphasis, he leaned forward and slowly trailed his fingers across her half-exposed breasts.

'Now why are you getting dressed, don't you want that swim? I will stand guard while you bathe,' said her audacious husband watching her confusion as she reached for her clothes.

'No thanks, Gavin, I have lost the urge to swim this morning,' and Helen, too, found herself smiling at this incorrigible man, who never failed to disturb her.

'Then get dressed quickly, darling, before Ram Das sends out a search party. If they see you and me half undressed they will jump to the wrong conclusions, unfortunately,' said Gavin with his mocking smile.

It was then that Helen noticed that her husband had evidently left the camp in a hurry because, apart from his boots and breeches, he was naked.

Whilst she dressed, Gavin waded into the water and dragged the dead leopard onto the river bank, 'For nature's refuse disposal team - the hyenas and carrion crows,' he explained, as he returned to her side, his broad, tanned, muscular chest glistening now with droplets from the waterfall. Helen wondered if he was aware of his blatant, masculine sexuality and once again she felt a weakness in her loins and a stirring of her own longing, the same emotion this man had aroused in her on their wedding night before she had rejected him. Now she found herself, perversely, wishing that he would make love to her here in the lovely surroundings of this Indian forest.

He was smiling, his dark eyes twinkling with amusement as he came towards her and Helen blushed, wondering for a brief moment, if her thoughts had been so transparent. She tensed as he put his arm about her waist but it was only to guide her back to the camp, although he tightened his grip, almost as if he was afraid she would escape.

'What am I to do with you, my beauty? You are far too independent for a woman. You risked your life today by venturing away from the camp alone; faced untold dangers when you rescued your unknown Khan from Thuggees and without consulting your husband, opened a clinic for the poor, exposing yourself to all manner of diseases,' said Gavin, looking down at his wife with a half smile on his lips, as he listed her so-called transgressions.

'I am sorry, Gavin,' replied Helen, regarding her husband with a frown, as she registered the significance of these last words. 'I must be a nuisance, but I have always been used to making my own decisions and with all your work, I didn't think you would wish to be consulted about the clinic.'

Then, as an afterthought, Helen added, 'You should have married a more submissive woman.'

Gavin threw back his head and roared with laughter, 'Then I would have died of boredom. I think I prefer the shocks and inevitable grey hairs from life with you.'

The camp was just stirring when they arrived back and Ram Das ran out to make sure the *memsahib* was safe.

'You were right, Ram Das; *Memsahib* had decided to take a bath in the waterfall.'

Helen gathered from this exchange that it was the Nepalese servant who had raised the alarm, when he had seen Helen leave the encampment alone with her towel and gun.

It was the last day of the Shikar and everyone hoped that Sher Saitan would not disappoint them that night. Over breakfast, served alfresco as usual, Helen looked up to see Gavin staring at her quizzically and when she caught his eye, he smiled and raised one eyebrow, winking at her mischievously. No doubt he was still amused by the incongruous picture that morning of his defiant wife in her combinations and boots.

She noticed that the Comtesse de Colbert had observed their unspoken exchange of looks and wondered what that incorrigible French woman was thinking.

The last watch that night was reserved for Helen, Gavin and John MacGregor. They took their places on the *machan*s, the high wooden platforms in the trees camouflaged with brushwood from another part of the forest. Gavin had explained to Helen that this was necessary, as the slightest disturbance in the surrounding vegetation would alert the tiger to their alien presence. Would he come at last?

It was a bright moonlight night and Helen saw the little kid goat quite clearly tethered in the centre of the clearing, chomping contentedly on some grass. If the tiger came, she must save that little animal. She wondered if Gavin and John found that their eyes, too, played tricks. Every tree and shrub seemed to transform itself into the tawny body and broad, black stripes of Sher Saitan and Helen could swear fearsome, amber eyes were watching her from the forest.

Suddenly the little kid looked up and stopped chomping, then after a moment it started to bleat. Helen raised her rifle, releasing the safety catch on her gun, her finger poised on the trigger, her eyes glued to the forest edge. Branches snapped and suddenly the tiger was there, a form of pure symmetry, stealthily moving its four-hundred-pound body inch by inch towards its hypnotised prey, its belly almost touching the ground. A monkey raised an alarm in the treetops and Sher Saitan fearing, perhaps, that his prey would take flight, crouched momentarily on his muscular hind legs before leaping into the air, massive claws splayed and jaws open in a vicious snarl. Helen fired, aiming at the point just below its outstretched front leg. With a roar of pain and rage the big cat somersaulted backwards and plunged to the ground only inches from the frightened goat and then, surprisingly, he sprang up and ran back into the jungle.

'Stay where you are, Helen!' shouted Gavin, as she moved to climb down from her machan to follow the animal.

'I believe your shot found its mark, Helen, but it would be foolhardy to follow a wounded tiger until we have more light,' explained John more gently.

At first light, they were joined by Ram Das and a few beaters who had heard the shot. A trail of blood led them into the forest and there, several yards from the clearing, lay the massive beast, its head resting on its front feet as if asleep, the wind ruffling its neck hairs. Only the pool of congealed blood around the front of the body testified to its mortal wound. Helen felt guilty that it was her shot in the region of his great heart that had ended the hunting days of Sher Saitan. Never again would he roam this forest, hunt his prey or sleep under the cool trees. Never again would the jungle reverberate to his mighty roars, alarming the birds into instant flight, or transforming the monkeys in the tall trees into jabbering wrecks. The beaters tossed sticks and stones at the inert body to ensure that the animal was quite dead and then they tied the tiger's legs together on stout poles and carried it upside down towards the camp. What an undignified end to the life of this King of the Jungle, thought Helen, as tears sprang to her eyes.

Gavin saw her distress and silently put his arms about her shoulders, recalling his own remorse when he shot his first tiger.

Everyone was waiting in the camp to see the dreaded quarry. Tape measures were produced to measure the length of the beast, and exclamations of surprise were uttered at the accuracy of the shot.

Then the villagers appeared beating their *tablas* and shouting,'*Jai Sher Memsahib!*' for word had got around that the Resident's wife had killed Sher Saitan with one shot.

'They are saying, "Long Live Tiger Lady",' said the Nawab

The whole camp seemed to be in a state of euphoria and Helen was mobbed by laughing villagers who garlanded her with so many flowers that she felt quite overcome by their heady perfume.

The Nawab presented her with a superb hunting rifle imported from famous gunsmiths in England and the French Consul produced a case of champagne to celebrate the end of a successful Shikar.

'Speech, Speech!' shouted a voice and Helen found herself lifted onto a chair by Gavin, who thrust a glass of champagne in her hand and said, 'I am afraid you have to say something, my lovely *Sher Memsahib.*'

Helen looked around at all the excited faces and, smiling, said, 'I feel a fraud for accepting this honour because, although they will deny it, I know

169

that my two gallant companions, Gavin and John, allowed me to take the first shot. Nevertheless, on behalf of all of us, I would like to thank your Highness for this memorable Shikar and for presenting me with this superb hunting rifle.'

After breakfast, the camp broke up and with a feeling of anti-climax, the party returned to Mirapore.

Helen's memory of Sher Saitan was not to be forgotten. A few weeks later her trophy, the skin of the tiger expertly mounted by a taxidermist in Delhi, was sent to her by the Nawab.

Gavin was in his study when the package arrived and Helen brought it to him. 'Will you accept this skin from your tiresome wife, Gavin. It will look handsome, here in front of the fireplace,' said Helen, as she laid the trophy in front of the hearth and stroked the handsome head of the tiger, his last snarl captured forever by the skill of the taxidermist.

Gavin laughed, remembering his words at the waterfall. He came towards Helen and placing his hands around her tiny waist lifted her off her feet and swung her around in circles, shouting mischievously,'*Jai, Sher Memsahib!*' until she pleaded with him him to set her down.

'Gavin, stop it, you are making me so giddy!'

He set her on her feet, his dark gaze caressing her, his hands firmly on her shoulders, pulling her towards him. Then with one hand under her chin, he lifted her mouth up to meet his. His kiss was savage, but Helen, longing

170

for his touch, did not care as he forced her mouth open, his tongue thrusting, teasing, until she responded, whilst his hand cupped her breast beneath her thin blouse, his thumb caressing her taut nipple. Her arms wound about his neck and sensuously she moulded her body into his, feeling his unmistakable arousal, her own longing almost an ache in the pit of her stomach.

'Helen, my darling, you are so lovely', her husband was whispering huskily, his lips against her hair. 'Say you want me as much as I want you. Say it!'

Taking her silence for assent, Gavin lifted her in his arms and laid her on the tiger skin before the fireplace, unbuttoning her blouse and bending his head to kiss her lovely breasts. 'Don't move, my darling, I'll be only a moment.' He left her to lock the study door, but before he reached it, the door opened and Isabel de Silva stood in the entrance with a tea tray, taking in the unmistakable love scene with a glint in her dark eyes.

'Oh, excuse me,' she said, 'I wondered if you would like your tea in here.'

Helen, feeling like a harlot, jumped up and said angrily, 'No, No!' and without a backward glance at Gavin, she brushed past the woman and ran upstairs to her bedroom, turning the key in the lock.

Helen was unaware that downstairs, Gavin had grabbed the tray angrily from the startled Isabel and sent it crashing to the floor, shards of broken china flying in all directions. 'How dare you enter without first knocking!' said Gavin, a note of steel in his voice and anger in his dark eyes. Then Gavin rushed up the stairs after Helen. But her door, like her heart, was locked firmly against her imploring husband.

Chapter 10

Helen continued her work at the clinic and was surprised that Princess Muna no longer attended. The Arab doctor explained that she was being prepared for her betrothal to the Prince of Delhi but something in his manner prompted Helen to ask, 'Is the princess now reconciled to her forthcoming marriage, Doctor *Sahib*?'

'I do not think so; she is a changed person and is losing weight because she is not eating properly. Perhaps you can visit her and try to encourage her, Lady Helen.'

Helen accompanied the doctor to the zenana and was shown into an enclosed courtyard where the little princess sat strumming her sitar. She looked thinner and her dark eyes were circled with shadows. When she saw Helen, she put down her sitar and threw herself into her friend's arms.

'I am so glad to see you again, Helen,' said the young woman, trying to smile through her tears.

'You look tired, child. Have you been sleeping well?' said a concerned Helen, who had not expected to see such a change in Princess Muna after only a few weeks.

'Look Helen,' said the princess removing an ivory miniature from the pocket of her *kameez,* 'This is the man I am to marry!'

Helen took the miniature and saw the head and shoulders of a man already in his late forties with a thick-lipped sensuous mouth and cruel, black, downward slanting eyes, the ethnic legacy of his Mongol ancestors. But it was the fleshy face and puffy eyes, which portrayed a man who indulged himself to the full.

Oh my poor little princess, thought Helen silently. How can they give you to such a man?

'Now you see why I am so miserable, Helen. How can I look at those features and not remember the clean, noble lines of the face of the man I love,' whispered Princess Muna.

Helen turned at the sound of a tapping stick on the marble floor and was not surprised to see Begum Shalima leaning on the arm of a maid servant, her half blind eyes staring at the two women.

'I am glad you have been able to visit the princess, Lady French. Perhaps you can talk some sense into her. This melancholia of hers must stop. She is to be married into the family of our Moghul Emperor, a great honour.'

The Begum sat down on a stone bench and indicated that Helen and Muna should sit by her side.

'Let me tell you a story, little one. Years ago in the court of her father lived a young girl of just thirteen years old. She heard that she was to be married on her fourteenth birthday and even at that tender age, would become the wife of a famous prince. She was naturally sad that she would have to leave her doting parents and her beloved brother but she had read the chronicles of the Emperor Shah Jehan and his love for the Princess Mumtaz. Her girlish heart dreamed that a great romance such as theirs would be hers one day. Her prince sent her beautiful jewels to mark their betrothal and a portrait of himself, young and handsome, and every day she would look at this portrait and wonder if he would be her Shah Jehan.

'On her wedding day, the women bathed her in scented rose water, oiled her body with perfumes and dressed her in her wedding clothes and that night when her husband came to her chamber, he lifted her veil and she saw, not the young and handsome prince of the portrait, but the pockmarked face of a much older man. You see the portrait he had sent her had been painted in his youth.'

'Oh, how dreadful', said Muna. 'What did the princess do?'

'Nothing, my child. He was her husband and she bore him strong sons. In time, she even came to love and respect him, not with the blinding passion of Mumtaz, perhaps, but with the quiet love of a devoted wife. She found, instead of the fire of love, that even more powerful aphrodisiac - power. She became a strong influence in her husband's court and when he died, she was the power behind the throne of his heir.'

Audrey Blankenhagen

Helen realised that this was the story of Begum Shalima, herself, and she wondered if little Muna would have the same strength of character to overcome her adversity.

******

The evenings were now much warmer and Helen, partly to avoid Gavin, started to take a walk in the gardens after dinner.

The night was a particularly warm and balmy one and Helen returning to the house, saw the light in her husband's study. Gaslights had been fitted a few weeks ago in the Residency and Helen could see Gavin quite clearly working at his desk.

The scratch of his pen on the document he was writing was audible through the open window. Suddenly Gavin stopped writing, helped himself to a cigar from the box on the desk, lit it and walked over to the window. Helen stepped back behind a thick bush but hidden by the darkness of the night, she continued to observe her husband. Gavin's brow was furrowed as if he was deep in thought and his eyes were narrowed as he drew on his cigar. He was gazing upwards, as Helen often did, at the spectacular panorama of the everlasting snow-covered crests of the Himalayas, rising above the silhouette of black forested foothills surrounding the Valley of Mirapore.

Because of the warmth of the evening, Gavin was wearing only his tight doe-skin riding breeches and a white linen shirt unfastened at the neck. His

176

strong, muscled throat and arms were revealed by his open neck shirt and rolled up sleeves and a lock of dark hair had fallen over his forehead. Helen had an unaccountable longing to brush it back tenderly. Her emotions in turmoil, she closed her eyes and saw again in her mind's eye the deep cleft in Gavin's chin, as he had leaned towards her yesterday in that same room in which he was now standing. She recalled with a beating heart his firm, well-formed mouth seeking hers and his dark eyes, at first soft with tenderness, but soon dark with passion as his kisses became more urgent and his arrogant, male body told her how much he wanted her.

She opened her eyes and noticed that someone else had come into the room. Gavin turned as the door opened and smiled. Isabel de Silva was standing in the doorway with a tray and Helen heard her say, 'I have brought you your nightcap, Gavin.'

He motioned her to put it on the desk and as she turned to to leave the room, Gavin stopped her, 'Just a minute, Isabel...'

Helen fled; she could not bear to observe her husband's intimacies with his paramour and so she did not hear him say, just simply, 'I am sorry for my outburst yesterday, Isabel. It was unfair of me. But you must understand that it is essential my wife and I have some privacy when we are together.'

Gavin was a man of principle and it was not within his nature to bully his subordinates. He realised that his rage yesterday at this unfortunate woman was due to his frustration at an interruption, which had strangely angered Helen and driven her away from his arms.

If only he could have guessed that he had driven his wife even further away by this spontaneous kindness to the Goanese woman.

Helen rushed blindly towards the stable and buried her face in the muscular neck of Sultana. The little mare whickered gently as if she sensed that her beloved friend's heart was breaking and Helen stroked her velvet nose as the horse blew softly at her.

'If only we could ride away together up there to those snowy heights where our *Sunyassi* has gone and we will never come down to earth again, sweet Sultana.'

The gold embossed invitation to Princess Muna's wedding was delivered, personally, by the young Rohilla guard. His grey eyes were inscrutable and showed no glimmer of the pain he must be suffering, delivering this invitation to his beloved's wedding to another man. Helen, remembering her own heartbreak, identified Abdul as a fellow sufferer in the cruel stakes of love.

'Thank you, Abdul,' Helen said gently, taking the invitation from the young man. 'Please wait for my reply, but I will ask my servant to bring you something cool to drink whilst you are waiting.'

Helen understood from Gavin, that the Prince of Delhi's caravan was already on its way and the day before the formal wedding ceremony, the huge procession of richly bedecked elephants, uniformed cavalry, troopers of the Emperor's camel corps, covered palanquins, musicians, and foot soldiers poured through the gates of the City of Mirapore with noise and fanfares. Helen realised that the pomp and ceremony of this colourful pageant was an echo from the glorious past of the Moghul Empire and deliberately designed to belie the decline of this once powerful dynasty.

'A small contingent of British officials will be our guests,' said Gavin when he discussed the wedding arrangements with Helen, 'but will not include the British Resident to the Court of Delhi, as the prince who is marrying Princess Muna is not the Heir Apparent.'

The wedding was a lavish affair and in true Muslim tradition, the feasting was segregated: men banqueted in the large Audience Chamber and the women in the gardens of the harem, seated at little tables covered with lace cloths and lit by hundreds of coloured oil lights shining in arbours and trees.

Helen called on Princess Muna in her bridal chamber. She looked pale and distressed but whispered to Helen, 'I have requested that the consummation of my marriage should not be celebrated until we arrive in my husband's apartments at the Court in Delhi.'

Helen, astonished, enquired, 'Did the prince agree, Muna?'

'Yes, because I asked my father to tell him that it is my wish that any issue from our consummation should be conceived in his father's, the Emperor's Palace, to protect his right to the succession. The Heir Apparent has only one son and he is very sickly, so it is possible that a son from our marriage will succeed to the Delhi throne.'

Muna's strange request regarding her marriage consummation and her belated acceptance of this union, troubled Helen slightly, but perhaps the story of her great grandmother's own marriage and the Dowager's statement that power was a more potent aphrodisiac than love, had steeled the young princess to accept her fate.

Two days later, Princess Muna set out from Mirapore in a covered palanquin in her husband's wedding caravan and Helen, who had said a tearful goodbye to the young girl, was astonished to find the princess calm and almost joyful.

'I believe I have misread Princess Muna, Gavin. She is more like her great grandmother than I believed. The girl that left Mirapore was not the shy, sad, little princess, but a proud, almost cheerful bride,' Helen remarked.

It was not long before the reason for Princess Muna's change of mood was tragically apparent. Helen's work was interrupted a few days later by an urgent summons to the palace.

Waiting for her on the steps of the zenana was the Chief Eunuch, Ibrahim. He looked serious as he said, 'This way please, Lady French.'

Helen was shown into the private audience chamber of the Begum Shalima, who sat on a raised divan, her head bowed and her old hands clutching a telegram. It was a few moments before she looked up to acknowledge Helen's presence, her half blind eyes wet with tears.

'Can you read Urdu, Lady French?' she said curtly. 'Perhaps I had better tell you what is written here, so you will have no doubt concerning the dishonour which has overtaken my family.'

"Princess Muna fled Stop Rohilla guard also missing Stop Villagers report two riders answering their description seen making for mountains Stop Search party following Stop Prince Hassan."

'You are her friend, Lady French. Do you know anything about her liaison with this man? I believe he was the guard who usually accompanied you and the princess on your rides,' said the old woman, her blind eyes now staring at Helen as if they were trying to read her soul.

'Are you suggesting that I encouraged any intimacy with this guard, Your Highness? Muna was veiled whenever we were together and never left my side during these rides. Why do you connect this man with a romantic liaison? Could he not have kidnapped the princess?'

Helen's voice was severe and cold and she realised that she could give no hint of her knowledge of Muna's affection for Abdul and the girl's unhappiness at her arranged marriage. If they found Muna, her honour could be saved only by a case of kidnap. Anything else would mean disgrace and perhaps death.

'I wish that was the case, Lady French, but Muna's maidservant has confessed, under questioning, that she delivered love letters for the princess and this guard, Abdul.'

'Questioning? you mean torture, Begum Shalima,' said Helen coldly, 'Confessions extracted under this sort of coercion are often worthless. I am surprised that you can believe this of your beloved great granddaughter.'

'*Feringhi* ideals are not Moslem standards and I must blame myself for allowing the princess to be so much in your company. You may go, Lady French,' and the Begum rose and left the chamber, her back straight and haughty, almost as if she had no need of the support of a stick, or her maidservant's arm.

Helen sought out Gavin in his study as soon as she returned home. He looked up from his work and saw his distraught wife standing in the doorway.

'Helen, what is the matter?' he said, coming towards her and taking both her hands in his.

'Princess Muna has escaped from the wedding caravan with her lover, the Rohilla guard called Abdul and the Begum blames my influence for this disgrace,' said Helen, fighting back the tears so close to the surface.

'Does she, by Jove! I will soon put the arrogant Dowager right on that matter. But come, sit down, darling, and tell me everything that you know,' said Gavin, guiding her to an armchair.

Helen found herself unburdening herself to Gavin with every detail of the rides, the picnics and her stern advice to the young, flirtatious princess when Muna had told her about her love for the young guard and their clandestine correspondence conducted through her maidservant.

'I suspect they tortured that poor servant to extract her confession,' Helen said bitterly, her voice breaking at the thought of this needless cruelty, and in an effort to fight back her tears, she bit her lower lip.

Gavin, who had been standing with his back to the fireplace, listening to Helen's account, took just two strides to reach his wife and lifted her into his arms. Her pent up emotions, her anger at the Begum's audacious dismissal and her fears for Muna, found relief in sobs, as he held her close and stroked her hair. Once again, Helen was that little girl in an English forest enclosed in the safe haven of her big cousin's arms and listening to his deep reassuring voice calming his 'little sweetheart.'

A week later, the search for the lovers ended and Mahmoud Bin Said, looking suddenly stooped and very much older, came to the Residency to break the news to Helen and Gavin. The Arab doctor told them that the Prince of Delhi had offered an enormous reward for information concerning the runaways and they were betrayed by the headman of a village, where they were resting, before continuing their journey.

'I am afraid, the Rohilla soldier was executed by the guards from the Delhi Court and Princess Muna...'

'What about the princess?' interrupted Helen quietly, fearing the worst.

'She was made to watch the execution of her lover before she was brought back, bound in ropes, to Mirapore.'

'My God, how did they execute him?' asked Gavin.

'By impalement, the Moghul punishment for treason. I fear that it has driven the little princess half out of her mind,' said Mahmoud Bin Said, a shudder passing through his tall frame.

Then turning to Helen, he said, 'If you could come to the palace with me, you may be able to help her, Doctor. She needs a woman's touch now and, preferably, a Western woman, who would not remind her of her own people.'

Gavin insisted on accompanying his wife to the Palace. 'There are many things that I would like to clear up with the Nawab concerning this matter, so I will accompany you and my wife to the palace, *Effendi.*'

Mahmoud Bin Said bowed in acceptance. Gavin's reluctance to permit his wife to venture unaccompanied into a Court, which he now considered barbaric, was understandable.

Helen and the Arab doctor were taken by the Chief Eunuch to Muna's apartments. Bars had been fitted to the windows and armed eunuchs stood outside the door leading off the inner courtyard. The room was dark when Helen entered, only tiny, clay lamps placed very high on the topmost beams, illuminated the chamber. It took Helen's eyes some time to accustom themselves to the gloom but then she saw little Muna, sitting quietly in a sort

184

of rocking chair, crooning tunelessly to herself, her beautiful eyes blank and staring at the ceiling. A tray of food lay untouched on a table by her side.

'Muna, my poor child,' sobbed Helen as she knelt by the chair and took two, little cold hands into her own.

Muna stopped staring at the ceiling and looked at Helen as if she did not recognise her, then she smiled and started rocking and crooning again.

'How long has she been like this, Doctor? Has she eaten or drunk anything?'

'She was like this when they brought her back,' replied the Arab doctor. The palace guards were instructed to take her to Delhi, but Prince Hassan insisted that she should recuperate in familiar surroundings before rejoining her husband. As for food, I believe all she has taken is a little water.'

'Please bring me some *dhai* and honey. I will see if I can tempt her to eat,' instructed Helen.

The little princess submitted to Helen's administrations, sipping each spoon and then crooning and rocking before she took another. The simple meal seemed to take ages and suddenly Muna focused on Helen's wedding ring.

'You are married, beautiful doctor, to a man you love, I know. I, too, am married to Abdul, my handsome Rohilla. We are going to his country far away,' mused Muna, an almost beatific smile playing on her lips.

A voice behind Helen spoke harshly in Urdu. Helen turned and saw the Begum, her face twisted with anger.

'How dare you speak of this man! Haven't you brought enough disgrace on your family, Princess!'

Before Helen could stop her, Muna grabbed the bowl of curds out of Helen's hands and flung it over the old lady, shrieking, 'You killed him, you and my father, killed him because you could not bear to see me happy.'

Then turning to Helen, she said in a voice filled with rage and anguish, 'They made me watch while they murdered him. Do you know what they did to my Abdul?' The Begum tried to silence her, but Muna insisted on continuing. 'The *Angressi* must learn what Moslem princes do in the name of justice!'

Muna continued her voice now filled with hatred, 'They tied him face downwards on a saddle and thrust an eight foot pointed stake through his anus until it came out of his chest. His cries of pain, Oh Allah, were terrible to hear and I fainted before they ceased. When I was revived by water in my face, I saw that they had driven the stake into the ground and left him hanging there, his beautiful face contorted with pain and his perfect body hanging limply on that unspeakable gibbet.'

Then as if she could still see her tortured lover, Muna walked up to a marble column and started gently to stroke and croon to the cold marble.

186

Helen turned angrily on the Begum, 'Why did you have to remind her of that horror? We were just getting her to eat something. Her mind had temporarily blocked out that horrendous scene she had been forced to witness. She was remembering her dream of love, a necessary safety valve if we are to save her reason.'

'Your husband is waiting for you, Lady French. Leave the princess to our own doctor,' commanded Begum Shalima and Helen nearly laughed unkindly at the old Dowager's efforts to appear regal with streaks of *dhai* dripping down her face. What sort of woman was this who put family honour before compassion for her beloved great granddaughter?

Gavin held Helen close, as their carriage made its way across the causeway, and she told him, in a voice broken with emotion, about Muna and the terrible memories of her lover's execution.

'The Begum was unspeakably cruel to the child, Gavin. Did her father really order her to witness that impalement?'

'Apparently not, although he did not try to stop it. It was at the command of her husband, the Moghul Prince. I have told the Nawab that the Company will strongly disapprove of this summary execution and the manner in which it was carried out and a full report will be made by me to the Governor General.'

'Will they be able to stop Princess Muna being forced to join her husband in Delhi? She has suffered enough and I am sure she will be treated as an outcast in the Badshah's Court.'

'The Company will be reluctant to interfere in what is an internal matter for Mirapore and Delhi, who have suzerainty in feudal matters, but I will insist that no supplementary dowry is paid to the prince, which he is now demanding from Mirapore,' said Gavin.

Helen was not allowed to visit the princess again. It was rumoured that she lapsed each day deeper into madness and was refusing food. Inevitably, news came of her death, brought to the Residency by the Court Physician.

'Sir Gavin and Lady French, I am sorry to be the bearer of sad tidings, once again. Our beloved Princess Muna died last night in her sleep, but I am sure that you, who knew her so well in happier days, will be glad for her release from a life of further misery at the Court of Delhi. Before she became too weak, she gave me this book as a gift to you, Dr. Helen. She said it is her translation from the Persian of the love poems written by her ancestor, the sixteenth century prince, to his beautiful dancing girl, whose tomb is sited in your garden.'

Helen took the little, red, leather-bound book and opened it to see Muna's rounded handwriting on the fly leaf with the inscription: "To my dear friend, Helen, in remembrance of our friendship and another tragic love story."

Tears made the writing swim before Helen's eyes until she could see in her mind's eye the sweet face of Princess Muna, as she galloped by Helen's side, glancing occasionally at the handsome Rohilla guard who was trying, desperately, to avoid those lovely, laughing eyes.

'I will treasure this gift in remembrance of a beautiful and delightful girl whose own love story was as tragic as her ancestor's,' said Helen. 'Thank you for bringing it to me, Doctor Sahib.'

The dignified Mahmoud Bin Said smiled one of his rare and beautiful smiles and said, 'I, myself, have decided that the time has come for me to become *Hadji* by making a pilgrimage to Mecca and so I must bid you, my dear and honoured friends, farewell. I will not be returning to Mirapore but you, my friends and Princess Muna, will always hold a special place in my heart.'

Before he departed he bowed in the way of his people, touching his breast, lips and forehead to bid them farewell with those wonderful Arab words. *'Alaikum Alsalãm'*

Helen had a strange feeling that Mahmoud Bin Said knew more about the little princess's death than he was prepared to admit. The thought struck Helen that she may have been poisoned. Whatever had occurred, she had to agree with her Arab colleague that death was a happy release for little Princess Muna.

Chapter 11

Helen missed the old Arab physician at the clinic They had formed a mutual respect for each other's skill and Mahmoud bin Said, unlike many of her European fellow practitioners, had no difficulty in accepting, from the first, that her sex did not preclude her from being a first-class doctor and surgeon.

The work at the clinic was as heavy as ever and Helen was now assisted by a Parsi, Doctor Patel, who had been engaged by Mahmoud Bin Said a few months ago and the nursing staff had been increased by two Eurasian nurses.

Gavin was called once again to the Punjab for negotiations between the Company and Sikh leaders and the morning he was leaving, he came to the stables where Helen was grooming Sultana. She did not hear him come in and was startled when she looked up and saw him leaning against the stall watching her with a cryptic look in his brown eyes.

'Sorry I startled you, Helen,' he said, his eyes admiring the tableau of the beautiful woman and her pretty mare. 'You two make such a pretty picture, I was reluctant to interrupt. So you groom Sultana, yourself, every day?'

'Yes, it is the best way of bonding with her and she loves the attention,' replied Helen.

Gavin came into the stall and took the curry brush from his wife. He placed both his hands on her shoulders and turned her to face him. 'And what about bonding with your husband, sweetheart,' he said softly, that enigmatic look still in his eyes and a smile twisting his lips.

Helen looked up at him, all too aware of his disturbing proximity - the faint smell of sandalwood and tobacco from his clothes, his dark eyes with those impossibly long lashes and that cleft in his chin which she longed to kiss.

Her green eyes looked into his, and she wondered what she should say, but before she could reply he said, 'I have to go away for about a week to ten days but when I return, I am taking some leave to take you away on a holiday. We have a houseboat on Lake Dal in Kashmir, which you will love and after this business with Princess Muna, you need a well-deserved rest.'

'The clinic...' Helen started to say, but Gavin placed a finger on her lips to silence her.

'Now, Helen, I won't take no for an answer. You will have time, when I am away, to make the necessary arrangements for the clinic and it is important that we spend some time alone together. I must find out why you have erected this barrier between us, my green-eyed minx,' he said, now tracing the contours of her face gently with his fingers, as if he would etch them on his memory. He drew her closer within his arms and lifted a strand of her lovely hair to his lips. He bent his head and kissed the delicious

192

hollow in her throat, visible above the open-neck of her silk blouse and unfastening the top buttons, buried his face in the scented cleft between her breasts, his breathing now quickening. Gavin lifted his head and Helen saw his eyes dark with passion and instinctively swayed towards him. His mouth was on hers and he was kissing her with savage sensuality. Then he let her go and she stepped back putting her fingers on her ravaged lips, her green eyes soft with wonder.

'Just a little souvenir, little sweetheart, so you won't forget your husband,' and with a roguish chuckle and a pat for Sultana, Gavin left her feeling drained and unfulfilled. Why did he always manage to break down her defences, thought Helen, chiding herself for her weakness and wondering how she would be able to resist him when they were alone together in Kashmir. Strangely, she had to admit, that thought both disturbed and thrilled her.

The days before Gavin's return passed slowly even though Helen tried to fill them with her work at the clinic, visits to the fort to see Agnes and her little goddaughter, baby Helen Brown, and, occasionally, rides and fishing trips with John MacGregor. She always felt so comfortable in the big Scotsman's company. He never tried to make love to her, although she often caught his look of tenderness.

One day when they were riding back to Mirapore after visiting the fort, John asked her, 'Are you happy, beautiful Helen? I cannot help noticing that sometimes there is a look of sadness in your eyes.'

Helen smiled at the big, blond man and thought how uncomplicated life would have been if she had fallen in love with him instead of Gavin. He was such a good friend and suddenly Helen wanted to share some of her burden with him; to confide in him her suspicions concerning her husband's secret life, which were driving her mad.

'Do many Englishmen take Indian mistresses, John, especially when their wives are still in England, or dead?'

John MacGregor started and looked at his riding companion quizzically, 'Where did that question come from, Helen? I know it is not just idle curiosity. You are not that type of person.'

'I was just wondering what a man like Gavin would do after his wife died. He was widowed for a few years before our marriage. Like any normal man, he would have had his needs, especially in an environment such as India where the very atmosphere is charged with the erotic,' said Helen, feeling herself flush to the roots of her auburn hair at her almost indelicate conversation.

'Your husband is a man of discrimination, Helen. But surely you do not believe he has a mistress now?'

Then seeing the look of distress in her eyes and the tears which were not far behind, he dismounted and lifted her off her horse. He tethered the two animals nearby and came back to Helen, who was standing gazing, unseeingly, at the stream at the foot of the mountain, gurgling over its boulder-strewn river bed.

John took her hands in his and turned her to face him, asking again, 'Is this what is making you so unhappy? Why do you think your husband has an Indian mistress? You are thinking of Isabel de Silva; am I right, Helen?'

Tears were now glistening in Helen's eyes as she said, 'So even you have noticed, John. How many others know of this, this liaison?'

'I know nothing of any liaison and there has certainly never been any gossip about Gavin and this woman, either before or after your marriage. It was just that I had noticed how she looks at Gavin when she thinks she is unobserved, but I am sure the attraction is on her side, alone. Your husband has eyes only for you. One has only to look at him to see how besotted he is with you, Helen, and I know, only too well, what that feeling is,' chuckled John, wiping the escaped tears off Helen's cheeks with the cushions of his thumbs.

'I feel she resents me and I know she was very close to his first wife, Maria. So perhaps it was only natural that Gavin should turn to her when Maria died. She never fails to interrupt us when we are alone,' explained Helen.

'No doubt she does resent you, or would resent any woman he married, because Gavin is a very attractive man, damn him,' laughed John, 'and I have no doubt the little Goanese woman is in love with him, herself. But if she worries you, why don't you discuss this with Gavin? Promise me you will do so when he returns from this trip.'

Helen smiled at her friend and on an impulse reached up and kissed his cheek, 'John MacGregor, you are the sweetest man I have ever known and I hope and pray that one day soon you, too, will find the love of your life, because that woman will be very fortunate indeed.'

The Scotsman helped Helen mount Sultana, and as he looked up at her, she saw, once again, the pain in his blue eyes that told her more than any words to whom his heart was already given.

The summer days were now getting very warm, although Helen was assured by her European friends that here in the valley of Mirapore with its Alpine climate, the heat was never as stifling as in the plains of India. The monsoons were not very far off and all nature seemed to be waiting with bated breath for the rains, even the call of the jackals seemed louder at night, as if they, too, were waiting in anticipation of the coming monsoon.

Then the storm broke. Helen and Rosita watching from her bedroom window were lost in wonder at the force of their first monsoon, which dwarfed anything they had ever experienced in England. Lightning leaped in forks across the mountain tops and filled the valley below with sheets of electric light. The thunder roared and rolled from the peaks, echoing across the valley as if the gods were shouting their anger from their mighty mountain tops at these insignificant humans who had dared to scale their heights. Then the rain began. At first dimpling the dry dust of the pathways and then escalating into a deluge.

Rosita, never very comfortable in storms, slept that night in Helen's bed and Helen was glad of her company and wondered if Gavin was dry and safe.

Two weeks after Gavin's departure, a hot and very wet Ram Das appeared in the Clinic compound on his little mud splattered mule.

'Memsahib!' he shouted as Helen rushed to meet him, a feeling of gloom clutching her heart at the frantic expression on the servant's face.

'What is it, Ram Das? Has something happened to Gavin *Sahib*?' Helen almost shrieked.

'Yes, *Memsahib*, Afghan tribesmen have taken him hostage. The *Sahib* gave me this piece of paper and a newspaper cutting, which I have to take to the fort, but I had to see you first.'

Helen snatched the paper from Ram Das. It was in Gavin's writing.

'Dear James,

These chaps have taken me hostage in exchange for their leader, who is being held in Fort William by the Governor General. Please do not give in to their demands. Our negotiations in the Punjab and Afghanistan are at a very delicate stage. The release of their leader will foment trouble for the ruler, Dost Muhammad Khan, who as you know, is now our ally against Czarist influence in Afghanistan. Ram Das has a newspaper cutting of the man who is responsible for my kidnap. I filched this from his tent when he was not looking. Apparently he came to India to visit his leader in prison earlier this year, when the press took this picture.'

Helen looked at the almost crumpled cutting and saw the face of the Afghan Khan whose life she had saved from the Thuggee assassins and a glimmer of hope lightened her fearful heart.

'Ram Das, do you know where they are holding my husband? I think I know a way to save Gavin *Sahib*, but it is important we leave without delay. I will arrange for this message to be sent to the fort by one of the sentries on duty at the Residency.'

Having been assured by Ram Das that he would be able to recognise the area where they were captured, Helen sent for a sentry at the gates of the Residency.

'Please take this without delay, Corporal, to Sir James Cameron but give this letter first to Lady Agnes. The Afghans are holding my husband hostage on the borders between Afghanistan and Kashmir.'

Seeing Helen's obvious distress, the soldier said, 'Don't worry, milady, we will get him back alive and well from those damned *Afridis*.'

After much argument from Rosita and Isabel against her decision to travel to Afghanistan, Helen and Ram Das set out on the three fastest hill ponies Ram Das could buy, one each for themselves and a third for the baggage. She hoped that her letter to Agnes, reminding her of the incident with the Khan and his promise to assist her if she ever needed his help, would explain her reasons for the journey.

'Dear Agnes,

My intervention with this man, whom you will remember promised to help me if I needed his assistance, stands more chance of achieving Gavin's release, than an attack by British troops, which may even precipitate his murder. I hope, dear Agnes, you can persuade Sir James to delay his military intervention until I have had time to reach this Afghan leader, Abdul Muhammad Khan.'

On the journey, Ram Das explained that after his meetings in the Punjab with the Sikh leaders, Gavin had decided to visit Kashmir to make arrangements for his holiday with Helen. A few miles from the border with Afghanistan, they were set upon by armed tribesmen and taken prisoner.

'The *Sahib* fought like a lion', explained Ram Das, not disguising the pride in his voice, 'but he was overcome and ordered me to drop my *kukree,* which I had drawn in his defence. We were taken by the tribesman to this Afghan Khan who forced my *Sahib* to write this note about their demands.

There was this newspaper cutting pinned to the wall of the Khan's tent that the Sahib quietly removed and passed to me, unobserved by the Afghans.'

'Was the *Sahib* injured, Ram Das?' asked Helen, feeling an intense pride in her husband's brave resistance, but fearful that he had been wounded.

'Just a few cuts and bruising from the skirmish, but he seemed well enough when I left him.'

Helen and Ram Das travelled all day and rested themselves and the ponies for a few hours each night, usually in a *Dak* bungalow, as long as they were in British protected territory. At Rosita's prompting, Helen dressed as a man and knotted her long hair in a topknot on her head, which she covered with a solar topee. They caused little comment from native fellow travellers, who were not surprised to see the effeminate Englishman and his servant travelling alone. The English were a race apart and nothing they did surprised the Indians. As soon as they came near the border, Ram Das suggested that Helen should now wear the *shalwar kameeze* of a northern Indian Muslim woman and travel in purdah and he purchased a green tunic, embroidered in gold, matching trousers and a black *Burka* that covered her from head to toe - a stifling, but even more effective camouflage.

The scenery across the border began to change. The mountains were indeed high but the landscape lacked the lush vegetation of the Himalayan foothills. The ground over which their ponies picked their way, was strewn with rocks and boulders and only a few stunted trees grew wherever there was a source of water. Sheep and goats grazed on the almost barren mountain sides, foraging for whatever hardy plants grew in this harsh ground that was covered, in the main, by powdery white dust from centuries of erosion. The dust coated their clothes and Helen longed to tear off her enveloping shroud and immerse herself in any little stream they passed.

The villages were scattered, the people very suspicious of these strangers, but Ram Das at last recognised the narrow, boulder-strewn ravine at the end of which stood a small settlement.

Forgetting their agreement not to address her as *'Memsahib'*, he said excitedly, *'Memsahib*, this is the place where the *Sahib* and I were ambushed and that is the village to which we were taken.'

'Hush, Ram Das, remember that I am not your *memsahib*,' said Helen, quietly.

'We are being observed,' whispered Ram Das. 'Look there is a mirror flashing a signal to another at the end of this valley and I am sure there is a warrior behind every boulder on these hillsides,' and Helen's eyes followed the surreptitiously, pointed finger of her servant's hand resting low on the pommel of his saddle.

As if by magic, wild looking men suddenly appeared, firing guns in the air and surrounded the two strangers. They were well armed with rifles, bandoleers of ammunition and dangerous curved knives tucked into their belts. Ram Das shouted to them in their language, *'Pushto'*, which he had learned during his Army service on the North West Frontier. Helen heard him mention the name of Abdul Muhammad Khan and turning to Helen he said, 'Show them the ring,' remembering, thankfully, not to address her as *memsahib* on this occasion.

Helen stretched out her hand from under the *burka* with the Khan's signet ring displayed on her little finger and suddenly realised that it was not only the ring with its conspicuous engravings, but her white hand and manicured fingernails which caught the attention of the Afghans.

'Who is this woman and what is her business with the Khan?' asked one of the tribesmen, his dark eyes trying to pierce the veil of the woman before him.

'Her business is the Khan's business and he would not be pleased if you delayed our meeting with him,' answered Ram Das sharply.

The men spoke together for a few minutes, each head turned to stare at the veiled woman and then the Afghan who had questioned them, indicated that they should follow him.

They brought them to the village and led them to a small hut in which an old crone was kneading coarse flour for bread. The hut was sparsely furnished - a string bed covered by a ragged flowered quilt, a few cushions and rugs and dented pots and pans on a rickety wooden table. The leader of their captors spoke briefly to the old woman, who went out and then he turned to Ram Das and said, 'Wait here with this woman, and I will bring the Khan to you. My mother will bring you food and water presently.'

He left them alone, but Helen noticed that two of the armed warriors squatted just outside the hut. The old woman returned with freshly baked, large, *Chappati* breads, a bowl of curried goat and a brass jug of water. Helen rolled some of the curry in the bread and turning her back to the inquisitive old woman, lifted her heavy *Burka* sufficiently to feed herself. The meat was very strong and stringy despite the spicy seasoning, but Helen was hungry and ate ravenously.

The old woman suddenly burst into high pitched laughter and said something to Ram Das who was also eating his food. He ignored her comments, but when Helen asked him what she had said, he replied in English, 'The old woman believes you must be very ugly to keep yourself veiled even when you are eating. I thought it best not to satisfy her curiosity.'

The old woman soon tired of staring at these strangers and left the hut, probably to tell her neighbours about the ugly woman who was her guest.

A few hours passed and Helen wondered if the Khan would send for them before evening. Ram Das suggested that she should try and get some sleep. Helen realised, suddenly, how tired she was, her weariness brought about not only by the journey, but by anxiety for Gavin. They were now alone, so Helen removed the heavy Burka covering her green and gold *shalwar kameeze* and lay down on the flowered quilt. She had no idea how long she had slept until Ram Das shook her awake. Helen sat up with a start and saw a man standing at the foot of the bed. His face was in shadow, although a kerosene lamp had been lit and placed on the wooden table. He lifted the lamp and came towards her and Helen saw that it was the man she had saved from the Thuggees.

'Ah, the beautiful houri from Paradise!' exclaimed the man with an impudent smile playing on his lips. 'What fortune has made our paths cross again?'

Helen stood up quickly and adjusted her creased clothes before she replied, 'I come to ask for your assistance, Khan *Sahib*, because you gave me your ring and told me that I could rely on your help if I ever needed it. You are holding an Englishman hostage. That man is my husband and I beg you to release him.'

The Afghan, stroking his full beard with one hand, regarded Helen with a strange glint in his dark eyes. Then at last he said, 'A woman as brave as you, who would risk her own life to save her husband's, is a pearl without price. It would be easy to grant your request if I was the only one to make such a decision, but I must consult my fellow leaders first.'

'Please, Khan *Sahib*,' said Helen, desperate to convince the Khan that he alone should decide, because she feared his fellow warriors would not agree to lose their valuable bargaining chip. 'My husband has already advised the British Commander in the letter he sent with his servant, not to agree to your request and I must tell you that the British do not make bargains with kidnappers, even if it means the death of the hostage. But I have not come empty-handed. Here is a great deal of money and a priceless emerald necklace which will buy you food and guns and whatever else you require,' pleaded Helen, putting the wad of notes and the beautiful emeralds, which had been her wedding gift from Gavin, on the table before the Khan.

The rebel leader fingered the notes and the necklace and then he looked up at Helen, his dark eyes holding hers for several moments before he said, 'You saved my life, beautiful lady, and I am honour bound to give you your husband's in return, because I am certain that if the British do not agree to our terms, my people will kill him. He, too, is a brave man. Wait here, I will bring him to you later tonight but you must leave immediately, because there will be some of my comrades who will want to bring him back.'

Then he picked up the money and emeralds and left and Helen and Ram Das waited in trepidation. The Khan's final words left no doubt in Helen's mind that her instinct, personally to call in her debt with the Khan before the British soldiers stormed the village, had been right. Silently she prayed that the Khan would keep his word and bring Gavin to her and she knew that without her husband, life would be worthless.

It was very dark when they heard voices outside the hut and when the curtain covering the low doorway was pushed aside, Gavin still manacled, entered with the Khan. Helen gasped in surprise, because her usually immaculate husband was almost unrecognisable with several days growth on his chin, eyes bloodshot from lack of sleep and a bloodstained bandage around his forehead covering, no doubt, a deep wound.

'Helen, what on earth! Ram Das what is my wife doing here?' shouted Gavin, addressing his servant, but staring at the vision in the garments of a Muslim woman with her beautiful auburn hair tumbling about her shoulders.

Before Ram Das or Helen could answer, the Khan replied, 'Your wife is responsible for your release, Englishman. She has given me something very precious and the bargain was your liberty. So brave and beautiful a woman is my houri from Paradise, and I must tell you that I am tempted to keep her for myself.'

Helen drew in her breath at these words and said, 'Khan *Sahib*, that would be against the teachings of your Koran to take another man's wife.'

'Yes, my beautiful houri, you are right; as a devout Muslim, I would offend our laws whilst your husband is alive, but his death would release me from that obligation.'

Then clasping Helen's hand in his own he said softly, staring hungrily at her with his hawklike eyes, 'Don't worry, if I killed him, I know you would hate me and that I could not bear,' and taking the emerald necklace from his pocket, he clasped it about her slender throat, his fingers lingering on her soft skin.

'The money I will keep, my beautiful *memsahib*, for my people are hungry, but these are yours and your husband's life discharges my debt to you. Now go quickly, all three of you; your horses are tethered outside. Do not stop till you cross the frontier,' and saying this, the Khan cut Gavin's bonds and turning on his heel left the hut, bending his tall, lean, frame to exit the low entrance.

Gavin had said nothing during this exchange and Helen, whose instinct was to run to him and clasp him in her arms, saw instead the glint of anger in his eyes and was surprised at the severity of his voice when he addressed her at last, 'Let us go, as your Afghan friend commanded, before your sacrifice on my behalf is worthless!'

They rode all night, just stopping once to water the ponies at a tiny stream and as dawn broke over the mountains, they came to the borders of Afghanistan and India. Throughout the ride, Gavin had not uttered a word, nor even deigned to answer Helen's question about his wound, except with a shrug and a brooding look in her direction. She wondered at his anger with her. Would he have welcomed martyrdom in his country's cause and did his anger arise from frustration at her efforts to save him: or was there another reason? When they were safely over the border, they stopped to refresh themselves and have a simple meal in a wayside inn and then continued their journey to Kashmir.

Helen was puzzled by Gavin's morose silence and before they reached the Residency houseboat on Lake Dal, her mood, too, had changed from gratitude for the Khan's magnanimity and relief that they were all safe, to anger at her husband's unwarranted stubbornness.

Chapter 12

Despite the atmosphere between Gavin and herself, Helen could not help being entranced by the spectacular Vale of Kashmir and could well understand the Emperor Jahangir, two centuries ago, whispering the name of Kashmir with his dying breath.

The beautiful Lake Dal, the summer retreat of Moghul Emperors in the past and now of the British, was spectacular. Its waters, with its unusual floating gardens, formed a perfect setting for the moored Residency houseboat, the only type of property, Gavin had told her, that the Princely Ruler of the State permitted foreigners to own.

Helen was surprised how well furnished and spacious their houseboat was, its design copied by the English from their houseboats on the River Thames. Constructed entirely of wood, the rooms had walnut panelling and ceilings. A large, open drawing room, with elegant furniture, crystal wall lights mounted on the panelled walls alongside beautiful paintings of Kashmir and floors covered with thick Kashmiri carpets, added to the air of luxury. An equally well furnished and elegant dining room, two cosy bedrooms and a bathroom with the latest Victorian fittings, including a large china bath standing on clawed feet, completed the stylish accommodation.

The drawing room led onto a shaded verandah, with a wooden carved fretwork balustrade running all along the front of the boat. Moored alongside the main boat was the kitchen boat which also housed the servants and a rowing boat, comfortably cushioned, called a *shikara,* which was manned by a young Kashmiri, whose only duty was to row them around the lake, or to and from the mainland.

The servants in the kitchen boat, a cook and his wife, were also the caretakers of the houseboat and it seemed their sole aim in life was to cook delicious meals and pamper the Resident and his guests.

After a very welcome bath, Helen opened the wardrobe in the bedroom and found some pretty muslin day dresses and a yellow silk Japanese kimono, clothes that had evidently belonged to Maria. She chose a pale cream dress embroidered with posies. Maria had, obviously, been the same height as Helen, but the bodice of the dress was a little tight, clinging to Helen's more curvaceous figure and she recalled the nude portrait of Gavin's first wife depicting a woman with small breasts, a tiny waist and voluptuous hips.

The meal was ready for them when Helen joined Gavin in the dining room. He, too, had bathed and shaved and discarded the bandage around his head, revealing a very red, three-inch knife wound.

'Gavin, would you like me to redress that cut? It should be kept clean until it has healed completely,' said Helen, approaching her husband to inspect the rather angry wound.

'Don't fuss, Helen, I have had worse injuries than this in the past.' There was a glitter in Gavin's eyes which were as hard as steel as he looked at the woman standing in front of him, as if he was seeing her for the first time and Helen was very aware that his angry mood had not changed.

The meal progressed almost in silence except for polite conversation, mainly on Helen's part, about the beauty of Kashmir and the comfort of the houseboat. Was this the congenial holiday Gavin had promised her, when he had held her in his arms that morning in the stables, before he left on his ill-fated trip? The man opposite was almost a stranger, allowing only a taut smile to register occasionally more, she believed, for the servants' benefit than hers. What had caused him to turn on her like this? True, she had been the first to raise a barrier between them when she had refused him his conjugal rights but in the days and months that followed, Gavin had been a pleasant and affectionate companion.

Helen suddenly felt bone-weary: the events of the past few days were taking their toll and Gavin's inexplicable coldness towards her was more than she could bear.

'I'll have an early night, if you don't mind. Perhaps, tomorrow, I will return to Mirapore with Ram Das. You seem to prefer to be on your own.'

Gavin looked up with a frown and said curtly, 'I am afraid you will have to put up with me for a few more days, Helen. Ram Das has already set out on his return journey to Mirapore with a message for Sir James. I expect your friend, John MacGregor, and a few soldiers will be here soon to escort us back to Mirapore. Now if you will excuse me, I must prepare my report on my recent negotiations with the Sikhs.'

Gavin walked out on to the verandah without another glance at Helen. She too rose and thanked the cook and his wife for the delicious meal and went to her bedroom. She took off Maria's dress and put on the kimono, the silk feeling cool against her bare skin. From the bedroom window she could see the spectacular mountain, Nanga Parbat, the ninth highest, Gavin had informed her, in the Himalayan range, the setting sun blushing its peak to a rosy hue. Kashmir was made for lovers but the man she loved suddenly seemed so far away. She heard the servants leave and Gavin's voice bidding them 'Goodnight' and Helen knew that they were now quite alone. Would Gavin come to her to-night?

Helen waited, lying on the top of the bed, eschewing the sheets because of the warm night and wearing only the silk kimono. It was dawn when she awoke, the pale morning light drifting through the open window. A man was standing at the foot of her bed looking down at her. He was naked from the waist up and with a start Helen recognised her husband. His hair was dishevelled, his eyes bloodshot and the cut on his forehead bleeding slightly. He had obviously torn off the dressing and reopened the wound.

Gavin's tall figure seemed to dominate the room. He stood watching her, with arms folded across his broad, bare chest, observing the way the silk of

212

her kimono clung to her tantalising body, the nipples of her full breasts pointing seductively through the thin garment. He was smiling, almost leering, and suddenly he reached out with his strong brown arms and pulled Helen to her feet.

The smell of whisky invaded Helen's nostrils and she knew that Gavin had been drinking heavily. Suddenly she was afraid. Never had she seen her husband the worse for drink and the look in his eyes showed no gentleness, only a burning lust. His hands were unfastening the kimono and he drew back slightly without releasing her, devouring her naked body with his eyes and Helen was reminded of a slave dealer assessing the merits of a potential slave.

'Yes', he said, almost reluctantly, 'you are the most desirable woman I have ever seen. Your lovely, auburn hair framing that perfect face and a body that even Venus would envy; your beautiful eyes which change colour with the clothes you wear, sometimes green as emeralds or turquoise as the sea, eyes that could steal a man's soul if he was not aware of the falseness underneath all that beauty.'

Helen flinched as Gavin's trembling hands touched her hair, her face, her breasts as he defined her charms, ending with those unkind words.

'Gavin, you are drunk, you don't know what you are saying,' said Helen, cut to the quick that her husband should accuse her of duplicity. She tried to shake off his strong arms, but he held her tighter, laughing cruelly at her discomfort.

'Come, my little whore, you give to other men what you refuse your husband, but to-night I am determined to take what is mine by right. I have been too patient, too gentle. Obviously, in the light of recent events, your preference is for a rougher lover!'

While he was speaking, he had lifted Helen in his arms and laid her on the bed. Still holding onto her with one hand, he divested himself of his breeches and, completely naked, knelt over her. Helen closed her eyes, slightly shocked at the sight of his aggressive manhood; his face so close to hers, twisted with desire as he swept her body with kisses and caresses, stopping only to whisper loving endearments interspersed with insults. This was a Gavin she did not know, ruthless and determined, but his caresses were inflaming her and despite her indignation, she found herself entwining her arms about his neck, allowing herself to be carried along on the wave of his ecstasy. His savage loving was a far cry from the tender, controlled passion he had displayed in the past but, Gavin, her love, her husband, was at last making her his.

'Gavin, why are you punishing me like this? This is not how it should be between us,' Helen heard herself pleading, but he paid no attention. He continued to kiss and caress her, smiling as he saw her response to each touch of his lips and tongue, as if he was deliberately playing her body to achieve a crescendo of love, like a virtuoso plucking the strings of his violin. She responded to his every touch and she heard him say hoarsely, 'I am the only man for you, Helen French, the only one who can send you to paradise like this,' as if he was challenging her to recognise his expertise as a lover.

Helen felt his lips caress her breasts, his tongue licking her nipples to hardness and then as she arched her back to thrust her breast into his mouth, she winced at the slight pain when she felt his teeth. He was laughing, hoarsely, as his fingers explored the sensitive, secret places of her body and she groaned with ecstasy, her body writhing under his lover's caresses, aware only of the unimaginable pleasure Gavin was giving her. Then the seducer became the seduced, as Helen, shyly and tentatively, encircled his arrogant manhood with her fingers and whispered, 'Gavin, oh my lover.' She heard his involuntary gasp of pleasure and, instinctively, arched her body to meet his own. With an oath he drove hard into her and froze.

She cried out at the sudden pain and felt him still within her and murmur against her mouth, 'Helen, oh my little sweetheart, what have I done?' She felt him quiver with strain and saw his eyes mist over with emotion, but he was inside her, part of her now and no matter how sharp the sudden pain had been, she knew she wanted his loving to continue. Her green eyes widened as she held him enclosed within her and her body responded to the sensations he was creating, as he gently stroked and caressed her. Then arching her body convulsively, she once more invited his deeper possession. Her sweet, hot, moist, tightness overwhelmed him so completely that with a cry as old as primeval man, he drove deeper into his woman until their bodies were swamped with the scents and euphoria of their mutual climax.

When the waves of passion ended, Helen heard Gavin's voice, as if from a long way away. She was conscious of the rapid beating of her heart, or was it his, as he lay collapsed on her shuddering body. She felt him move away and when she opened her eyes, he was stumbling towards the door. What was wrong? Why did he leave her so soon? Had she disappointed him with her inexperience? Helen, perplexed and feeling that she had been used, was suddenly ashamed and angry, sobs tearing her body as she buried her face in her pillow. How could she have given herself so completely to this man, who had betrayed her?

The day went by with hardly a word from Gavin. Apart from breakfast, he locked himself in the other bedroom to work on his report and instructed the Kashmiri boy to row Helen around the lake. Helen, too, wanted to keep her distance and when the boy suggested she should hire a pony and guide to take her trekking into the mountains, she jumped at the opportunity. The magnificent mountain scenery, the snow-clad peaks and the carpet of wild summer flowers filling the valley floor, could not ease her pain. She stopped for tea at a Swiss style hotel and when she could not prolong her absence any longer, she hired a *shikara* to take her back to the houseboat.

Gavin came that night to her bedroom but he stood awkwardly inside the doorway for a moment before coming towards her. He took her arm and guided her to the window seat, sitting beside her and keeping hold of her hand.

'I believe I owe you an explanation for my brutish behaviour last night, Helen,' he said quietly.

'You were drunk, Gavin, but I do not understand why you had to insult me and treat me like a bazaar woman,' and Helen, with perverse pleasure, watched her husband wince. 'Is that the sort of woman you want in your bed?'

'Of course not,' Gavin stood up and walked away from her, his hands held behind his back, clenching in agony as he continued, 'I was angry, jealous, if you like, because I believed you had given yourself to the Afghan leader in exchange for my freedom. I remember his words as clearly as if they had been etched in stone, "She has given me something very precious and the bargain was your liberty." As he gave you back your emeralds, I could only assume that you had slept with him in exchange for my liberty. He was obviously enchanted with you. Please forgive me.'

'The Khan was the man I rescued from the Thuggees in Mirapore and 'the precious gift', to which he referred, was his own life,' explained Helen quietly.

She watched her husband's broad back and suddenly thought of Isabel de Silva. No Gavin French, you are not going to be forgiven so easily, what about your own duplicity, but Helen did not utter these words, instead she said, 'Even if I had given myself to the Khan to save your life, you should have been grateful, not treated me so unfairly. But what made you change your mind about my morality?'

Gavin turned to face his wife again and said quietly, 'I knew when I took you last night that I was the first. Can you forgive me?'

Helen looked at her husband's pale, drawn face and she should have felt compassion, but Isabel de Silva's image kept intruding and she did not know whether she loved or hated this handsome man standing so dejectedly in front of her.

She said, half to herself, 'You men are all the same, one rule of morality for your wives, but another for yourselves. Even Princess Muna had to die to wipe out the dishonour she brought to her dissolute Prince, who would have continued in his profligate ways even after he took her to his bed.'

Gavin looked puzzled and his eyes narrowed. 'What has Princess Muna's marriage to do with us? I have explained the reason for my brutish behaviour to you last night, which I regret with all my heart. I hoped you could forgive me but it seems you are determined to continue this war between us. Well so be it, I will not grovel,' and with those words Gavin French, his arrogant male pride ruffled, stormed out of Helen's bedroom, banging the door behind him.

The next morning Helen awoke to the beautiful sunrise over Dal Lake, the sunshine turning the waters of the lake into burnished gold. Fishermen were casting nets from small boats, birds hovering to share their catch and in the distance she could hear the call of a *muezzin* summoning the faithful to prayer. It was a beautiful day.

Gavin, too, seemed to recover his self-control and surprised Helen by suggesting that he should show her some of Kashmir whilst they awaited their escort from Mirapore.

'I am taking you on a visit today to the beautiful Shalimar Gardens and some of the other sights for which Kashmir is famous. I am sure you will wish to use these few days before we return to Mirapore to see more of this beautiful State.'

Gavin was an attentive and congenial host and the upheaval of their recent encounters was almost forgotten by Helen, as he took her arm and guided her from one exquisite sight to another. They picnicked in the lovely Shalimar Gardens, built by the Moghul Emperor, Jahangir, for his queen, Nur Jehan, and were entranced by the terraced Nishat Gardens designed by her brother Asaf Khan. They walked around the bazaars of Srinagar and

Audrey Blankenhagen

took a boat across Lake Dal to Nagin Lake to visit Hazratbal and the famous mosque in which is housed a hair of the Prophet Mohammed.

That evening after a typical Kashmiri meal of several courses, Gavin took Helen on a *doonga,* a pleasure boat, where musicians sang love songs to the accompaniment of Kashmiri musical instruments.

The night was lit by soft moonlight, the scenery around them exquisite and Gavin put his arm around his wife's shoulders as they reclined on comfortable cushions and listened to the haunting melodies. His lips brushed her hair and when she looked up at him, she saw that unique smile of his that always reminded her of 'The Buccaneer', the subject of a painting, which had hung in her father's study. Gavin's smile was the same as that bold man's - bright and audacious.

'Are you enjoying yourself, little sweetheart? There is so much more of this lovely part of India, which I would like to show you. I promise I will bring you back here one day. Would you like that?'

'Oh, yes, very much and I would like to bring dear Rosita with us, Gavin,' smiling up at her husband, her beautiful eyes no longer flashing anger at him and Gavin recalled how dark they had become with passion when he held her in his arms, not so many hours ago.

His own eyes darkened as he looked at her, remembering her cries of ecstasy, her sweet voice calling his name and suddenly he wanted her again and was forced to withdraw his arm from her shoulders, because the touch of her was more than he could bear.

His gesture was not lost upon Helen and she wondered if he regretted his display of affection towards her. The barrier between them was as high as ever and Helen, too, moved slightly away finding Gavin's proximity very disturbing.

That night as she lay in her bed, through the thin walls of the bedrooms, she could hear Gavin pacing up and down in his room like a frustrated, caged prisoner. Was he, too, longing for love? Then why did he not come to her again, take her in his arms and drive her to distraction? But she waited in vain and when his pacing stopped, she knew he would not seek her out that night. He had been disappointed in her; she was not comparable to his first wife, the voluptuous Maria. She hated herself for being so inexperienced in the art of pleasing a man. Her puberty had been spent in studying medicine, passing exams and becoming a doctor. But how was she to learn how to please her husband if he did not teach her?

At last asleep, her cheeks wet with tears, she did not hear the quiet footsteps of Gavin as he came into her room and stood at the foot of her bed watching her. She looked so vulnerable lying there in all her beauty, one round breast escaping from her night dress, her beautiful hair fanning out on the pillow and he stooped and kissed her gently, afraid to awake her in case he saw, once again, the contempt in her eyes.

221

Last night, he had taken her savagely, wanting to hurt and humiliate her in his jealous rage but when she had responded so passionately, whispering his name and touching him shyly, his control had snapped and he took her unexpected virginity so ruthlessly. He should have known; he recalled how amazed he had been when she responded to his every touch, as if she had never been touched before. He saw the desire in her emerald eyes, eyes which had haunted him in his dank prison in the Afghan village and he thought of her looking at the Khan with that same wide-eyed passion, and almost hated her. Only when his passion was spent and he felt her quivering body beneath his, and looked up to see her eyes closed, long, damp lashes hiding their expression, that he cursed himself for his brutality. He stumbled from her room, not wanting to face her contempt and just outside the bedroom door, heard her distressed sobs. How she must have despised him.

Now, looking at her lying there, with the moonlight shining on her loveliness, he remembered his delight when he first saw her standing in the doorway of the Residency, with the sunlight outlining her figure through the thin stuff of her dress. She was so beautiful and as the days and months went by, he found himself more and more entranced by her, not just by her beauty, but by her intelligence and, yes, even though it had irritated him many times, her independent spirit.

Helen was like no other woman he had ever known and he knew that he had never loved this way before. He had no false modesty in denying his own appeal to women. There had been many lovers before Maria, his first wife, who attracted him because she, too, was different. It was only after their marriage that he realised just how different Maria was and the direction of her sexuality, which had repulsed him.

But Helen, from her instinctive responses to his love-making was, without doubt, a passionate woman yet to be awakened to her full potential and he was determined that he would be the man to turn that key, despite her efforts to keep him at arm's length.

'Be warned, my beautiful Helen,' Gavin whispered to his sleeping wife, 'when we get back to Mirapore, things are going to change between us and I will woo you until you are mine and mine alone.'

Chapter 13

The escort from Mirapore, soldiers from the Sikh platoons and John MacGregor, arrived the next morning. The little houseboat was quite crowded and the cook and his wife almost overwhelmed with this sudden influx of British military power. John, with his usual Scottish bluffness, embraced Helen and turning to Gavin said, 'What a woman you have here, Gavin. To ride into the remote Afghan mountains to barter for her husband's life is truly in the spirit of our own Flora MacDonald. Lassie, you had us all worried sick!'

Gavin smiled, his mouth twisting wryly in acknowledgement of the Scotsman's words, but recalling his own churlish behaviour and jealousy, he drew Helen into the circle of his arms and said softly, 'I will never forget what my wife did for me, John.' Then whispering into her ear so that she, alone, heard his words, 'and how I repaid her.'

The journey back to Mirapore was long, but uneventful. Helen rode between John and Gavin and listened to their conversation about the Santal tribal rebellion in Bengal against British efforts to control them and to tax their land.

'There has also been unrest in the Bengal Army whose sepoys are reluctant to be sent to Burma over the *Kala Pani,* as they call the ocean.

224

Why they should consider the colour of the sea 'black', when it is either blue or grey according to its moods, is very strange,' commented John.

'Perhaps it is because the Europeans came by sea to conquer this sub continent, whereas all the other invaders came overland from the North. I have also heard it said, by some of the more conservative Indian rulers, that the British sent their young Indian princes overseas to be educated in our schools and universities and they returned more English than the English, changes which their parents could not understand. Perhaps 'black' reflects their apprehension,' said Gavin.

Helen looking at the tall, bearded Sikh soldiers riding ahead of them could not believe that these splendid warriors could be anything but loyal to the Company they served.

'Do the Indians really understand us?' questioned Helen, remembering the Begum Shalima's words of criticism. 'We keep ourselves segregated in our homes, our clubs and our cantonments, as if we are afraid to be corrupted by their culture and we may give them the impression of arrogance, even of disdain.'

Gavin looked at his wife, surprised that she, after so short a time in India, had observed something, which many an old Indian hand failed to see.

'You are quite right, Helen; our segregation might strengthen our position as rulers, but it does nothing to endear us to the people of this

225

ancient land with its long history and its vast differences of castes and creeds. I despise the protocol and prejudice, which creates such a barrier between the Indians and the British. As Lord Bentinck said, "We must never forget that we rule India for the Indians".

Helen, hearing Gavin's words, felt a deep respect and admiration for her husband and was not surprised that Gavin's understanding and love for the Indian people made him one of the most effective ambassadors for the Company.

At last they arrived at Mirapore and were greeted with rousing cheers by the sentries at the gates of the Residency. Their arrival had been announced even before they entered the City gates and Rosita and Isabel were standing, expectantly, on the steps of the house, with all the servants lined up on either side like a guard of honour.

Helen had barely dismounted when she was clasped to the ample bosom of a tearful Rosita, who laughed and cried as she thanked God for bringing her dear child safely home and she was not content until Gavin, too, had been encompassed in her motherly arms.

Noticing his wound, she broke into a stream of Spanish, thanking all the saints that he was still alive.

Gavin laughed and lifting her off her feet said teasingly, 'With all those saints to protect me, how can I fail to return to you, *querida* Rosita.'

THE CURSE OF KALI

Then seeing Isabel's quiet, tearful emotion when she said, 'I, too, have prayed for your safe return,' Gavin put his arm around the little Goanese woman's shoulders and smiling, said gently, 'Thank you, Isabel. You see, all your prayers have been answered; we are both safe and well.'

Helen felt a stab of pain as she saw Gavin's gesture, wondering if he was deliberately suppressing his desire to hold Isabel de Silva close in his arms.

She looked towards John MacGregor, who was smiling sweetly at her, no doubt guessing her thoughts about Gavin and Isabel and she wanted to run to him and feel the safety of his arms as she had on the night of the storm at sea and hear his strong voice soothing away her fears.

John was their guest that night and after dinner, he and Gavin talked late into the night.

The next morning Helen was awakened by a flock of noisy mynah birds imitating the calls of other birds in the mango trees outside her bedroom window. She stretched and walked to the window to watch the squabbling colony and noticed on her dressing table a single red rose and a blue velvet box. A note was propped up against the box and it read, '

'My sleeping beauty, you looked so lovely and peaceful this morning that I did not have the heart to awake you.

'I hope you will like this little gift which I meant to present to you on our holiday in Kashmir, but you were so angry with me that I felt the gift would have been misunderstood.

'I have to go back to the Punjab again, but John and a platoon of Highlanders will be accompanying me at the insistence of Sir James, so I shall be quite safe.

Until we meet again,

Your loving husband.'

Once again the unmistakable flourish of Gavin's signature ended the little note and Helen wondered when he had crept into her room to leave the beautiful ruby and diamond bracelet and the red rose.

She picked up the lovely flower and placed it against her lips, remembering her husband's kisses and their angry night of passion on the houseboat, which had left her emotionally confused.

'What an enigma you are to me, my darling husband,' Helen whispered to her reflection in the mirror. 'If only you could love me as much as I love you, Gavin, because there is no room in my heart for any other man.'

After her morning ride on Sultana, who showed such equine delight when Helen greeted her in the stable, Helen felt restless. The day promised to be humid and the cool of the marble mausoleum seemed to be the obvious place to read the little book of the Khan's love poems, translated so lovingly by Princess Muna.

Helen entered the little *chaatri* and noticed a trug of flowers at the foot of the tomb. She wondered why they had not been arranged in the crystal vase that had been provided for this purpose.

She sat down on the stone bench and opened the book to the first poem and a picture of the grieving Khan contemplating his lover's resting place was not hard to imagine, as Helen read the poignant words of love he had dedicated to his dead beloved. She thought, too, of the beautiful Princess Muna, who had come into her life for such a short time and left it so tragically. She hoped that the long dead Khan and the little princess were at last reunited in Paradise with their respective lovers.

The faint sound of a flute reached Helen's ears and she wondered where she had heard that refrain before. A rustling noise and sudden movement in the trug of flowers caught Helen's eye. Her blood froze; the head of a cobra rose amidst the blooms and started to sway to the melody of the pipe. Then she remembered where she had heard that music before. Men with dancing bears and snake charmers often called at the fort to entertain the children and it was the snake charmer's flute that she could hear now. She had also been told that when the music stopped, the snake was at its most dangerous.

The snake continued to sway, its flat head moving to the tune of the pipe, its hooded eyes watching her. Helen stood up cautiously and moved slowly towards the door of the *chaatri,* praying that the music would continue to hypnotise the reptile until she had reached the exit. Suddenly the door flew open and the gardener stood there with a trug of flowers in his hand. His eyes opened wide as he saw the swaying snake and he rushed back into the garden shouting, '*Sarp, Sarp!* Helen was too terrified to call him back and then Ram Das was there with his *kukree*.

'Don't move, *memsahib*,' he whispered and stealthily approached the trug with its deadly occupant. A quick flash of his curved blade and the decapitated cobra was writhing in its death throes.

Helen sat down on the stone bench, her legs refusing to bear her weight any longer until she noticed the gardener looking fearfully over Ram Das's shoulder. 'Why did you bring another trug of flowers, *mali*? Did you not remember the first trug?' asked a puzzled Helen.

'*Memsahib*, I did not bring those other flowers in here. I have only just cut these fresh blooms for the vase and came to arrange them, when I saw the snake.'

Ram Das had picked up the dead cobra and replaced it in the trug.

'*Memsahib*,' he said, 'something is not quite right here. I too heard the snake charmer's music even before the *mali* shouted, "*Sarp, Sarp!*"' If you will excuse me, I will find the snake charmer and bring him back for questioning. Why should he be in the Residency grounds charming snakes?'

Helen picked up her book of poems and rose to leave the mausoleum, when Isabel de Silva appeared in doorway. She took one look at Helen's white face and the dead snake in the trug and shouted, 'Oh my God, have you been bitten, Helen?'

'No, Isabel, thanks to the deftness of Ram Das's *kukree*.'

Ram Das searched the grounds of the Residency, thoroughly, without success and was told by the guards at the gates that no snake charmer had, or would have been allowed to pass them. It was a mystery and Rosita, particularly, was very anxious.

That evening she came to Helen's bedroom and told her of her own strange experience whilst Helen and Gavin were away in Afghanistan.

'I went to your bedroom to repair the lace on one of your shifts, when I heard chanting that seemed to come from the mausoleum. I looked out of the window and in the moonlight I saw a woman's figure, and yet it was not a woman, because it was slithering like a reptile towards the monument. It may have been clouds crossing the moon, but the figure was suddenly huge and black, like an enormous shadow. I was so afraid, I fell on my knees and prayed to Our Lady to save me. When I opened my eyes and looked out of the window again, there was nothing, even the chanting had stopped.'

Helen listened to Rosita and then told her about her own experience on the first night of their arrival in Mirapore.

'I believe, *querida*,' said Rosita, 'that something evil is in that monument. This is a strange country full of idols and mysticism. To-morrow I will visit my friend, the Senora Hernandez, and ask her to let us borrow her Catholic chaplain, Father Carlos. He will exorcise any evil there is, I am sure.'

'Oh, Rosita, do you think we should reveal our fears to the Spanish Consulate? Besides this is a Muslim mausoleum and the Nawab may not appreciate an infidel defiling the tomb with the Christian rites of exorcism.'

'He need never know. I will ask Father Carlos to call at the Residency, as if he is visiting me and then I will take him quietly to the tomb when no one is around. If there are any repercussions, then you can blame your superstitious Spanish companion,' said Rosita.

Father Carlos visited the Residency whilst Helen was at the Clinic and she heard from Rosita, later, that he had performed the rites of exorcism, but it was his firm belief that the evil was not in the tomb, but came from another source.

It was six weeks since their return from Kashmir and Helen awoke one morning feeling quite nauseous. She wondered if a stomach bug was the cause, but a brief look at the calendar confirmed the lateness of her period. Could she be pregnant, or had her recent stressful episode with the snake upset her cycle? She would have to wait and see.

Helen had taken Sultana for a gentle ride, aware that if she was pregnant, strenuous riding would not be advisable. The forest paths were

232

cool and sitting astride a horse enabled horse and rider to approach even the shyest animal before it took fright and fled. Helen had halted Sultana near a clearing and was admiring the little spotted deer grazing on the edge of the thicket. Suddenly the animal looked up, a look of anxiety in its alert eyes and Helen reached for her gun in its gunboot, strapped to the offside of her saddle, but the sound which disturbed the deer was not a predator but the hoofbeats of another horse.

The rider came galloping into the clearing and Helen's heart jumped for joy when she recognised Gavin and Sultan. He whooped for joy when he saw her and vaulting off his horse even before the animal had stopped, Gavin bounded towards Helen pulling her from her saddle into his arms and claiming her mouth with a kiss so passionate, it left her breathless.

'My darling, little sweetheart, have you missed me as much as I have missed you?' he said, huskily, when his mouth finally released hers, but before Helen could reply, he was kissing her again, whispering endearments and torturing her with his hands and his lips on her body.

Then the rain began to fall, large drops which threatened to drench them and Gavin lifted Helen in his arms and ran for the shelter of the tree with the densest foliage, a large banyan, its spreading branches forming a perfect shelter.

They were both laughing now and as Helen leaned against the sturdy tree, Gavin's strong body formed a barrier between her and the rain.

233

'Shall I tie you to this tree, little sweetheart, and rescue you again when it is dark?' chuckled Gavin and Helen knew that he, too, was thinking of that evening so long ago in the English woods.

Helen looked up at his dark, teasing eyes, his wet tousled hair and reached up to kiss the cleft in his chin, an impulse she soon regretted, because Gavin was suddenly serious, 'Helen I want you so much, tell me that you want me too,' his fingers already unbuttoning her shirt. With a low moan he kissed each naked breast, his tongue circling the dark pink areola, before taking the sensitive tips into his mouth. Helen felt her pulses pounding, her body shuddering and she knew that she had no resistance left and would soon become this man's creature as much as Isabel de Silva.

'No, no!' she heard herself protest.

Gavin released her and stood back, his jaw set, a fierce look replacing the love in his eyes. He bent over her once more and said angrily, 'So you are determined not to forgive me, Helen. I will not beg, nor will I take you again without your consent. But remember this, I am a man with a man's needs and if my wife rejects me, there are other women who would gladly welcome me to their beds.'

Without another word or glance in her direction, Gavin mounted Sultan, who was grazing nearby with Sultana and rode off leaving Helen shaken and angry.

She heard herself sobbing and shouting to the trees. 'Yes, I know Gavin French, you have another woman who will always welcome you to her bed but I will not play second fiddle, even if I am carrying your child.' But Helen's heartbroken sobs and her words of reproach echoed through the forested foothills and were carried by the winds to the high peaks of the Himalayas and beyond, but they did not reach her husband's ears.

Gavin did not appear again that day, locking himself in his study, ostensibly for work and ordering his meals to be served there.

Helen asked for the carriage to take her to the clinic and there she immersed herself in work until late evening. Then bone weary and with a feeling of deep depression, she ate a light supper and retired for the night.

A worried Rosita watched the pale face of her beloved child as she brushed her hair and knew that something had upset her. Was it Gavin's fault? Yet when he had returned that morning, the first thing he did was enquire after Helen and hearing that she was out riding, had barely stopped to change his clothes before setting out to find her, his eagerness all too obvious to Rosita.

'Is everything all right, *querida mia*? You look so pale and tired,' she asked.

Yes, I am fine, dear Rosita, but I am very tired. There was a lot of work at the clinic today. I think that is enough hair brushing for tonight. I'll feel better after a good night's rest,' said Helen, as she kissed Rosita on her cheek and climbed into her large bed.

The next morning, Gavin watched his wife from his study window climb into the phaeton. She was carrying her medical bag so he guessed she was on her way to the clinic. He noticed that Helen looked pale and cursed himself for upsetting her the day before. Why did he threaten her with another woman? His heart was filled only with thoughts of her but she had made him so angry, at first looking at him as if she loved him and then rejecting him when she had aroused his passion. No other woman had ever had this effect on him, driving him to despair and frustration and yet he would give his right arm if she would only love him as he loved her.

Several days passed and Helen and Gavin were like polite strangers when they met, which was not often as they avoided each other as much as possible. Helen was glad when Gavin had to leave Mirapore with the Nawab to inspect the Company's plans to build a railway to connect Mirapore to other hill stations in British India.

She knew that Gavin had used all his diplomatic skills to persuade the Nawab that a railway link would be mutually advantageous to Mirapore and the Company, and he was determined to guide the ruler through these final stages.

The monsoon had been intermittent this year and the few early storms had not filled the nullahs to irrigate the land in village India, bringing a threat of famine to the drier regions. Here in the foothills, there was enough rain and the Nawab had made a good profit selling the bountiful produce of his valley to Indian merchants. Gavin had pointed out to Mohammed Hassan Khan, that when the British completed their ambitious plans to link all India by rail, a railway link would, in times of drought, bring in even more revenue for the State. Its produce could be transported direct to the dry kingdoms of the wealthy Rajput Princes, cutting out the middlemen, rich *bunias* who made an enormous profit.

Helen continued to feel lethargic and she finally had to admit that it was not only her difficult marriage, but pregnancy which accounted for her state of mind. Morning sickness was now the norm and it was this latter symptom that she could not hide from Rosita's sharp eyes.

'Helen, *querida mia*, I believe that you are going to have a baby. You must tell Gavin when he returns. He will be thrilled.'

'No, not yet, I will tell him when I believe the time is right. Please do not say anything to anyone, Rosita,' implored Helen and Rosita knew that her child had good reason to keep her husband in the dark. The barrier which she had noticed between these two seemed higher than ever and she was afraid to delve deeper, feeling powerless to help her beloved child with something she knew only husband and wife must solve. That they loved each other, she had no doubt, but something was keeping them apart.

Rosita felt that it was the evil she had sensed which was blighting the lives of these two beloved people and, once again, she asked Father Carlos to bless the whole area.

Helen came home from the clinic, hot and tired, to hear voices raised in anger coming from the tomb. She opened the door and was surprised to see Rosita and Isabel shouting at each other and a very embarrassed Father Carlos trying to calm the two angry women.

'What is going on here?' exclaimed an irritated Helen.

'Mrs. Llewellyn is defiling this tomb by inviting this priest to perform his mumbo jumbo not only here, but in the house and in the gardens,' yelled an unbelievably rude Isabel, her eyes glaring at Rosita and the priest and her little fists clenched as if she would like to strike them both. Helen was taken aback at the ferocity of Isabel's attack, especially as the woman had always been so meek and subservient.

'You realise that they are putting Gavin in a very difficult position as the British Resident to a Muslim court,' she continued, now addressing herself directly to Helen.

Helen, stung by the woman's arrogance and rudeness, said with an icy voice,'You forget your position, Isabel. Sir Gavin does not need your sympathy. He is diplomat enough to deal with any problem. Now, as to the question of Father Carlos's blessing, I believe even Islam believes in the might of Allah over *Saitan* and if Mrs. Llewellyn, as a good Catholic, wishes her priest to bless our home, then she has my support.

'Please leave us, I wish to speak to Father Carlos and Mrs. Llewellyn.'

Isabel de Silva left the tomb, but the anger and spite in her face was apparent for all to see.

'Please excuse my housekeeper's behaviour, Father. I thought as a Goanese, she would be of the Catholic faith and pleased to have your blessing,' said Helen.

'I do not understand the woman, myself,' said the priest. 'Rosita and I were speechless when she burst into the tomb and harangued us. As for being a Catholic, I do not believe that is her faith, Lady French. As I have told Mrs. Llewellyn, the evil she senses is not in this tomb but elsewhere. Nevertheless, I have faith that the holy rites I have performed will keep its malign influence at bay, at least in the Residency and its grounds.'

Chapter 14

Two days after the awkward scene with Isabel de Silva, Rosita fell ill. At first she was merely out of sorts, feeling queasy and with a loss of her usually robust appetite. Helen wondered if it was the sudden heat and insisted that Rosita should rest in her bedroom, cooled continuously by the *punkah* and dampened blinds at the windows. However, her symptoms became more acute. Rosita complained of tingling in her mouth, dulled sight and hearing and Helen noticed that her breathing was difficult and despite the heat, she was shivering. Helen suspected that her beloved friend had been poisoned.

Her first task was to give her a strong emetic and regardless of the heat, to keep Rosita warm. The *punkah* was stopped and the wet blinds removed and when the vomiting ceased, Helen made Rosita drink a glass of strong brandy. She seemed to be better by evening but Helen, nevertheless, sent Ram Das to fetch Dr. Graham from the fort.

'I believe you have diagnosed poisoning correctly, Helen. Mrs. Llewellyn's symptoms suggest some sort of poisonous irritant, but what?' questioned the Scottish doctor.

'I'll have to monitor her breathing, carefully. If she continues to vomit, I'll administer the emetic by enema. Do you agree?' Helen asked Dr. Graham,

'Yes, that would be the best and perhaps a more drastic antidote will not be necessary if the poison is flushed out of her system. I'll call again tomorrow, if she is no better.'

Rosita had a restless night and by morning, her breathing was once again difficult and it was clear that despite all the treatment, the poison was still in her system.

Helen, at her wit's end, remembered Dr. Patel at the clinic. The Parsi physician had specialised in tropical diseases and poisoning from snake bites and perhaps he could identify this poison.

Dr. Patel, to Helen's surprise, listened to Helen's description of the patient's symptoms, took one look at Rosita and then starting searching her room.

'What are you looking for, Doctor?' enquired a puzzled Helen.

'A plant ... ah, here it is, just as I thought.' He picked up a potted plant which stood concealed behind Rosita's dresser and looked deceptively innocent with its profusion of pale yellow flowers.

'This plant is of the monkshood family but even more toxic. Your description of the lady's symptoms - tingling of the mouth and throat and impairment of sight and hearing - are common indications of poisoning by this plant, but how was the poison ingested? That is what we must find out,' said the Parsi doctor.

241

'But I ordered all plants to be removed from Mrs. Llewellyn's bedroom when her breathing became impaired,' said Helen, wondering why this particular plant was secreted behind the dresser and how it had come into Rosita's possession.

'I have some tincture of belladonna at the clinic that is the antidote, Lady French. But we must hurry before Mrs. Llewellyn's lungs collapse. Be prepared to give her artificial respiration if her breathing fails before I return,' said Dr. Patel as he hurried out of the room.

His horse must have had wings, because he was soon back with the tincture. Helen measured out thirty drops, the first dose she administered by enema because Rosita was still nauseous and when in twenty minutes Rosita's breathing was less strained, she repeated the dose by mouth every half hour.

At last after two hours, Rosita's colour returned, her breathing was back to normal and an exhausted Helen turned to Dr. Patel, 'How can I thank you, Dr. Patel? You have saved my dear friend's life. I knew it was some sort of poisoning but never dreamed it could have been caused by a plant. I am afraid my medical knowledge failed me when it was most needed.'

'Do not blame yourself, Doctor French. I worked for a while amongst the tribal peoples of Assam and this plant was used extensively against their enemies. I soon came to recognise the symptoms, but not before I had lost a few patients, myself. I believe it is important that you discover how the plant came into Mrs. Llewellyn's possession and how she might have ingested the poison.'

For the next two days, Helen hardly left Rosita's side, except to prepare nourishing broths for her. She was still so weak and Helen was afraid to leave her alone, or to designate the preparation of her food to anyone else.

Gavin returned and found his wife sitting beside Rosita's bed exhausted and trying desperately to keep awake. He had returned by way of the fort and been advised by Dr. Graham of the near tragic events at his home.

'Helen, how is Rosita? Dr. Graham told me what had happened,' and forgetting their bitter quarrel, Gavin knelt down beside his wife and took her in his arms.

The strength of his arms, her weariness and her sudden relief that he was by her side again, swept away all Helen's reserves and her pent up emotions gave way to desperate sobs, that seemed to tear at the core of her being as she clung to Gavin.

Gavin rocked her gently, 'Hush, my little sweetheart, our darling Rosita is going to be fine and I am here now to look after both of you. You are so exhausted and must sleep.'

Gavin lifted his wife in his arms and laying her gently on the chaise lounge, plumped up a cushion under her head and covered her with his jacket. The smell of sandalwood and tobacco filled Helen's nostrils and it was as if Gavin was still holding her. Half asleep she murmured, 'Don't leave us Gavin, I am afraid someone is trying to...' Her words trailed off as she fell into a deep sleep and Gavin wondered why his intrepid Helen was afraid. What had happened here whilst he was away?

Rosita recovered but was unable to explain how the poisonous plant had been secreted in her room and had no recollection of even seeing it.

Helen recalling Isabel's acrimonious argument with Rosita, had her suspicions that the Goanese woman was in some way responsible for her friend's illness, but she had no proof and Isabel seemed as alarmed and distressed as everyone else at Rosita's illness. How could she inform Gavin of her suspicions? In his defence of Isabel, he might reveal the depth of his feelings for the woman, which Helen would be unable to ignore and which she was not yet ready to face.

But events in a few days time soon persuaded Helen that it was not only Rosita's life, but her own which was endangered.

The weather had been very warm, the air still and sultry, the sky tinged a greenish yellow. Helen was half asleep on the chaise lounge in Rosita's bedroom in the afternoon, when the settee suddenly tipped over and she was hurled across the room. She reached out her hands to stop herself hitting the wall and then became aware that the bedroom floor was heaving and tilting and Rosita's large oak bed was sliding dangerously towards the window. The house was swaying and trembling as if a giant hand had it in its grasp and was shaking it vigourously. Sounds of falling masonry and

244

splintering glass could be heard from somewhere in the house, combined with the unearthly sounds of human and animal cries of terror.

Rosita's bed had come to rest just feet from the window and the poor woman was sitting bolt upright with a look of abject terror on her face, praying loudly in Spanish and exhorting God, the Virgin Mary and all the angels and saints to save them.

Helen cupped her hands over her head for protection from falling plaster and like a drunk reeled over to Rosita's bed. She knew that they were not safe in these upstairs rooms and would have to make their way down the staircase to the comparative safety of the garden. The tremors had stopped momentarily and half dragging, half carrying Rosita, Helen tried the door but the frame had buckled and the catch was jammed.

Even as she looked around for some implement to force the catch, the door burst open and Gavin stood there, white faced and dishevelled, surveying the two terrified women and the chaos of the room.

'Quick, Helen, give Rosita to me. I will carry her downstairs and you must follow me closely. This old house is built on solid foundations, but another tremor may bring the roof crashing down,' said Gavin, his usually calm voice now reflecting the urgency of the situation.

The hallway was full of dust from falling plaster and broken glass and Gavin urged Helen to step carefully. Here and there, the balustrades had twisted and broken and Helen following closely behind her husband, prayed that the calm would continue until they had reached the bottom of the stairs.

All the servants were already out on the lawn and Ram Das brought a chair from the verandah for Rosita.

Helen became aware of the distressed neighing of the horses and ran towards the stable block, where she guessed the syce was trying to calm the nervous animals.

Gavin had already gone on before her and was shouting instructions to the syce. Helen saw him come out of the half-ruined building with one of the horses and then the earth began to shake and twist again and she was knocked to her knees.

Gavin was shouting, 'Christ Almighty, Helen look out!' Helen felt a hand in her back and half turning around, saw Isabel de Silva just behind her, the woman's amber eyes glinting malevolently, her teeth bared in a cruel smile. Helen looked down and perceived, too late, the fissure opening in front of her. The pressure on her back intensified and Helen found herself falling into the yawning chasm. Desperately she struggled to hold onto the crumbling sides of the rift, when suddenly her arms were almost pulled from their sockets by strong, brown hands lifting her. Ram Das, with almost superhuman strength, was dragging Helen out of the abyss, which even as they watched, was closing again.

246

Then Gavin was kneeling beside her, gathering her trembling body into his arms. His face buried in her hair, she half heard his sobs of relief as he realised how close she had come to being buried alive. 'Thank God, my darling, Ram Das was in time.'

She heard Isabel's voice, 'I put out my hand to stop her, Gavin, but she was already falling into the chasm.'

Helen realised that Isabel was endeavouring to conceal her malicious intent in case she had been observed, but Gavin did not seem to be aware of anything untoward. Everything had happened so quickly and he had been some distance away.

'How are the horses; Sultana must have been so afraid?' asked Helen, remembering that she was rushing to the stables before the second tremor.

'She will be fine, the syce is with them and he is expert at calming nervous animals, so don't worry, sweetheart,' said Gavin softly, gathering Helen even closer into his arms. She closed her eyes, relinquishing herself to his strength, reluctant to move from their safety. But there was no escape, as she became aware of the noise and cries of terror in the distance and she knew that people were dying in the city and villages and as their doctor, she must help them.

Gently pushing Gavin aside, she stood up and asked for her medical bag.

'I must help those people, Gavin. Stay here with Rosita and the others. Ram Das, my medical bag is on the hall table. Please fetch it for me.'

Gavin looked at his wife with pride. Despite her ordeal, she would not shirk her duty to others.

'I will accompany you, Helen. There must be something I can do to help. Ram Das, stay here and look after Mrs. Llewellyn. The worst is over now and God willing there will be no more aftershocks, but stay downstairs until we are back.'

Helen and Gavin picked their way on foot carefully over fallen trees and rubble and noticed that the palace seemed intact, although part of the causeway had disappeared under the waters of the lake. Most of the buildings in the European quarter were unscathed, except for broken chimneys and splintered window panes, but terrible cries of human suffering were coming from the native quarter and the villages outside the city.

Boats carrying the Nawab's Rohillas were just tying up to the jetty and, for once, British soldiers had been permitted into the City to help in the humanitarian search for life under the tons of wood and rubble that had once been shops and houses.

Gavin organised the wounded to be taken to Helen's clinic and the dead were laid out in rows in the grounds of the mosque for identification and burial or cremation, depending on their religion. 'If that can be ascertained in all this turmoil', he said.

As long as she lived, Helen would never forget the tragedy, signs of which were evident as she picked her way through the devastation to the clinic which, fortunately, still stood intact. She saw a mother holding her dead child, refusing to accept its death; a father digging with his bare hands to find his wife and family under the rubble of his hut; lost children wandering about dazed, looking for parents whom death had claimed. Here was a dead cow, already bloated in the heat, there a human arm sticking up from a chasm which had buried the rest of the owner, reminding Helen all too cruelly of her own narrow escape.

She and the other doctors worked late into the night, sewing gaping wounds, amputating limbs, setting broken bodies. Gavin came to her occasionally and gave her milky nourishment to keep up her strength. Never had he loved this woman more than now when she was dirty and bloody, dark circles under her beautiful eyes, working tirelessly to save these people she had come to love. Helen looked up and caught his eye. Why was he looking at her like that and what did that expression in his eyes mean? she wondered. He smiled, that special smile of his which always caused her heart to flutter, but she had no time to indulge her emotions. because one more patient was being placed on the operating table for her attention.

On one occasion, Gavin brought her an assistant, the beautiful Comtesse de Colbert. Blanche wore an apron over her pretty muslin dress that was soon blood-stained, but the lovely Creole did not flinch from

249

carrying buckets of soiled dressings to the makeshift incinerator, or endeavouring to make Helen's patients comfortable after their surgery. She sponged the dirt from the wounds the doctors were treating and knelt down beside the dying to give them comfort.

The tall, blond Scot, John MacGregor, rolled up his sleeves and used his great strength to carry the wounded into the clinic, or transferred patients after their surgery onto straw mattresses, which were laid out on every available space of floor in the little hospital.

It was the early hours of the next morning when the last patient was brought to the doctors - a small boy rescued by British soldiers from an air pocket deep beneath the rubble of his home. He was traumatised, but still breathing and had suffered a cracked collar bone, which Helen knew would heal naturally. They nicknamed the little orphan 'Lazarus', because of his remarkable rise from the dead. Not far from where he lay, the soldiers told Helen, they had found the crushed bodies of his family.

There were so many homeless people and orphaned children. Gavin had organised makeshift camps on the outskirts of the city for the families and the Army had set up soup kitchens serving milk, *dhal* and *chappatis*. The Nawab had promised to rebuild his people's homes as soon as possible and Blanche was organising places in the Catholic Mission for the little orphans.

Little Lazarus was more fortunate. The syce's wife, a pretty doe-eyed woman of about twenty-five called Lalitha, who could not bear children, herself, pleaded with Helen to be allowed to adopt the little fellow.

'Well as long as no other relative comes forward to claim him, Lalitha, I see no reason why you cannot take him home,' replied Helen to the Indian woman whose eyes lit up with joy as she scooped little Lazarus into her arms.

It was very late that night when she and Gavin returned to the Residency. A hot bath and some food were all Helen could manage before she climbed into her large bed and fell asleep immediately, with Rosita by her side enveloping her in motherly arms, as she had done so often when Helen was a child.

The next day the storm broke, bringing welcome relief from the sultry heat, but causing more problems for the teams clearing the earthquake debris. More rain fell in a few hours than had fallen since the start of the monsoon season and the river was becoming dangerously high, another threat to the lives of these unfortunate people.

Amidst protests from the villagers, who were reluctant to move again, the British soldiers dismantled the tents and moved them to higher ground. Helen at the clinic was at last visited by the Royal Princes, whose presence in the aftermath of the earthquake had been prominent by their absence.

'We are grateful for your efforts on behalf of our people, Lady French. In fact, His Royal Highness, the Nawab, wishes to express his gratitude to all the British community for their heroic efforts,' said Prince Hassan, rather pompously.

Helen, remembering his grandmother, the Dowager Begum's criticism of the British, wondered if she, too, would be grateful to the despised Angressi.

Chapter 15

Life, after the terrible disaster of the earthquake, was returning to normal. The people had started to rebuild their homes and shops, financed to a large extent by the Nawab. Even most of the damage to the Residency, which was quite slight in comparison to other parts of the city, had been repaired and her beloved horses now, thankfully, quite recovered from their ordeal, had been rehoused in newly-built stables.

Helen made several trips to the homes of victims of the earthquake on whom she had operated, and was touched and surprised how, even the limbless with true Indian fatalism, were learning to adapt.

Two months had elapsed since Helen missed her first menstrual cycle and she was now certain that she was pregnant. Suddenly, she recalled the look in Isabel de Silva's eyes during the earthquake and the unexplained poisoning of Rosita and she was determined, for the sake of her unborn child, to remove the woman from the Residency. She decided to tell Gavin about her pregnancy and at the same time to speak to him about sending Isabel de Silva away. A generous annuity could be arranged for her, so that she would not be destitute, but both Helen and Rosita would feel safer if the woman was not around.

Gavin had moved his office to the guest house, whilst the wood panelling in his study (which had been damaged by the earthquake) was repaired. His response, 'Come in,' to the knock on the door was followed by a surprised, 'Helen!' as his lovely wife entered the room.

Helen was wearing an apple green, muslin dress, similar to the one she had worn on that first day he had seen her in Mirapore, which seemed so long ago now. Her auburn hair had been lifted off her neck in burnished copper ringlets and tied with a green velvet ribbon which matched her large, long-lashed, emerald eyes and her creamy skin was now faintly tinted with gold from the Indian sun. Her beauty was as breathtaking as ever, and Gavin despite his intentions to fight her attractions, because of her continued rejection of him, found himself rising from his chair and moving towards her.

'To what do I owe this unexpected visit from my wife? I have hardly seen you lately,' he smiled and took her hands in his, his eyes narrowing quizzically.

'I need to talk to you about something, Gavin, something which may or may not please you.'

'How intriguing,' quipped her devastatingly, handsome husband, as he led her to a comfortable leather sofa.

Helen sat nervously on the edge of the sofa, whilst her husband leaned his tall frame against the mantelpiece, a cigar clutched between his teeth, his bearing that of a man completely at ease with himself whilst Helen, herself, felt her own nerves stretched to breaking point.

'Well, Helen, what is this piece of news you are not sure I will like?' Gavin's dark eyes watched her with an expression she could not decipher.

'I am pregnant,' she blurted out and Gavin throwing his cigar into the fireplace was soon kneeling at her feet, clasping her in his arms, the joy in his face unmistakable as he cried out, 'My God, sweetheart, how could you believe I would not be pleased! How long?' he questioned, his brown eyes dancing with golden lights, as he looked adoringly at the prospective mother of his child.

'I believe I am two months' pregnant, so if I go full term, the baby should be born in February. But I have something else to discuss, Gavin,' said Helen, wishing to bring her overjoyed husband back to reality, because he was now sitting by her side on the settee, his arms drawing her into their circle, pressing her back against his strong chest as his lips caressed her soft neck and his hands moved down to the swell of her breasts.

'H'mm, what else do I need to know, my little sweetheart?' murmured Gavin huskily, as one hand cupped her full breast and the other moved across the slight curve of her belly.

'I do believe your lovely breasts are a little fuller, my darling.' Gavin teased, 'but I need to examine you more closely,' and twisting her around, he pushed her gently down on the settee, his mouth silencing her protests, his hands sliding her dress off her shoulders. Helen saw her husband's dark eyes linger for a moment on her naked breasts before he bent down to take each rosy nipple into his mouth. She felt again that surge of weakness, that irresistible need for him and it took her all her strength to push him away and to jump up from the settee. She walked to the window, adjusting her dress, determined to put some distance between herself and her husband in order to steady her own raw emotions.

Gavin, too, rose and came towards her, reluctant to let her go, and when he would have taken her in his arms again, she said, imploringly, 'Please Gavin, let me speak.'

She felt him tense and move away.

'Are you not pleased to be carrying my child, Helen? Is that what you want to say?'

'Oh, Gavin, of course not. What I want is for you to get rid of Isabel de Silva,' Helen said, more abruptly than she had intended.

Gavin started and leaning towards Helen, as if he had not quite heard her words, asked, 'Isabel? Why? Is there something wrong with her work. I have always found her to be most efficient and loyal.'

'Oh, it is not her work; I can't fault her there and as for her loyalty, perhaps that is reserved solely for you, but certainly not for me, I am afraid. In fact, I suspect she is involved in some unholy cult and may have had something to do with Rosita's illness. Only a few days before Rosita took ill, Isabel had been extremely vociferous in her condemnation of Rosita inviting a Catholic priest to exorcise the tomb and...'

'I know about that,' Gavin interrupted. 'Isabel told me and she also expressed deep remorse at upsetting you and Rosita about the matter. It seems she was afraid the Nawab's family would object to the desecration of the tomb by an infidel rite and the matter would be an embarrassment to me as Resident here.'

'Indeed, so once again our loyal Isabel had to report to you about my actions,' said Helen, not bothering to cloak the sarcasm in her voice and remembering that it had been Isabel's tittle tattle, which had given Gavin cause to be jealous of John MacGregor. 'And did you agree with her, Gavin?'

'I dismissed her fears as unnecessary. The Residency is British ground and the Nawab cannot interfere with what is done here. Personally, I did think that Rosita's anxieties over something sinister in the tomb were a bit illogical, but she is Spanish and very superstitious and if it gives her piece of mind for a priest to bless the place, I can see no harm in it. But why do you want to dismiss Isabel from our employ? There is really no proof that she was involved in the poison Rosita ingested. You have not given me a good enough reason yet, Helen.'

Gone was the softness in Gavin's face. His expression was now serious, the face of the British Resident intervening between two protagonists and wanting to learn all the facts before he made a judgment.

Helen was furious, her face drained of all colour as she glared at her husband, her lips curling in contempt when she replied, 'I wonder why you are so defensive of Isabel de Silva. I can see you can believe no ill of her. Perhaps you should examine your own feelings for the woman, Gavin French, and when you have made up your mind, let me know.'

With these cutting words, Helen moved towards the door, but Gavin caught her arm and pulled her around to face him, his face contorted with anger.

'What the hell do you mean, Helen? What are you implying?'

'That she is your mistress and has been, perhaps, even when poor Maria was alive,' Helen heard herself retaliate angrily.

Gavin's hands bit into her shoulders as he glared at his wife, his eyes flashing with anger, 'How dare you make such a scandalous suggestion. The woman was devoted to Maria and it was Maria's last wish that I should give her employment, as long as I was in India and find her a suitable position when I left. Isabel de Silva has always been loyal to both Maria and myself and I can only think that it is your present condition that is making you so uncharacteristically unfair, Helen.'

'My condition, I would remind you, my devoted husband, is a result of lust, not love,' sneered Helen, watching Gavin flinch as, with these words she viciously reminded her husband of his brutal lovemaking in Kashmir. 'Don't worry, I will bear your child, Sir Gavin French, but you will never be welcome in my bed again,' and Helen tore herself from her husband's hands and stormed out of the guest house, not noticing the figure in a sari crouching in the shrubbery beneath the open window, listening to every word she and Gavin had exchanged.

She did not see Gavin again that day. He took his meals in the guest house on a tray and, for all she knew, even spent the night there because she did not hear him moving about in the adjoining bedroom.

Once again, they were like strangers, passing each other occasionally with only a brief nod of acknowledgement. As far as she was concerned, Helen felt that Gavin's refusal to believe her about Isabel de Silva's machinations, was proof of his feelings for the woman, despite his anger at her accusation.

Then Isabel vanished without any explanation and Gavin glared at Helen over the dining table when the housekeeper's disappearance was reported by a servant. Apparently she had taken all her possessions and her room was empty.

'Do you know anything about this, Helen?' Gavin asked curtly.

'You mean, have I dismissed her without your consent? Of course, not. But I am sure she will return to you. Where else can she go?' replied Helen with biting sarcasm.

Isabel de Silva did not return and Helen felt it was all her fault and although he did not say so, it was evident that Gavin believed she was responsible.

When Rosita asked her if there was anything amiss, Helen only shook her head and smiled sadly, but the Spanish woman was too astute to miss the signs of heartbreak in her beloved child. She watched her pushing her food around her plate without any appetite, the dark circles under her lovely eyes, which became deeper by the day and the brave, little smile she forced her lips to make whenever she saw Rosita studying her. Rage, that her sweet child who was carrying his child, should be treated in so cavalier a manner by her husband, forced Rosita to interfere against her better judgment.

On the third day of what was now obviously a deep estrangement between husband and wife, Rosita waited for Helen to leave for the clinic and then stormed into the guest house to confront Gavin.

'Hello, Rosita, what is the matter, you look so upset?' he said, as she came into the room, barely waiting for his permission to enter.

'Yes, I am upset and disappointed in you, Gavin. Why are you so cold towards my precious Helen? Do you not know she is carrying your child and should be loved and protected? What could be so terrible that you have turned your back on her?'

'Please sit down, Rosita,' said Gavin gently, guiding the distraught Spanish woman to the settee. 'I hate to see you so upset. Yes, I know about Helen's pregnancy, but it seems she is not too happy about her condition and is prepared to invent some cock-and-bull story about Isabel de Silva to justify her unhappiness. Did she tell you that she believes the poor woman is trying to harm you and is involved in some devil worship? She even accuses me of adulterous relations with our housekeeper,' explained Gavin, the bitterness in his voice barely concealed.

Rosita sat in shocked silence as she heard Gavin's words and then she said quietly, 'She is right about Isabel de Silva's involvement in some black art. I, too, have witnessed something demonic, an evil influence that changed the woman from her mild, quiet personality into a black, reptilian demon. Let me explain, Gavin, because I can see you find this hard to believe.'

Gavin listened in astonishment as Rosita came to the end of her description of her own and Helen's experiences and he thought of what he had read when he first came to India, about the demonic possession of some members of a Cult which worshipped a certain goddess and chose the Left Hand Path to avoid their karma. What the hell was the goddess's name? Then he remembered - 'KALI'!

'Oh my God, Rosita, if this is true then my family's history, my ancestor's strange Will would make sense,' muttered Gavin, his practical mind still

261

refusing to accept the malevolent influence of an eighteenth century curse on his family.

'Apart from trying to poison me, which we cannot prove conclusively, did Helen tell you about the snake which menaced her in the tomb, a snake which had, obviously, been introduced there deliberately? Also there was the incident that occurred during the earthquake. Helen felt sure that Isabel's hand was at her back pushing her into the abyss which had opened suddenly at her feet and if it was not for Ram Das's prompt action, she would have been buried alive,' said Rosita, as she saw Gavin blanch under his tanned skin, his eyes widen in astonishment and then flash with rage.

He stood up and strode towards the window, his hands clenching spasmodically behind his back as if he was struggling to control a strong emotion. At last he turned to face Rosita.

'No, Rosita, Helen did not mention these threats to her life; she just told me that she wanted me to dismiss Isabel de Silva and when I asked for her reasons, she accused me of ... well adulterous relations with the woman, which angered me. Rosita, you must know how much I love Helen but I am unable to break down this hideous barrier between us. Sometimes I believe she is sorry she married me.'

Gavin slumped into the settee near Rosita and buried his face in his hands, his elbows resting on his thighs, his body bowed as if the burden of his love was weighing him down and Rosita put a soothing hand on his dark hair as sobs shook his tall frame.

'Only you can break down this barrier, Gavin. Go to her when she returns from the clinic and convince her of your love for her. If she believes (and, incidentally, she has never mentioned her suspicions to me) that Isabel de Silva is your mistress, then only you can make her see that this is false,' advised Rosita, her heart aching for this man and her beloved child, Helen, whose powerful love for each other was destroying them, as she had foreseen.

Helen had already returned from the clinic, they were told by the gardener, when they went to find her in the stables. In fact the *memsahib* had saddled her horse and gone out somewhere, ordering the syce to accompany her on one of the pack horses.

'Gone riding!' exclaimed Gavin and then turning to Rosita with barely concealed anger in his voice said, 'You see, as a doctor, Helen is well aware of the dangers of horse riding in her condition, but she is prepared to risk her own and our child's life just to spite me. Are those the actions of a loving wife, who is happy to be carrying her husband's child?'

Rosita saw the pain in Gavin's eyes and for the first time she felt that the trouble between these two was as much, if not more, Helen's fault. The girl had always been independent and at times headstrong, traits that her beloved father and Rosita, herself, had never discouraged, but now she was

263

married, why could she not accept her husband's right to be master in his own house.

Helen returned after several hours and Rosita heard her ordering one of the servants to bring a light supper to her bedroom, because she intended to retire early.

Rosita was about to follow Helen when she heard Gavin's study door open and saw him stride up the stairs. She would not interfere. It was time for her headstrong child to face her angry husband and Rosita trembled for her beloved.

Helen had removed her divided skirt and sat down to remove her riding boots. She was just undoing the buttons of her silk blouse, when Gavin burst into her bedroom. She saw at once the angry flush on his face, the steel cold expression in his dark eyes.

'Don't you ever knock, Gavin?' asked Helen, recalling another occasion her husband had come into her bedroom uninvited.

Ignoring her remark, Gavin came towards his wife, his hands lifting her to her feet, his fingers clamped hard on her shoulders. 'So you decided to try abortion by horse-riding, did you Dr. Helen!' Gavin accused, his lips twisted contemptuously, conveying in those few words his belief that she knew exactly what she was risking. 'So much for your promise to bear my child.'

'Don't be absurd. I rode carefully and the syce accompanied me.'

264

'What was wrong with taking the carriage to wherever you felt compelled to go?'

'Where I was going, there is no track for carriages,' and realising that this explanation was not enough to satisfy her irate husband, Helen went on to explain. 'I went to the temple of Kali behind the waterfall in the forest, because I hoped Isabel's brother would be there.'

'Isabel's brother, Vincent de Silva? I did not know you knew him and what...'

Gavin was not given a chance to finish his sentence. Helen pulled herself away from his restricting hands and walked wearily to the window. She was suddenly very tired and wanted an end to this conversation as soon as possible.

'I met him once long ago when I was visiting another temple and he tried to coerce me into following him to the temple of Kali. But that is a long story and I am too tired to indulge your curiosity any further, Gavin. I hoped he would know where Isabel was and I would have asked her to return to the Residency, for your sake. But he was not there.'

Helen's back was turned to her husband and he could not see the tears sparkling in her eyes

'Bring her back, for my sake? Bloody hell, Helen, you wanted to get rid of her and now you risk your own and our child's life on this stupid whim. Look at me, woman,' Gavin demanded almost arrogantly.

Helen turned and Gavin's heart softened when he saw the tears in her eyes and her brave attempts to fight them. She looked so tired, yet incredibly lovely, standing there framed in the window and he could not fight his impulse to take her into his arms.

'Helen, Helen,' he whispered into her hair, his arms holding her gently. 'I want you to take things easy now, if not for my sake, then the sake of our child. Isabel has decided to leave and there is no need to scour the country looking for her. I will make some enquiries and make sure she is not financially embarrassed. Now you must rest because I can see you are very tired.'

Kissing Helen lightly on her lips, Gavin left the room and Helen, unable to control the bleakness in her heart, lay down on the bed and sobbed quietly into her pillow. That Gavin would find Isabel, she was sure, and now that his wife suspected their relationship, he would install his mistress in a secret location where he could visit her clandestinely.

Before she closed her eyes, Helen recalled her abortive visit to the temple. The syce was reluctant to accompany her at first and when they approached the entrance to the temple, a cave behind the waterfall, he was trembling with fear.

'You stay here, syce, with the horses. I will see if de Silva *Memsahib's* brother is inside.'

'No, *memsahib*', the frightened man whispered as Helen dismounted and shook his head from side to side accompanied by a similar movement of his hand, (a strange gesture which Helen had observed was used exclusively by Indians when they tried to express some emotion). 'Please don't go in there. I have heard...' What he had heard, Helen did not stop to find out.

Helen picked her way carefully behind the waterfall, along a narrow ledge slippery from the spray, which led to the opening of the cave. It was dark and dank inside and it took some time for her eyes to become accustomed to the darkness and then she shook with fear. At the end of the cave was an enormous, black figure mounted on a dais, its blackness glistening in the lights of the clay lamps at its feet, as if it had been smothered in grease. A hag with fangs and a protruding tongue, red as if she had supped on blood, naked except for her ornaments of skulls and severed hands, was staring at Helen, with bulging eyes. The giant figure had four arms which seemed to sway from her black body, one was holding a pickaxe, the other a noose. One leg was raised in the motion of a temple dancer, poised as if it would stamp down to the clash of tablas and cymbals to perform the *Bharata Natyam*. Was it her imagination, or did the figure move and Helen heard the clink of anklets worn by Indian *nautch* girls and she could have sworn two hands of the Goddess started to move in the traditional gestures. With a thrill of fear and fascination, she approached the idol.

It was suddenly very cold in the cave, yet Helen was sweating. She reached into her jacket pocket for a handkerchief and her fingers closed on the holy beads given to her by the old Sunyassi. She lifted them out and, unaccountably, raised them to her lips. Almost immediately the Goddess was nothing more than a stone idol, black and ugly, but only a pagan statue, garlanded with her terrible ornaments.

Helen left the cave quickly, not understanding what she thought she had seen, and returned to the very relieved syce and the horses, but the experience seemed to have drained her and she fell into a heavy sleep in which she dreamed Isabel de Silva was dressed in the costume of a temple dancing girl, anklets and glass bangles clinking as she swayed seductively in front of Gavin, whose hands were reaching out to pull the sari from the dancer's naked body.

Chapter 16

As if to assuage her unhappiness, Helen plunged once more into her work at the clinic and, accompanied by Doctor Patel, visited the villages that were now rebuilt in the valley beyond the city. Most of them consisted of mud huts with thatched roofs but a group of them were situated well away from the others, with their own water supply.

'I am afraid, Doctor French, even in this mainly Muslim state, the Hindus observe their caste system. The houses you see across the river belong to the 'Untouchables', who by circumstances of their birth, must always be casteless.'

'Yes, said Helen, 'I am always surprised by this aspect of Hinduism. In the West, we have class distinction, but a man can lift himself by education and wealth, even buying vast estates and titles as our eighteenth century Nabobs demonstrated.'

Helen followed Dr. Patel through the villages and remembered that he was not a Hindu but a Parsi, one of the oldest religions in the world. His people, the Arab physician Mahmoud bin Said had told her, came to India in AD 632 and because they had never proselytised, had no religious conflict with any of the other Indian religions. Helen knew that the Parsis with their fair skins and Western ways were popular with the British, who admired them for their business acumen and philanthropic culture.

269

People of another nationality were now leaving Mirapore. The Spanish Consulate was being closed and Don Hernandez and his family had been recalled to Madrid.

'You British have left us very little leeway on this sub-continent, so we must concentrate on our South American colonies,' he laughingly told Gavin.

A farewell dinner was to be held in the Consulate and the invitation included the British Resident, Sir Gavin, Lady French and Senora Llewellyn. Helen knew that Rosita would be sad to see her fellow countrymen leave. After all her years in England, she had been pleased to speak Spanish again and spend time in the Spanish ambience of the Consulate on her weekly visits to Senora Hernandez who was, herself, a Southern Spaniard from the same region as Rosita.

Rosita had been busy making the dresses for the dinner. She had found some beautiful midnight blue velvet for Helen, which she made up in subtle drapes to disguise her swelling stomach and a low cut bodice to accentuate her magnificent bosom. Rosita's own dress was plainer, in black taffeta, but beautifully cut to minimise her bountiful figure.

Gavin could not take his eyes off his wife that evening. It seemed he was not alone, for every man in the room admired (and Gavin had no doubt lusted after) the beautiful Lady French. The colour of the midnight blue velvet was a perfect foil for her magnolia cream complexion and auburn hair, which Rosita had dressed in a heavy chignon low on the nape of her neck decorated by a small garland of creamy jasmine flowers around the coiled hair. Perhaps it was her approaching motherhood, but Helen had a bloom, the subtle feminine appeal of the everlasting Eve, which was hard for any man to resist. Gavin watched her as she smiled and mildly flirted with her admirers, her graceful posture giving no hint of her condition.

Her dinner companion was John MacGregor and Gavin felt a stab of jealousy each time his wife smiled at the handsome Scot, who had never been able to hide his admiration and fascination for Helen.

Helen saw Gavin's eyes on her and John MacGregor and wilfully turned all her charm on the hapless Scot. She leaned towards him and Gavin was well aware that the soft curves of her bosom and the scent of the perfume she dabbed between her cleavage, would be intoxicating to the Scot. Gavin saw him blanch and whisper something in Helen's ear, which obviously delighted her as she laughed and had the grace to blush.

After a sumptuous dinner, many speeches and a tearful farewell to their Spanish friends, the guests departed.

Helen allowed Rosita to unfasten her dress but when her Spanish friend unpinned her hair and took up the hairbrush, she said, 'Not to-night Rosita; you, too, must get your beauty sleep. Goodnight, *querida*,' and with a kiss on her cheek, a hug and an insistent hand on her elbow, Helen escorted Rosita to her bedroom door.

271

Helen was now alone and with a sigh, she undressed and stood naked before her cheval mirror studying the slight swell of her belly and the fullness of her breasts. She looked down, her hand stroking her abdomen and whispered, 'Goodnight, my little one.'

She smiled at the stirrings of her motherly emotions but when she looked up again at her reflection in the mirror, she gasped, because Gavin was standing behind her. He was watching her, remembering how every man and particularly the Scot, had lusted after her that evening and his eyes flashed with anger. Helen turned and reached for her wrap, but Gavin took it from her hand and turning her around to face the mirror again, said with a cynical twist to his lips, 'Why cover yourself from your husband, madam, when you have permitted every man, and particularly your Scottish friend, to peer down your bodice this evening. Why pretend to be so modest now?'

Before Helen had time to protest, Gavin swung her around to face him and fastened his lips hard on her mouth. Then he lifted her in his arms and carried her to the bed, kneeling over her, glaring at her, his insane jealousy provoking him to prove that he was her master.

Gavin's lovemaking was savage, more domination than love, his mouth bruised Helen's lips and his hands were rough on her body. At last he took her with clenched teeth and a reckless frenzy, more to satisfy his own hunger than to pleasure her. When at last he was satiated, he collapsed

272

heavily on her, his heart pounding against her breast, his hair damp with sweat.

Unaccountably, Helen's anger melted away and she felt a strange tenderness for this man who had set out to dominate her with his arrogant masculinity, but now lay weak and helpless on her breast. She knew that it was her own deliberate flirtation with John MacGregor that had driven Gavin to make love to her so savagely. She lifted her hand to stroke his damp curls and at her touch, he looked up, astonished to see the look of tenderness in her green eyes, which had flashed anger at him only a short while ago.

'My God, Helen, you made me forget myself again. I am sorry if I was rough, but you drive me to distraction. Why must it always be like this between us?'

Then, as if to compensate for his roughness, Gavin took her in his arms once again, kissing and caressing her slowly and deliberately. He lay her back on the pillow and wound her long hair around his own neck.

'You are so beautiful, my darling, but you must remember you belong to me and me alone,' he murmured, pressing kisses on her eyes, on the little hollow at the base of her throat where a pulse was beating rapidly. One of his hands cupped one breast, whilst his tongue licked and teased the taut nipple of the other. Gavin's hands were lover's hands, tender and reverent, sliding over her body, stroking her belly and the mound of damp, dark auburn curls beneath and then his sensitive fingers invaded her intimately until she was aflame with her need for him and she cried out, 'Gavin, oh Gavin, please!'

'Please what, my love, make you mine again? That is just what I propose to do,' whispered Gavin huskily, his own body now hard with desire as he looked with wonder into the emerald depths of his wife's beautiful eyes. Helen held her arms out to him, her legs opening seductively to receive him and when he entered her, she wrapped her limbs about him, her body arching convulsively as waves of rapture overcame them both and they cried out, simultaneously, as they reached that exquisite pinnacle of love.

That night for the first time in their married lives, Helen slept in her husband's arms. He drew her back towards him until her soft curves fitted perfectly into the angles of his hard body, as if they were two parts of one whole and she drifted into sleep, feeling one of his hands cup her breast and the other caress her stomach and heard him whisper, 'Sleep, my little sweetheart, my love, my darling wife, the beautiful mother of my unborn child.'

The next morning when she awoke, Helen was alone again and she remembered that Gavin had to leave early to accompany Prince Hassan to the outlying borders of the mountain State. The earthquake had caused landslides in the hills and some of the villages had been crushed. Help had been sent, but it was important that the people saw, for themselves, their Ruler's concern for their welfare.

Helen found a note on her dressing table propped against a crystal bud vase containing a single red rose and she smiled tenderly as she read Gavin's words, 'Take care of yourself, little sweetheart, until I am back and I promise to take up where we left off last night.'

Your besotted husband!'

Helen smiled, seeing in her mind's eye, Gavin's dark, twinkling eyes and his audacious smile. Last night he had been at first a jealous and savage lover and then he had driven her to untold heights of rapture with his tender but passionate lovemaking. She had always loved Gavin French, first with a childlike adoration and now with a woman's sensual intensity. She looked down and cupped her belly with both hands, a madonna-like smile playing about her lips, still swollen from his kisses, as she remembered every delightful moment of the night she had just spent in the arms of the father of this child.

The warm days of the Himalayan summer continued and Helen, who had promised Gavin that she would not attempt to ride Sultana, nevertheless, visited the paddock daily to greet her equine friend. The little grey never failed to whicker with delight when she saw her mistress approaching and even if she was at the far end of the field with the other horses, Sultana would gallop up to the fence to greet Helen. She knew that

275

there was always an apple or crushed carrot treat in her friend's pockets but even when these were offered and eaten, the little mare was reluctant to leave her mistress, nuzzling her and blowing her sweet breath into Helen's hair.

Often Sultan trotted up for his share of the treats and fussing, but he didn't hang around after he was sure there was nothing more on offer. Helen laughed as he cantered off, 'What an example of cupboard love, Sultana. Your friend is not interested, now that I have nothing more to offer him.'

Helen's visits to the clinic were restricted to a few hours each day. Doctor Patel and the nursing staff had everything well in hand. She was still, however, asked to attend the harem women. She hated visiting the seraglio because it had too many memories of the lovely and tragic Princess Muna. The Dowager Begum was now totally blind and suffered from high blood pressure, but despite Helen's advice, she continued to eat large quantities of fatty food and smoke her *hookah*. She seemed to have obliterated her great granddaughter from her memory and had her apartments sealed.

One of the harem women told Helen, 'Nothing has been removed from Muna's apartments. They are exactly as they were when she was alive, but no one can enter now, because the doors are sealed. Some of the women have heard soft weeping behind the high walls surrounding her courtyard garden and the lilt of the sitar which Princess Muna loved to play. I believe, Memsahib, her spirit cannot rest or enter the cycle of rebirth. I am a

Buddhist and I pray to the Lord Buddha each night to help her attain Nirvana.'

Helen felt a deep sadness, as the Residency phaeton left the gates of the Palace.

As she recalled her conversation with the harem lady, she reflected on the fascination of India, its climate, its history, its ancient traditions and wondered, not for the first time, how the British had been able to gain control over such a vast and ancient country. The religions alone were divisive:- Hindus believing in Karma and Dharma and adhering to their unchangeable caste system; the Muslims' belief in their own spirituality which often lead to fanaticism, their religion, nevertheless, having a great deal in common with Christianity. Then there was the Buddhist, like the harem lady, who believed in the 'Middle Way', a path halfway between austerity and the indulgence of materialism. Helen had, of course, met the proud warrior Sikhs with their uncut hair covered by turbans, who had been taught by their founder, Guru Nanak, that God was the same no matter in which religion He was worshipped.

There had been many invaders of India but none like the British with their segregated clubs, judicial and administrative institutions, their vast army, most of which was Indian, controlled by British officers and their innate sense of superiority, born of a culture as alien to the Indian as theirs was to the British? Even here in Mirapore, the bungalows dotted about the hills belonging to the British had names like "Rose Cottage", "Beech Croft", and "The Oaks", as if these people from that little island off Europe were determined to leave their imprint even on their Himalayan retreats.

Helen had heard that Indian voices amongst the educated classes were now being raised against this dominance by the foreign, western John Company but here in Mirapore, she had felt no hostility from the village people as she tended to them in the clinic or in their mud huts in the villages. It never failed to surprise her how even the poorest villager would offer her a cup of tea or some sweetmeat and when she restored a sick child to health, a little present of silk or handcrafted earthenware would be laid at her feet with gratitude and respect.

That afternoon Helen was to take tea with her friend, the Comtesse de Colbert, at the French Consulate, which reminded her that the French were another European power that had endeavoured to control India through their own Compagnie des Indes Orientales. Their rivalry with the British was more fierce and bitter than with the Dutch and Portuguese, because their respective countries' hostilities in Europe lasted some seventy years, but thanks to the leadership and personality of men like Clive, Hastings, Roe, Charnock, Stringer, Lawrence, The East India Company became the dominant European Power on this vast Sub-Continent.

That was all in the past and now she was to take tea with her dear friend, the Comtesse de Colbert

Blanche, looking as elegant as ever, was standing at the ornate door of the French Consulate as the Residency phaeton drew up. She greeted Helen with a hug and taking her hand, led her into the beautiful blue and gold drawing room, which was her own private salon.

'Helen, you look ravishing. Being *enceinte* suits you, my sweet,' said the irrepressible Comtesse and seeing Helen's look of surprise explained, 'Your husband told me on the night of Don Hernandez's farewell dinner party, because I remarked that you were even more beautiful than the first day we met. You know, my dear, your husband, like all Englishman, is good at hiding his emotions under that cool, debonair exterior, but now he is like a little boy, bursting to tell everyone that his beautiful wife is carrying his child.'

The lovely Comtesse was pouring the tea into delicate Sèvres china cups when she remarked suddenly, 'I do envy you; I would have loved children but, unfortunately, I cannot conceive.'

'May I, in my medical capacity, ask if you have consulted a specialist? Sometimes a simple operation, or knowledge of the right conditions for conception, will overcome sterility in a woman, but both you and your husband should seek advice.'

'No, it is my fault, Helen. My husband was a widower when we married and had already fathered two children. He knew, of course, that I could never bear him children, but being the kind and loving man he is, this made no difference to his wish to marry me,' said Blanche.

279

Audrey Blankenhagen

'Then let me write to a colleague of mine in England who is in touch with an eminent gynaecologist. You are still too young to give up the chance of having children,' begged Helen, taking her friend's hand.

'I see, Dr. Helen French, I shall have to tell you all about my wicked past to convince you that no specialist, no matter how eminent, can help me.

'When I was a young girl, no more than sixteen years old, I fell in love with a dashing French officer. He was darkly handsome, like your Gavin, with the same charisma that made every woman shiver with delight when he walked into a room, whether she was fifteen or seventy-five, but it was me, Blanche Jaurès, who won his heart. He asked my parents for my hand in marriage and they would have consented, but my father discovered that François was part Huron, North American Indian from his mother's side and like all colonials, my father refused to dilute our French blood by marriage to François. François asked me to wait for him. He would return to Canada and make his fortune and when I was eighteen, we would be married, whether my father consented or not.

'Before he sailed for Canada, we made love and since then no man has ever been able to match my part American-Indian lover,' whispered the lovely Comtesse, with tears in her eyes.

'He did not return; his ship was hit by an iceberg just off Newfoundland: there were no survivors. I discovered soon after that I was carrying his child. I kept the secret too long until I was unable to hide my condition from my

280

parents. They were horrified, because no man would want to marry me now and I had to agree to a secret abortion. The surgeon tore my François's baby from my womb and made it impossible for me ever to bear children again.'

Blanche came to the end of her tragic story and Helen clasped the beautiful woman in her arms, her own heart breaking for the lovely Creole.

'You will keep my secret. I would not like to embarrass the Comte', pleaded Blanche de Colbert.

'You have no need to fear any indiscretion on my part. What you have told me is covered by the ethics of the Hippocratic Oath which decrees that patient/doctor confidence should be strictly observed - an ethic which is as sacred as the Roman Catholic Confessional,' replied Helen.

'Now that I have opened my heart to you,' said a smiling Blanche, taking Helen's arm. 'I hope you will not take it amiss if I give you a little word of warning. Do not try to make your husband jealous. No don't protest! Is that not what you were doing at the Spanish Dinner with that adorable Scotsman, John MacGregor? I could see how you flirted with the poor, besotted man and how your husband's hands were clenched on his knees, in fury. You know I was his dinner companion and was near enough to observe his suppressed anger.'

Helen could not deny her behaviour and admitted, 'I know it was very wrong of me and unfair to John, but Gavin had made me angry earlier.

Audrey Blankenhagen

Believe me, he left me in no doubt of his displeasure when we returned to the Residency that night,' confessed Helen, and her blushes left Blanche in no doubt how the lesson had been taught.

Chapter 17

The day of Gavin's return came at last and it was arranged by Lady Agnes Cameron that Helen should lunch at the fort and return with her husband, who would call there as customary, on his return from the Northern territories of Mirapore.

Helen dressed carefully in a cool amber silk dress, with a bonnet to match, trimmed with ruched amber silk around the brim under which her lovely auburn ringlets bounced playfully. She skipped down the stairs to the waiting phaeton and when she looked up with those long-lashed, emerald eyes to wave to Rosita standing on the verandah, the Spanish woman thought, as Blanche de Colbert had before her, that pregnancy suited her darling child. Never had she seen her looking so lovely and so happy.

Perhaps she had reconciled her differences with Gavin. Rosita had been astonished when he had told her that Helen had accused him of having a mistress, namely Isabel de Silva. She didn't care very much for the Goanese woman, believing her quiet, unobtrusive manner to be a cloak for a deeper and darker side of her personality but Rosita, herself, had never noticed any familiarity between Gavin and his housekeeper.

Gavin French was the only man her beautiful Helen had truly loved and Rosita had no doubt that that he, too, had fallen madly in love with his wife.

She watched the carriage disappear down the long drive and offered a silent prayer for the future of these two people dearest to her heart.

The syce, who tended the horses, was the carriage driver that day and Helen remembering that it was his wife, Lalitha, who had fostered the little orphaned Lazarus after the earthquake, asked how the child had settled in.

'He seems very happy now, Memsahib. At first, he cried every night for his parents and his sleep was disturbed by nightmares of falling roofs and the dark hole in which he lay until the soldiers dug him out. But when he cried out, Lalitha and I brought him into our bed and held him until the bad dreams disappeared. Now that fear has gone and he is a normal little boy again, who knows that he is loved by his foster parents. You should see him flying kites with the other servants' children. His laughter is a joy to hear.'

The carriage left the north gate of the City skirting golden-green paddy fields and orchards, heavy with fruit ripening on the trees. This valley, she had been told, was famous for its apples and pears. The path then followed the winding mountain road above the river which, at this point, flowed rapidly through a narrow cleft in the valley floor. The mountain track to the fort was just wide enough in parts for the carriage and horses. Dark-green, forested hillsides rose steeply on one side of the path, whilst on the other side, the land plunged precipitously into the fast flowing river below. It had rained during the night and Helen noticed, with relief, that the syce was driving very carefully.

She always loved this journey especially when she, herself, was on horseback: the sound of the river in its quieter moments, gurgling and rippling over its boulder strewn bed, the dark green, pine forested hill slopes and there beyond the tree line, the snow capped peaks of the mighty Himalayas, rising from fifteen to twenty thousand feet towards the brilliant blue Himalayan sky, today dappled with fluffy clouds. At times, of course, the mountains were masked by mists which drifted down to the lower peaks, hovering like fluffy cotton wool above the valley.

To-day the river was in a more turbulent mood, the recent rainfall swelling its waters until it roared through the narrow gorge. When she looked out over the sides of the track, she saw the dangerous torrent below and was glad the syce had the horses well in hand. Suddenly the carriage stopped and Helen heard the syce's voice raised in alarm.

'Why are we stopping, syce?' shouted Helen and leaned sideways to look out of the carriage window. A man appeared suddenly in the opening, a man dressed in black with the ends of his turban draped over the lower half of his face to conceal his identity. All that she could see were his peculiarly, light coloured eyes.

'What do you want; who are you?' demanded Helen, but before she could utter another word, the man jumped into the carriage and threw a black cloth over her head, blotting out all light. Helen felt herself pushed roughly to the floor of the phaeton. Someone shouted something in a language she did not understand and she felt the carriage moving again and the weight of her captor's feet on her back. She was stifling under the cloth and tried to remove it, but the feet kicked her and she heard a voice, a somewhat familiar voice, command in English, 'Lie still, Lady French, unless you want me to render you unconscious.'

Helen could hear the whip being used on the horses and their almost uncontrolled flight. What had they done to the poor syce, she wondered, for this driver of the phaeton was surely not her careful servant. She tried to ask her captor, but her words were muffled by the cloth over her head and he didn't hear her, or refused to answer. The erratic movement of the carriage wheels on the rough track and her bowed position on the floor, were making her very uncomfortable and she clutched her stomach as if she would cushion the effects of this nightmare journey on her unborn child.

Suddenly the carriage stopped and hands were lifting her and then she was once again set on her feet and the stifling cloth removed from her head. Helen looked around and saw she was in a courtyard. She was pushed towards the open door of the house and made to lie on a cushioned divan in the room beyond. Women in saris were crowding around her, undressing her until she lay there white and naked. Someone produced a jar of aromatic oil and proceeded to massage her body, someone else painted the soles of her feet and the palms of her hand with a red dye and placed a red tikka mark in the centre of her forehead. Then hands pulled her to her feet and wrapped a diaphanous, white sari around her body. Her hair was loosened from its ringlets and brushed into a shining cape down her back and about her shoulders and hibiscus flowers were pinned behind her ears. She smelt of attar of roses and sandalwood and the strong perfumes began to give her a sickening headache.

Helen pressed her fingers against her throbbing temples as if to dislodge the pain and realising she had a raging thirst, asked for a drink of water,

'*Pani*, please,' and one of the women brought her a glass of iced lassi. She drank the cool, yoghourt milk gratefully, but almost immediately felt giddy. Everything around her was revolving and before she passed out, Helen realised that the drink they had just given her had been drugged.

She was lying down now, but it was as if her body floated above the woman on the divan. She could hear music and see flashing lights and her floating body had no weight but glided gently towards the rainbow lights at the end of a tunnel where Gavin was waiting, his arms open to hold her, his kisses burning her flesh. His mouth was saying something, but she could not hear his words because the music filled the room, but his eyes were black as coals and burning into her soul and then it was not Gavin, but the black goddess Kali, lifting her arms, bending her leg in the movement of the *Bharata Natyam,* her terrible red tongue lolling from her mouth, her black eyes flickering as if she was alive.

Helen saw that she was now in a sort of grotto, lit by kerosene torches and flickering clay oil lights. She could hear the faint sound of the waterfall in the background, but this vast cave was not the small, dank one she had visited earlier. Indians, men and women, were seated cross-legged in a semi circle around the ebony black idol and Helen, herself, was now lying on a raised stone dais in the centre of the circle. A low chanting was coming from the people and Helen heard the words, 'Kunkali, Kunkali, our Dark Mother.'

Helen looked again at the terrible Kali, the flickering torches casting a shadow of the idol on the wall behind, and as she looked, the shadow seemed to grow and dominate the cave. Was she still hallucinating from the drug they had given her, but even though she found she was not bound, Helen could not move a muscle.

Then the music stopped and a man dressed in a hooded white cloak stepped onto a cotton sheet, which one of the worshippers had spread before the idol. He raised his hands as if in benediction of those around him and said in English, in a voice which seemed strangely familiar to Helen.

'Brothers, today I will speak to you in English and not *Ramasi,* our secret language, which some of you have yet to learn. Our Cult, which has been blessed by our Goddess Kali for centuries, has been brutally destroyed by the British and many of our brothers have betrayed us to save their own lives. Amongst these, I regret to say, was my own ancestor,

Chandra Lal, who sold his soul to the Englishman called William French.' There was a murmuring amongst the followers as the name 'French' was mentioned and the man in the white cloak continued,

'Yes, you recognise the name, brothers. That man was the ancestor of the Resident at the Court of the Nawab of Mirapore, Sir Gavin French, and the husband of the English woman who is our captive to-day and who will be our instrument of vengeance in the name of our Dark Mother.'

Once again the voices of the crowd were raised in unison, 'Kunkali, Kunkali. Let us do her will, *Huzoor* of Thuggees.'

The leader raised both arms for silence and continued,'You all know how our cult came into being, but today I will repeat that wondrous saga so all our followers may know how blessed we are.

'In the beginning the Creator created mankind but the Demon of Blood and Seed killed his creations as they were born. Then Kali, the wife of our Lord Shiva, took her sword and killed the demon and drank his blood which turned her skin blue black, but some of the demon's blood was spilt on the earth and the demon's seed sprouted and more demons sprang up to kill the Creator's creations.

'Kali worked hard, slashing with her sword, but as many demons as she killed so many more sprang up from their blood split on the earth, until Kali was tired and lay down to rest. Drops of sweat fell to the ground, as she wiped her blue black arms with her handkerchief and the Creator took pity on her and made helpers from her sweat. She gave these men her handkerchief and told them to strangle the demons so that their blood would not fall to the earth and multiply and when the men had done her will and returned her handkerchief, she said. 'You have saved mankind and all men shall be yours. Keep the rumel and use it to kill and to live.'

Then taking a bag near the feet of the goddess, the leader emptied the contents of raw brown sugar lumps onto the sheet and said to the crowd, 'This is the sweetness of Kali. Take and eat. You are hers and she is yours and from this day, we will be her servants again, and wield the sacred rumel to kill the British.'

The sugar was collected in the bag again and passed round to the seated followers who were chanting, 'Kali, Kunkali, to-day you will be avenged!'

The music - the clash of cymbals, the beat of tablas and the clinking sound of brass anklets and bracelets worn by Indian dancing girls, started again. A glistening, naked woman appeared, her long black hair greased and hanging like snakes about her slender shoulders, her toes splayed, one leg lifted in imitation of the dancing stance of the goddess. Helen, with a start, recognised the dancer - she was Isabel de Silva. Isabel was obviously drugged, her eyes enormous in her small, dark face, her pupils mere pinpoints. Her foot stamped down in the movements of the temple dance and her hands, wrists and neck moved to the beat of tablas. It was not

Isabel de Silva but Kali, herself, who danced, anklets clinking, the terrible head moving stiffly from side to side, backwards and forwards in time to the music.

Then it was Isabel again, spinning wildly like a whirling dervish until she gasped and fell in front of the goddess, a violent tremor shaking her small body.

Another figure jumped into the circle and knelt over Isabel, the man in the white cloak which he discarded to reveal that he, too, was stark naked, his hands reaching for the woman's breasts, his lust displayed in his erect penis. The couple writhed on the floor and touched each other obscenely and Helen was shocked when she realised that the man was Vincent de Silva. So he was the man who had kidnapped her, his light eyes and the voice she remembered from that other temple. Suddenly, Helen recalled Maria's painting of the lovers and she felt sick with disgust. Did Gavin's first wife know of these siblings' incestuous relationship, or was their unnatural behaviour just another part of the depraved Left Hand Path that these followers of Kali followed?

Helen closed her eyes and heard herself praying loudly, trying to drown out the fanatical calls of the Kali worshippers, now roused to fever pitch, as they watched the incestuous gyrations of the couple on the floor.

'Hail Mary, Full of Grace, the Lord is with Thee, Blessed art Thou amongst woman and Blessed is the Fruit of Thy womb, Jesus. Holy Mary,

Mother of God, Pray for me, a sinner, now and at the hour of my death,' intoned Helen, to the prayer she had learnt from her beloved Rosita.

Then she heard herself almost shouting the Lord's Prayer and as if in answer, the music stopped and the Kali worshippers were silent. The naked figure of Vincent de Silva approached her. His hands reached out and tore the white sari from her body, leaving her as naked as himself. He was salivating and even though he had coupled with his sister a few moments ago, Helen noticed, with a terrible dread, that he was quite capable of violating her.

He was climbing onto the dais, his hands pulling her legs apart when a sudden commotion made him jump to his feet and turn around. A tall rider on horseback rode into the circle scattering the screaming worshippers. The horse reared on its hind legs and at the rider's signal, brought them down on the body of Vincent de Silva, as he stood in open-mouthed terror. He fell backwards, his chest crushed by the iron hooves. Helen screamed as the Horseman of the Apocalypse, for so she believed this apparition was, dismounted and came towards her.

With relief she saw that it was Gavin, who lifted her in his arms and cried, 'Oh, my darling Helen, have they hurt you?' Helen was sobbing, partly from relief, partly from the strain of her ordeal and Gavin held her closer in his arms whispering into her hair, 'Hush, my little sweetheart, I am here now and you are safe. My God, if anything had happened to you, I don't think I could have borne it.'

Then Gavin became aware of her nakedness and taking off his shirt, draped it around her.

Suddenly they heard John MacGregor's shout, 'Watch out, Gavin!' and when they both looked up, they were momentarily mesmerised by the sight of the small, mad figure of Isabel de Silva, as she rose from her brother's crushed body and came towards them. She looked like a demon, her mouth snarling, her lips stretched across her pointed, feral teeth, a long sharp knife held murderously in one raised hand, and then she screeched, 'Kali, be avenged!' The knife was inches away from Gavin when a shot rang out and the woman fell, a look of incredulity on her face.

John MacGregor was by their side now, his gun still smoking from the fatal shot that had killed the demon that was once Isabel de Silva.

'The soldiers are rounding up the Thuggees and will look after the bodies of these two,' John said grimly, pointing his pistol in the direction of the naked corpses of the sister and brother. Isabel had fallen on top of the crushed torso of her brother and it appeared that even death could not separate this unholy pair.

Gavin mounted Sultan and asked John to pass his wife to him. Tenderly, John lifted Helen and placed her in front of her husband on the horse and with one arm holding her tightly, Gavin rode back to the Residency followed by John MacGregor and Ram Das.

Helen leaned back against her husband's naked, broad chest and closed her eyes remembering that gentle beech and oak forest of England where Gavin had held his little seven-year-old cousin in his arms, much as he was doing now, and carried her to safety away from the trolls and witches of her childhood nightmares.

Chapter 18

Rosita was leaning over Helen when she awoke in her own bedroom at the Residency. The overpowering oils and red dye had been washed from her body and she had been changed into a cool, cotton nightgown.

'She's awake at last, Gavin,' said Rosita and Gavin, who had been standing by the window, was across the room in rapid strides to kneel by his wife's bedside.

He reached for her hand and turning the palm over kissed it tenderly. 'How are you feeling, little sweetheart? Doctor Graham has examined you and he insists that you stay in bed for a few days longer. The shock you have had has been enormous. You will heed his advice, won't you, my darling?' he pleaded.

Helen knew, even though Gavin had not said so, that they were thinking of the risk to her unborn child. She put her hands over her belly and smiled sweetly, her lids heavy again with sleep.

It was in the night that the pains erupted. Helen had been dreaming of a dark, dank cave and a man prostrate before the ferocious effigy of the Goddess Kali. His fingers were clutching at the black feet of the idol and he was crying out for her mercy. Kunkali looked down at him unmoved, her blood red tongue slithering from her fanged mouth, like a serpent. Two of her four hands, not holding the pickaxe and rumel, moved towards the suppliant and a snake wound itself around the man's neck, tightening its coils until his choking gasps were stilled.

Then Helen awoke screaming as terrible pains racked her body and she knew that she was losing her child.

Gavin was there and Rosita and soon both Doctor Patel and Doctor Graham, but Helen knew that there was nothing they could do. Kali had been avenged. Gavin's heir was being strangled in her womb.

They removed the bleeding remains of her child and as if in a dream, Helen heard Gavin pleading with the doctors to save her life. Why, she wondered? Did he believe that she could bear him another child, another child to be taken by the terrible Goddess in retribution for the avarice of Gavin's ancestor? No, never again would she allow them to murder her unborn infant.

It was this thought that stayed with Helen when she at last recovered. She looked pale and thin and her eyes were as empty as her heart when she looked at her husband. Gavin saw this look and was perplexed.

He came to her that night, 'Let me lie beside you to-night, my darling. I only want to hold you in my arms to comfort you. No, don't turn away from me,' he pleaded and Helen hearing the hurt in his voice, felt a savage compulsion to wound him even more, as they, the demons of Kali, had tortured her child.

THE CURSE OF KALI

'Leave me alone, Gavin. I am not ready to risk another child. Perhaps, I never will be,' and with a stubborn finality, she turned her back on him.

The days and nights passed and despite his pleading, Helen continued to reject Gavin's love.

'I can't get near her, Rosita. She just pushes me away. It is as if she blames me for bringing her to India, for not heeding this Curse of Kali, for endangering our child,' he said to the Spanish woman one day when they were alone.

'When I think of what might have happened to her, I blame myself for not taking that diabolical Curse seriously. Just think, Rosita, if the relief guard riding to the Residency had not found the half-stangled syce in time for us to learn of her kidnap and the location of the secret Temple of Kali, which they had visited previously. How can I ever forget the sight of that monster intent on raping her and his half-crazed sister rushing at us with her knife,' said Gavin, his white knuckled hands clenched in agony.

'Did you not have any inkling about Isabel's associations with this cult, Gavin?' asked Rosita.

Gavin was standing at the window of his study, watching his wife walking in the garden. Rosita had brought him a tray of tea, but the cup she had poured for him was untouched.

He turned to Rosita when he heard her question and moving over to the mantelpiece, helped himself to a cigar from a box of carved walnut wood.

He took his time lighting it, and Rosita wondered whether he would answer her question.

Then he said quietly, 'How could I know? Isabel had worked for Maria, as a lady's maid and our housekeeper. They were inseparable but it was Maria who warned me of Isabel's profligate brother, Vincent. It seemed he was light-fingered and several valuable trinkets went missing from the Residency after his visits to his sister. But apart from banning him from coming here, there was no reason to believe him to be any more dangerous than a petty thief.'

'Why did Maria not bear you a child, Gavin? She was very beautiful,' asked Rosita. Gavin started and looked questioningly at her.

'How did you know what she looked like, Rosita? There are no portraits of Maria here in the Residency.'

'Isabel showed Helen and me a self-portrait of Maria, which I believe you had asked her to destroy after your first wife's death. There were also other very erotic paintings of Indian women and one of the Goanese brother and sister naked in a most unnatural embrace,' said Rosita, blushing when she remembered her shock on seeing the pictures.

'What happened to the paintings?' asked Gavin sharply, his brow furrowed in annoyance.

'Don't worry, Gavin, Helen insisted that Isabel should burn them, but she pleaded to keep the portrait of Maria, which she took away from the Residency.'

Gavin sat down in an armchair opposite Rosita, drawing on his cigar, his eyes narrowed against the smoke. After some moments he said, 'My relationship with Maria was a very strange one, Rosita. When we were married, I thought I could love her. She was beautiful in an exotic way, but very secretive which I mistook for shyness. However, soon after we were married, I discovered that her sexual tastes were not for men, but for women. It was not entirely her fault. She told me that her Nepalese ayah had, from a very young age, introduced her to the lesbian love immortalised in the poetry of Sappho of Lesbos.'

'I am so sorry, Gavin. Did you never try to change her? You are a handsome and charming man and I notice very attractive to women,' said Rosita with a smile.

'The only time Maria would let me make love to her was when she had taken some sort of drug and then she became another person - strange, erotic but very coarse in her lust, almost evil ... well, she revolted me. It was when I discovered her habit of visiting the bazaars to paint and sleep with young Indian prostitutes, that I decided enough was enough. I was considering asking her for a divorce, when she contracted smallpox from the bazaars and died.'

'And then your father suggested you should marry Helen,' continued Rosita. 'You know she has loved you since she was a child,' and when Gavin looked up in surprise, Rosita went on, 'Helen has no secrets from me, Gavin. I heard all about your dramatic rescue of her from the English forest when she was a little girl and I saw how avidly she followed your career in the East India Company as the years went by. I knew when Sir Terence asked her to consent to be your wife, she would not hesitate, although she pretended to need time to consider his proposition.'

'Then why did she tell me that she only married me for my position and title? Yes, she said that on the day after our wedding,' said Gavin, when he saw Rosita's disbelief etched on her expressive face.

'No doubt it was because she believed you still loved Maria, or more likely, that Isabel de Silva was your mistress. This was one secret Helen kept from me, although I knew something was wrong between you two.'

'Rosita, I fell in love with Helen the moment I saw her. How could I do otherwise? No other woman has ever moved me the way she has and yet she is so stubborn but before this terrible catastrophe, I believe she was coming to accept my love for her and for her alone. Now I think she hates me!' said Gavin grimly, his eyes dark with misery as he bowed his head between his hands. Rosita stood up and came to stand beside him. She put her hand on his dark curls and said gently, 'Don't give up on her, Gavin. Give her time; like any woman who suffers a miscarriage, she is confused and bitter about the loss of her baby. I have always believed that you two are soulmates and one day your love for each other will win.'

A polo match was arranged in the grounds of the Nawab's palace, the Nawab's team challenging the British. It was a warm day and Helen, dressed in a cool white dress, held a white lace parasol over her head, as she sat in a covered pavilion between Agnes Cameron and Blanche de Colbert.

Helen's eyes turned often to the dashing figure of her husband, dark and strikingly handsome in his cream riding breeches and polo shirt. His athletic figure, dark brown curls, damp with sweat, tumbling over his forehead and his grace as a rider playing the game with skill and daring, made him undeniably attractive and Helen could not fail to observe the many women watching him.

She caught his eye at one point when he was changing ponies and he lifted one shoulder in an ironic shrug and smiled that wicked, impudent smile that always set her heart thumping. Then he was back in the fray of the polo field and Helen's blushes were not lost on her friend, Blanche de Colbert.

'In society in France, *ma petite*, it is considered bad manners for a husband to be so much in love with his own wife,' joked the effervescent Creole.

****

It was in May 1857, when a telegram arrived at the fort informing the Resident and Brigadier General Sir James Cameron that Indian army sepoys had revolted in Meerut, killed their officers and British civilians in the town and were marching on Delhi to rally behind the Moghul Emperor, Bahadur Shah II, against the British.

It was decided to play down the revolt for fear of arousing passions amongst the Indian troops at the fort in Mirapore. Gavin called on the Nawab to ensure that there would be no question of his loyalty to the British.

In his capacity as Resident, he wrote to the Governor General, Lord Canning, in Calcutta, 'Most of the royal princes realise that their own sovereignty depends on their treaties with the British, in the absence of which there would be a return to the chaos, the fear and insecurity which followed the fragmentation of the Moghul Empire after the death of the last great Moghul, Aurungzib, in 1707. I believe that we will have no trouble with Mohammed Hassan Khan in Mirapore, although his son, Prince Ali and his ambitious French mother, must be carefully watched.'

Then over the ensuing months, the news of the spread of the revolt - the occupation of Delhi by the mutineers; the siege of the Residency in Lucknow where many of their friends resided; the treachery of Nana Sahib and his slaughter of British men, women and children in Cawnpore - reached the Europeans in Mirapore and brought feelings of disquiet and fear.

Precautions were taken to ensure that the troops at the fort remained uncorrupted by the mutineers. Gavin introduced a system of permits at the borders of the State and British soldiers were stationed, with the reluctant consent of the Nawab, at border points. Letters to the Indian troops at the fort were opened in case mutinous rebels communicated with them. John Lawrence, the powerful Administrator of the Punjab, assured Gavin that the Punjab would remain peaceful and that he could rely on his Sikh troops' loyalty.

Then Lord Canning commanded John Lawrence to send troops to the aid of the Delhi Field Force that was pinned down on the ridge facing the city. Lawrence's Punjabi troops, under the command of Brigadier John Nicholson, began to cross the Sutlej and Brigadier General Sir James Cameron was ordered to swell these forces by his Sikh and Highland troops under the command of Captain John MacGregor. John's promotion had been confirmed from Calcutta only a few weeks earlier, to the delight of all his friends.

Gavin was uneasy. Only a small force of loyal Gurkhas and a few British troops were left to defend the fort. The check points were now guarded by the Nawab's Rohillas, Afghan mercenaries who had little reason for loyalty to the British, pondered Gavin.

Audrey Blankenhagen

Sir James Cameron and Gavin followed the course of the mutiny. Standing over a map, spread out on a table, Gavin's fingers traced the large region of India, centred around the holiest places, which was now in the hands of the mutineers and when details of the murder in Cawnpore of women and children reached them, there was a sense of horror.

'It seems Major General Sir Henry Havelock's relief forces arrived too late to prevent the bloody massacre of two hundred British women and children,' said Sir James, an expression of deep sadness on his old campaigner's face, as he handed the despatch to Gavin.

Gavin, concerned for Helen after the recent loss of their own child, kept the worst reports from her.

The Residency at Lucknow was relieved by Henry Havelock after a siege of eighty-eight days, and Gavin brought the good news to his wife who knew many of the British families living in that town.

'Our half-starved friends are now safe, thank God,' said Gavin, 'but we do not know how many have survived the relentless barrage and pounding of the Residency walls.'

Telegraph lines, cut by the mutineers, were now being repaired and news of the British Army's courageous assault against Delhi came through. Prayers were offered at the fort's little chapel for the safety of Captain John MacGregor and their Highland friends, who were part of Nicholson's four columns, fighting their way, street by street, through the city against tremendous odds.

In September, Gavin had news of the British sacking of the city and the subsequent occupation of the Royal Palace by Brigadier Archdale Wilson. He told Helen, 'Delhi is now firmly in the hands of the British. I understand the princes of the Royal Court have been executed for their part in the rising and the Old Emperor has been imprisoned.'

'So Princess Muna's husband must be amongst the executed royal princes,' said Helen with a strange feeling of satisfaction that the man, who had caused so much pain to her friend, was now dead.

Another name, Sir Colin Campbell, the recently appointed Commander-in-Chief, India, began to appear in dispatches. Campbell turned his attention to Oudh, which was the home of a large proportion of the high-caste sepoys recruited by the British Army. These men were now mutineers and rallied behind their King of Oudh, who had refused to sign the treaty surrendering his State to the British in 1854.

At last, letters from John MacGregor were received. Apart from two Highlanders slightly wounded, he and all his troops were safe and well. They were marching with Colin Campbell to relieve Rohilkand, the neighbouring province to Oudh. John feared that because of delays in the fighting and, subsequently, the orgies of retribution, drunkenness and looting by some British troops (which their commanders seemed unable, or unwilling to curb) many rebels had been allowed to escape. They fled to forts of rebel Princes whose own States had been annexed by the British under Lord Dalhousie's Doctrine of Lapse.

'It may be best if all British civilians and any Europeans living in Mirapore were moved to the British fort for protection. Large forces of these mutineers are on their way to the foothills and others have fled to Central India, where the revolt is still to be subdued,' John warned.

Gavin collected Helen and Rosita and with their horses and one carriage, made their way to the fort, where Lady Agnes had prepared quarters for them. Ram Das, the *syce*, his wife, Lalitha and little Lazarus, accompanied them, because the syce explained, 'My loyalty is with you, *Sahib*, and not with these mad men. What will they do when they have gained their freedom? Will they give us work and put bread in our children's mouths?'

Gavin had already organised the transport to the fort of British civilians living in and around Mirapore and at the request of the French Consul, arranged for the escort of the Comte and Comtesse de Colbert and their servants to quarters in the fort.

'These mutineers are hardly likely to love the French any more than the British, Gavin. We, too, are a Western colonial power in their country,' explained the Comte.

Chapter 19

Two days after their arrival at the fort, the sentries in the watch towers alerted the Command to the large force of rebel sepoys marching into the Valley of Mirapore. They appeared to march in good order with regimental pennants flying. Their voices singing, incongruously, familiar British army marching songs were carried on the wind to the fort.

'No upstart force this', observed Sir James, training his telescope on the rebels, 'but well-trained, former Company Army infantry and cavalry, now led by non commissioned Indian officers. One can scarcely believe they have only recently murdered their British officers and families.'

It was midday when Helen noticed that Gavin and Ram Das were missing. She had a terrible presentiment that they were still in the city of Mirapore, now about to be occupied by the mutineers and her fears were confirmed by Sir James.

'Yes, Helen,' he replied. 'Gavin felt that as Resident, he should be at the Nawab's side to broker any negotiations with the rebels. The Nawab is pro-British, but for how long? Gavin is determined to prevent the Nawab going the way of the Rani of Jhansi and proclaiming his State independent. I have heard that the small British community in the fort at Jhansi were massacred, as at Cawnpore, despite being promised safe passage.'

Helen was suddenly very afraid and sought out Rosita. She clung to her Spanish friend sobbing, 'Why must my husband put his duty before everything else? He is in mortal danger if the Nawab is persuaded by the rebels to support them. Oh, Rosita, I love him so much and we have been unhappily estranged since my miscarriage.'

'I know, *queridisima*, Gavin told me how deeply hurt he was by your rejection. *En verdad* he loves you as much as you have always loved him. But dry your tears, little one. You should know by now that your husband is a brave and resourceful man and will not endanger his life unnecessarily.'

Still kneeling by Rosita's chair, Helen lifted her tear-stained face and asked quietly, 'Tell me what he said to you, Rosita ... about me.'

She listened in silence as Rosita told her about her conversation with Gavin, his love for Helen and his hurt by her continued rejection of him. He blamed himself for not taking the Curse of Kali seriously and putting Helen's life in danger with Isabel de Silva.

Helen listened in surprise when Rosita told her about Gavin's unfortunate marriage to his first wife, Maria, and the discovery of her lesbian tendencies that had revolted him, especially when he learnt of her visits to the bazaars to sleep with Indian prostitutes.

'He was even contemplating divorce', said Rosita, 'because it was a matter of time before Maria's lifestyle became public knowledge amongst the British community here in Mirapore and in the Company administration in general. That would have made it impossible for Gavin to continue as Resident. I believe it was fortuitous for Gavin that Maria contracted smallpox and her death relieved him of the trauma and disgrace of divorce, especially the hurt he would cause her parents for whom he held a deep affection and respect.'

That night was a sleepless one for Helen and she was awake with the early dawn to stand on the ramparts to watch for Gavin and Ram Das. It was late afternoon when two riders approached the portcullis of the fort and Helen recognising Gavin and his servant, almost tripped over her long, dark grey, worsted skirt racing down the much trodden, centuries old, granite steps to arrive, breathless, just as the heavy gate was swung open.

Gavin looked surprised to see his wife standing there, her auburn hair flying about her shoulders, her beautiful face flushed above the white lace collar of her dark grey blouse. But it was the look in her emerald eyes which were shining with love that took his breath away.

He vaulted off his horse and ran towards her, enfolding her in his arms, his face buried in her hair as she, and she alone, heard him whisper, 'My little sweetheart, my little love, did you miss me?' An embarrassed cough nearby brought the lovers abruptly back to earth and Gavin reluctantly released his wife when he saw the soldier waiting patiently.

'Yes, sergeant?' Gavin enquired.

The sergeant saluted smartly and said, 'Compliments from Sir James, sir. He asked me to fetch you as soon as you returned.'

'Yes, sergeant, I intended to report to Sir James as soon as I got back, but I was pleasantly distracted.' His wink and impudent smile brought blushes to Helen's cheeks, as Gavin bent down and kissed her on her lips before moving away with the sergeant. Helen picked up her skirt and made her way back to her apartments with as much dignity as she could muster, not daring to turn round to observe the guards at the gate who, she guessed, would be smirking and nudging each other in the manner of soldiers.

It was over dinner in the officer's mess that Gavin gave an account to his fellow officers and their wives of his dealings with the Nawab.

'The Nawab, at my insistence, sent his Rohillas to deny entry to the rebels who were encamped outside the city gates and to demand their surrender. He warned them that any forced entry would be met by equal force and his treaty with the British would ensure that Company's troops would be called to his assistance.

'I have not, of course, informed the Nawab of our depleted forces here at the fort: he believes we are at full strength. He is also aware that a large force of loyal Sikh troops from the Punjab is on its way to Mirapore. Here again, I did not mention to the Nawab that dispatches for aid to John Lawrence in Lahore have only just been sent by Lord Canning, our

Governor General in Calcutta. The Nawab believes that Sikh troops are even now crossing the Sutleg.'

'Good, Gavin', said one of the Highland officers, 'these rebel chaps know how fiercely they have been dealt with in Oudh by our forces. Will they pack up and leave now, do you think?'

'I am afraid not,' said Sir James, 'there is a further setback, which Gavin will now explain.'

'Whilst I was in conference with the Nawab and Prince Hassan, the Chief Eunuch of the harem, Ibrahim, asked to speak to the Nawab privately. It appears that Begum Shalima's spies have discovered a plot by Prince Ali and his French mother to deal directly with the rebels who believe, with justification, that to surrender would mean certain death at the hands of the British. In exchange for their help in seizing the throne, Prince Ali has given them carte blanche to storm the fort and slaughter the Europeans before the arrival of any British relief forces.'

'Did his father arrest Prince Ali and his French mother, Gavin?' enquired Lady Agnes.

'Unfortunately, we were too late', replied Gavin. 'The prince and his mother had already left the palace with an escort of bribed Rohilla guards to negotiate with the Rebels. The Nawab and Prince Hassan pleaded with me to leave with Ram Das, as they feared that my presence in the palace would only complicate the position.'

'Well, gentlemen and ladies,' said Sir James. To be forewarned is to be forearmed and we know that a siege of the fort is imminent. We will resist until we are relieved. Fortunately, the Emperor Akbar built this fort to withstand siege and its walls are almost impregnable. On one side, the cliff face is perpendicular and the only road leading to the gates of the fort is well within the range of our guns.

'I will leave you ladies to organise the rationing of our food supplies, the medical team will be Doctor Graham and Helen, assisted at her request by the Comtesse de Colbert. And now, gentlemen, we must examine our defences and ammunition.' Brigadier General Sir James pushed back his chair and rose to his feet with the air of a man determined to acquit himself as military commander of the small British garrison at Mirapore.

It was late when Gavin came to their room that night. He looked tired and Helen, who had been entering her diary of events that day, seated at a little escritoire, stood up and came towards him.

'You look tired, my darling. Come, let me help you off with your boots. There is some hot water I ordered for your bath, but it must be cold now,' she said, turning and taking each booted leg between her thighs, as she had done so often for her father after they had been riding together.

When the boots and hose were off, Gavin stood up and allowed his beautiful wife to undress him, only stopping her by holding her hand when she would have removed his breeches. Then he laughed and allowed her to continue, stepping out of his breeches until he stood stark naked before her, his bold eyes no longer showing any sign of weariness, but glinting with amusement as he saw her blush at the sight of his erection.

'See what you have done, woman. That is what happens when you come so close to your husband. Don't you know how irresistible you are, sweetheart?'

Then lifting her gently, he carried her to their bed and removed the flimsy shift she was wearing, his hands, lips and tongue following every lovely contour of her body. He made love to her as he had never done before, now that he knew that his love was returned and Helen sighed with longing as Gavin's endearments, his kisses and his touch inflamed her senses. She felt that earthy sensuality that only this man could arouse in her and as his naked body moved over hers, flesh on flesh, she cried out her love and need for him, 'Gavin, my darling, how I love you!'

He kissed her swollen lips again hard and possessively, almost shouting in his rapture, 'At last, at last, my beautiful Helen, how I have longed to hear those words from your lips,' and lifting her hips towards him, he possessed her unable any longer to hold back his pent-up hunger for her.

As he lay spent on her breast, she whispered, 'My darling, is it always so wonderful between lovers?'

'No, little sweetheart, only between us because, as Rosita says, you are my soulmate,' and Gavin smiled as he enveloped her closer in his arms,

313

content at last that their misunderstanding was past and they could love each other without reserve.

Long after Gavin slept in her arms, Helen lay awake, listening to his even breathing and when she touched his face tenderly, he smiled in his sleep and Helen knew that whatever hardships overtook them in the days ahead, this moment would be theirs to treasure.

The next day was hectic; the fort was preparing for siege. The ramparts were thronged with soldiers, checking the heavy guns mounted on the walls and in the courtyard troops were testing their musketry and sharpening their bayonets and knives. Home-made bombs, infernal machines, huge stones and blocks of wood to impel scaling ladders, were assembled together with other missiles to be hurled on the heads of the invaders. One of the young officers, whose father had fought in Spain against Napoleon, made it his task to collect lime. This, he explained, had been thrown in the eyes of French soldiers who had succeeded in storming a fort defended by a handful of Wellington's grenadiers. The lime filled grenades were piled in strategic places on the ramparts and near the fort gates.

Helen and Doctor Graham prepared the little hospital, hoping that there would be few causalities. Lady Agnes and the officers' wives inspected the food stores, instructing the cooks to use only the perishable food first. The stores of fresh apples and pears were checked and each fruit was wrapped in paper to preserve and prevent contamination as it ripened. The floors of the cellars in the fort were cold stone and Agnes told Helen their supplies of salt beef, pork, fresh fruit, preserves, cereals, lentils and rice should keep well. There was plenty of flour for bread.

There was, however, only one well inside the fort perimeter, and because of the low rainfall that summer, it was not as full as they would have wished, but before the siege started, the soldiers had taken mules to the river below and filled as many water skins as they could to be stored in the cellars.

The fort was crowded, not only with soldiers, but with British civilians, merchants, women and children and other Europeans, amongst them the French Consul, his wife and their staff. In all there were about 3000 people, only half of these fighting men.

The Indian troops, mostly Sikhs and Gurkhas, renewed their pledge of loyalty and Sir James and Gavin had no doubt that they would not be betrayed by these splendid native soldiers.

That day Sir James told his officers, 'The relief force from the Punjab has been held up because Sikh troops sent for the relief of Delhi have not yet returned and John Lawrence is reluctant to deplete his forces further, until he is sure the Punjab will not mutiny. I believe we can hold out for at least three weeks but this is for your ears only, gentlemen. We do not wish to cause any anxiety amongst the civilians here in the fort.'

That night, under cover of darkness, the mutineers fires appeared in the valley below as they set up camp well away from the range of guns on the fort walls. Through their telescopes, the British officers saw the formidable numbers of rebel troops, former company sepoys, their numbers swelled by the Nawab's Rohillas. It was obvious that Prince Ali had succeeded in overthrowing his father and brother.

The morning saw a siege train of heavy artillery being hauled by palace elephants and despite heavy fire from the fort, native engineers began constructing battery positions to bombard the walls. As many unfortunate sepoys were killed by artillery fire from the fort, their places were taken by others, until it seemed to the British watching from the ramparts, that the rebels had a death wish.

If the fort had been at strength, Gavin told Helen, as she lay in his arms that night, the British would not have permitted the mutineers to enter Mirapore, but would have attacked them outside the city walls. She slept fitfully and when she awoke in the early hours of the morning, her husband was no longer by her side.

If she had known why, she would have been mortally afraid. Gavin, Ram Das and a platoon of Gurkhas crept out of the fort under cover of darkness. The Gurkhas silently drew their *kukrees* and slit the throats of the sepoy sentries whilst Gavin set charges to blow up the enemy batteries, so dearly erected by them a few hours ago.

When Helen saw him again, later in the morning, he was leaning against a wall in the courtyard eating *chappatis* and drinking mugs of tea with his Gurkhas. His short dark hair was tousled and there were powder marks on his face. Even unshaven and unkempt, he looked so handsome that her heart leaped. When Gavin looked up and saw his wife, his brown eyes softened and that buccaneer's smile twisted his lips. Helen had heard the soldiers talking about the attack on the enemy battery and she knew now that Gavin had been involved.

'What a sight to gladden a soldier's heart,' he said, coming forward to kiss his wife, but Helen's smile was strained and she caught his arm and propelled him a little distance from his troops.

'Gavin, you are not a soldier and should not be risking your life in these daredevil escapades. You are the Resident of Mirapore and surely there are trained officers to infiltrate enemy lines.'

His fingers touched her lips gently and he said, 'Hush, my darling, I was a soldier before I was appointed Resident. Besides, what can a Resident do in a fort besieged by mutineers; there are no ambassadorial duties for me here, my love, and Sir James needs every man who can fight. Even our gallant French Consul has armed himself with a rifle.'

Helen looked at Gavin, his brown eyes crinkling at the corners against the glare of the late autumn sunshine. She knew why she was bewitched by this man. His courage, his self-assurance, at times almost bordering on

317

arrogance and his powerful masculinity, were magnets that would draw any woman. Now, unshaven and battle-stained, he was smiling at her, almost like a mischievous boy begging forgiveness for a naughty prank.

Helen laughed at his expression and looked over Gavin's shoulder at the little brigade of Gurkhas, their wide, flat, Mongol faces wreathed in smiles, obviously enjoying the spectacle of their Sahib being taken to task by his wife and then she noticed the cut on Ram Das's cheek.

'I hope to see you later, Gavin, but please order Ram Das to come to the hospital for that cut to be stitched,' she said in her severest physician's manner and as she moved away, she heard Gavin telling the intrepid Gurkha, 'You heard the doctor *memsahib*, Ram Das, jump to it!'

Late that night, when Gavin came to their bedroom, Helen was already in bed. The night was quite cold and because fuel was rationed by order of Sir James, there was no fire burning in the small iron stove in the corner of the room. Gavin, who slept naked whatever the weather, pulled back the heavy quilt quickly, sprang into bed and drew his wife's warm body towards him.

'Keep me warm, little sweetheart,' he teased, his hands moving over her, bringing her the delight they always did. Helen was beginning to look forward to these nights in her husband's arms and his ardent love-making. She put her arms about his neck and drew his mouth down to her breast.

'Will you be leaving me again by morning?' she asked, running her fingers through his dark curls and down his strong back, making him gasp when she slipped one hand between their bodies and touched him intimately.

'No, sweetheart. I intend to make love to you all night. You know I can never get enough of you.'

They made love and slept only to wake and make love again and when Helen finally awoke with the the pink dawn light creeping though the latticed windows, she saw the dark eyes of her husband studying her with a quizzical look.

'Why are you looking at me like that,?' she asked sleepily.

His finger traced her lips still swollen from his kisses and then he gently picked up a strand of her shining hair spread out on the pillow.

'Why? Because you have the look of a woman who has been well loved. If I was not the first to ravish you, I would find myself wondering what previous lover had instructed you so well in the art of love. But then, they say that women with hair this colour are naturally sensual,' he smiled, his white teeth gleaming in his brown face as he lifted the lock of her perfumed hair to his lips.

Helen was to recall Gavin's remark with a warm glow several times during her busy day, and she remembered how she had been concerned that he would find her inexperienced as a lover. The love that she felt for her

319

handsome husband made her bold and almost wanton in their bed and she

knew, instinctively, how to please him.

Chapter 20

Despite Gavin's and the Gurkhas' valiant efforts to cripple the enemy battery positions, the bombardment of the fort walls was not too long delayed. Howitzers and mortars, with their high trajectories, found their mark over the ramparts and 24 pounder guns started to hit the thick walls.

It was decided that the women and children should be quartered in the more sheltered areas of the fort. Now even trips to the well were becoming hazardous from exploding shells and bullets from snipers, positioned on a ridge opposite the fort.

Some of the sepoys decided to storm the British defences and their slaughter from the fort's artillery gave the British the first clue of the inadequacy of the rebel leadership.

'It broke my heart, milady, to see the poor blighters pushed forward repeatedly by their leaders, only to be mowed down by our guns and still they came, until the mountainside was littered with corpses,' said a wounded Highlander, who Helen was treating in the hospital.

By evening, the sepoys came with white flags to collect their dead and wounded and the British observed a ceasefire until the last body was removed. Even though the air temperatures were lower in the Himalayan autumn, the ground on which the dead lay was still warm from the summer heat and flies swarmed everywhere, whilst vultures and carrion crows circled in the skies before swooping down to begin their macabre feast.

Helen issued strict instructions that all water was to be boiled for drinking, cooking, washing of food utensils and food, and prepared food was never to be left uncovered.

Despite her precautions, it was not long before the first cases of dysentery were diagnosed. Helen suspected that water had been drunk without boiling, or over-ripe fruit eaten. She started to prepare a room to barrier nurse the patients of this infectious disease and with Doctor Graham's consent, decided that only she and Blanche de Colbert would attend to the dysentery cases, to prevent the infection from spreading.

Although the bombardment of the fort continued, no further attempts were made to storm the walls.

'Perhaps they are waiting for our supplies of food and ammunition to run out,' said Sir James. 'Let us hope the reinforcements are here before that. The devils have cut our telegraph lines, so it is anyone's guess when the Punjabi relief force will arrive.'

Now, after two weeks of siege, rationing was introduced, one main meal a day for adults, two for the children and a light breakfast of chappatis and tea. Helen was concerned because the dysentery patients needed nourishment and she ordered a diet of rice water, light broth thickened with arrowroot and albumin water.

She had sufficient supplies of castor oil and opium to relieve the griping pains of the disease and carbonate of bismuth and extracts of ipecacuanha for their treatment, but in the event of an epidemic, even these supplies would be severely stretched.

The beautiful Comtesse de Colbert was a source of untiring support to Helen in the treatment of her dysentery patients and she told Gavin that night, 'My admiration for the lovely Blanche has never been higher. She rolls up her sleeves and never flinches from the unpleasant aspects of nursing dysentery sufferers.'

'She feels the same about you, my darling. Only today she told me how impressed she is with your medical expertise and skill,' replied Gavin, fondling his wife's exposed breasts and grinning at her wickedly and she knew that soon they would both forget that anything or anyone existed outside their world of love.

Helen was concerned about Rosita. Now sixty years old, her beloved companion was beginning to show her age and despite Helen's entreaties to take life easier, the Spanish woman was determined to 'pull her weight'. She had taken over the care of the children in the fort whilst their parents were engaged elsewhere. She was often found in the schoolroom teaching the children Spanish, or relating the wonderful folklore of her country and Helen recalled her own childhood, when she had sat at Rosita's knee and listened to these very same sagas.

The rebels were now constructing a large semicircular trench with salients and a protecting ditch beyond the range of the fort artillery and the British, observing through their telescopes, were well aware that the commander of the rebels was now preparing for assault. This work was carried out mostly at night but was hampered by defensive sorties through the fort's Sally port - a small gate set in the ramparts. These forays were designed not only to impede the investment, but to lower the moral of the rebel engineers, as their throats were slit by Gurkha *kukrees*, their sappers blown up by explosives and even entrenching tools were captured.

Helen knew that many of these sorties were led by her husband, because he would often return in the early morning dressed in a sepoy's uniform with his skin stained a deeper brown and his buccaneer's smile wider and more impudent when he greeted her. She was seeing another side to Gavin - a warrior who seemed to enjoy the thrill of battle, as if it was no more than a vigorous game of polo.

She, herself, had little time to brood. Grape shot and mortar fire were causing many casualties and dysentery was still a threat. One of the Gurkha children developed gangrenous chickenpox and its resemblance to smallpox caused a great deal of panic amongst the mothers of the other children, until Helen's diagnosis, confirmed by Doctor Graham, calmed their fears. The child was immediately put into quarantine and although a few milder cases of the disease occurred, strict quarantine and applications of soothing zinc

324

powder and ointments to the skin, soon brought the little patients back to health.

It was the fourth week of the siege when the reason for the apparent inaction of the mutineers became apparent. A large force of rebel reinforcements under the banner of a rebellious Maratha Maharaja, marched into Mirapore, bringing with them the Indian ruler's big brass 18 and 24 pounder cannon and more muskets.

Now there was no time to loiter. Sir James ordered the tightening up of the defences. The ditch surrounding the fort had been scarped and mines and shells buried and horizontal row of poles *(fraises)* constructed to impede assault ladders. The largest battery, projecting from flanking bastions in the rampart wall, would bring enfilade fire from its three guns on the attackers; *cheval-de-frise* - portable obstructions of sword blades - were constructed to block any breaches in the walls; more shells, combustibles and quicklime were assembled on the parapets.

The British women, formerly ladies of leisure employing cooks, *dhobis* and *ayas*, found themselves coping with all the tasks usually performed by these servants. Firewood was becoming scarce and as the distinct chill of the Himalayan nights heralded the approach of winter, mothers started to cut up their fur coats to make garments and warm moccasins for their children. People went to bed fully dressed, but the worst aspect was the lack of news from the outside world. The besieged wondered if the Mutiny had been put down elsewhere and when the promised relief forces would come to their aid?

The lower temperatures at least prevented the spread of diseases such as cholera, although dysentery was still a problem and the hospital was now filled with the wounded. Helen and Doctor Graham worked hard, removing bullets, performing major surgery but supplies of chloroform were now very low and the doctors feared for the fate of future amputees.

Now Helen hardly saw her husband. With dangerous sorties, sentry and other duties all the men - officers and other ranks - were preparing for the inevitable assault. When they did snatch a few hours together, their lovemaking took on a new desperate hunger for each other, as if each time would be their last.

The siege was now in its sixth week and the conditions in the fort were becoming squalid. The air was filled with the smell of death and gunpowder. Rationing of food was now tighter, most meals consisting only of *dhal* and rice and a little meat for the fighting men. In the first few days of the siege, the enemy gunfire was not too hazardous, but the mutineers started to use incendiary shells and even flaming arrows and their small arms fire often found its mark. The little graveyard soon began to fill up, not only with dead adults, but with new-born babies who died because their mothers' milk had dried up.

Several attempts to storm the ramparts were made, but the enemy assaults were repulsed by heavy fire from the garrison's batteries and the mutineers did not appear to have intrepid captains to lead by example. Trumpets blowing the advance and shouts of *'Chalo Bhai; Maro Feringhi Soor'* (Come on, brothers, kill the foreign swine) did not seem to have the desired effect on the rebels, when the British guns took their toll.

The Maharajah's brass cannon were now pounding away at the walls but the solid masonry stood up well and where breaches occurred, these were repaired immediately, despite heavy enemy fire.

It was a few days before Christmas. The women had tried to bring some festive cheer, especially for the children, by baking small cakes from their reserves of flour and holding carol services, but everyone was aware that time was not on their side and if they were not relieved soon, their lives would be forfeit. Before the telegraph lines had been cut and despatches from Calcutta delayed, the British in Mirapore had heard of the fate of their countrymen at the hands of the mutineers: Cawnpore, where defenceless women and children were butchered, Delhi where the Europeans in the palace were slaughtered by the knives and swords of mutinous cavalry, and the murder of inhabitants at every British station along the route of the mutiny.

Audrey Blankenhagen

Several of the married men made a pact with their wives to destroy each other if the enemy achieved a breakthrough and the wounded in the hospital asked for explosives to be set in this event.

Helen asked Gavin that night, 'My darling, will you shoot us, if I do not have the courage to take my own and Rosita's life?'

'Don't worry, little sweetheart, if there is a breakthrough, I will come to you and we will die together. But this is all nonsense we are speaking; relief will be here sooner than later. A brave Highland officer, disguised as an Indian and his Gurkha corporal have, some days ago, abseiled down the precipitous side of the cliff face and are on their way to seek out the British relief columns and warn them of our plight,' said Gavin, kissing his wife and holding her close in his arms.

The enemy were now entrenched not far from the fort, sapping ever nearer under cover of darkness and their guns were pounding the walls relentlessly. The British garrison, severely depleted even further by casualties, had to restrict their sorties to destroy enemy batteries and it was feared that if the siege continued much longer, they would run dangerously short of ammunition.

Now there was very little sleep for everyone. Mothers huddled with their children in basements, the men sharpened knives and bayonets and the officers buckled on their revolvers and swords, all prepared to repel the invader to their last breath. The constant pounding was at last having an

328

effect on the walls and crumbling masonry would soon make a breach wide enough for a breakthrough.

Once again, when the sun dipped below the highest peaks, enemy trumpets sounded the attack and this time drums and cymbals were added to the bloodcurdling sound of the sepoys' now familiar war cry, *'Chalo Bhai; Maro Feringhi Soor!'* Heavy fire from the ramparts showered the oncoming hoards, cutting murderous swathes through their ranks, but still they came.

Helen sort out Rosita and brought her to the hospital, so that Gavin would know where to find them both in the event of a breakthrough. Rosita sat quietly in a corner of the ward, running the beads of her rosary through her fingers and smiling bravely whenever Helen caught her eye. Why did I allow her to come with me to India? thought Helen sadly, looking at the beloved woman who had been mother and friend to her since her own mother's death.

It was a bright moonlight night. The mutineers had fallen back to regroup before an even more ferocious attack which, if sustained, would be impossible to repel. For a brief moment whilst they gathered, the sound of artillery was stilled.

Then, as if in a dream, the skirl of Highland pipes was carried on the winds to the ears of the desperate, besieged garrison and lookouts on the Keep were shouting, 'The Highlanders, the Highlanders!' Telescopes were raised and the sight of a large force of Colin Campbell's Highland Regiment,

329

pipers sounding the Highland Charge, brought tears of joy to the besieged. The ranks of mutineers, too astonished to turn their guns around on the Highlanders, were taken by surprise.

Sir James ordered the men of the garrison to break through the breached wall and the two forces - besieged and relief - routed the mutineers. The slaughter was horrific as swords and bayonets slashed their way through the demoralised rebels, who had seen victory snatched, so savagely, from their grasp at the very last moment.

The Maharajah, Prince Ali and his mother were captured outside the City gates by a Highland brigade positioned there to prevent the escape of mutineers. The Maharajah and the prince were brought back to the fort and held prisoner until a trial could be arranged. Prince Ali's mother was returned to the palace to be dealt with by the Nawab and Helen had no doubt, by the Begum Shalima.

Helen, herself, had no time to join in the celebrations. Too many injured needed her attention and she and Doctor Graham worked late into the next morning. When at last she emerged from the hospital, rolling down the sleeves of her white cotton blouse, she felt herself suddenly lifted off her feet by strong arms and looking down, saw the bearded face of John MacGregor grinning with excitement. John greeted Helen with such shouts of enthusiasm that every eye turned to see who the Scottish captain was whirling around, dancing the Highland fling and hollering with joy.

'Ah Helen, lovely, wee lass. How glad I am to see you safe and well!' and then to the astonishment of everyone, he kissed her soundly on her lips.

'John, you idiot, put me down and stop behaving like an overgrown puppy,' she laughed and saw over the Scotsman's head, her husband talking to Sir James and Colin Campbell. Gavin was about to light a cigar when he looked up and saw the reason for the commotion. He raised one eyebrow sardonically at the sight of his wife being enveloped by John MacGregor's bear hug, but now secure in the knowledge of her love for him, this time he was not jealous, only amused: how could he blame the giant Scot for loving his beautiful wife.

John MacGregor took Helen's arm and leading her towards her husband and Sir James introduced her to Sir Colin Campbell. 'Sir Colin, may I introduce one of our hard working surgeons, Lady French, the wife of our Resident.'

The formidable Commander-in-Chief smiled one of his rare smiles and raising Helen's hand to his lips said, 'I am honoured, Lady French. How fortunate you are, Sir James, to have such a beautiful surgeon. Our field surgeons are stout fellows, but hardly the stuff of dreams.' He laughed uproariously at his own joke and winked at Gavin, who was more than a little surprised at the gallantry and unexpected humour of this dour Scottish General.

331

Audrey Blankenhagen

That day there was rejoicing everywhere. Food was prepared from the fort's meagre supplies supplemented by geese, ducks and pigeons from the Maratha Maharajah's stores and quantities of beer found in his tent. It seemed this Indian Ruler travelled in opulent style, even to war.

Gavin and Helen listened in horror to John's accounts of the siege of Delhi and Lucknow and the tragedy of Cawnpore, where the troops had found bloody evidence of the massacre of almost two hundred, helpless, British women and children.

'Every British soldier who passed through Cawnpore and saw, for himself, the bloody evidence of the butchery which had taken place about the house and courtyard where these prisoners were held:- the tree from which Brigadier General Neill's troops cut down British women hanging by their hair; the well which had been crammed with more bodies of the women and children; bloodstains of children's tiny hands and feet on the walls; their little shoes and dresses and even their mothers' bibles and marriage certificates still strewn around the courtyard - could not feel anything but hatred for the perpetrators.

'I am not proud of the savage acts of awful revenge committed against the Pandies[2] by our own enraged troops, but when one visits Cawnpore, the British soldier's thirst for reprisals and his uncharacteristic lack of pity, are

---

2 British nickname for mutinous sepoy troops

332

understandable,' said John quietly, his fists clenched and his eyes closed, as if to shut out the terrible scenes he had witnessed.

Audrey Blankenhagen

Epilogue

Helen and Gavin continued to live in the fort for a few more days until the city of Mirapore had been cleared of rebels. More British troops arrived to bring the garrison back to its former strength. Sir Colin Campbell was then able to leave with his own force and to march back to Calcutta with the royal prisoners - the Maharajah and Prince Ali. Their fate was not long delayed. A telegram from Calcutta informed the Resident that both prisoners had been tried, found guilty of treason and executed by firing squad.

'They received a sentence far more lenient than the sepoys they had led,' remarked Sir James. 'Many mutineers were strapped to and fired from our cannons.' Then seeing the women's looks of horror, he explained, 'This was the way the Moghuls executed traitors: ironic, don't you think, in view of the mutineers' proclamation that the last of that Moghul dynasty, Bahadur Shah the Second, was the rightful Emperor of India and not the Empress, Queen Victoria.'

Gavin called on the Nawab to inform him of Prince Ali's sentence and execution. Mohammed Hassan Khan was sitting alone on his throne in the vast Audience Chamber, a man suddenly aged.

'He is my son and I will grieve for him, Sir Gavin, but it is hard to forget his treachery, not only to the British but to his own family,' said the Ruler of Mirapore.

Then, as if as an afterthought, he said, 'It is strange that it should be my son, Ali, who embraced everything Western, who was the one to betray the English Raj.'

The Begum Shalima's clinic continued to function under the direction of Doctor Patel, but there was an air of mistrust now between the Indians and the British and Helen found an unease amongst her patients. The Highlanders had set fire to many homes of villagers who had given sanctuary to rebel sepoys and Helen believed that the Indians now regarded the British as cruel and despotic as any of India's previous conquerors.

Even the Residency was no longer the beautiful place she had come to regard as home. It had been looted and defaced, its elegant furniture and priceless paintings piled up on the lawn and reduced to ashes by the mutineers.

The mutiny was over and the British were again firmly in control, but the Governor General, Lord Canning, decided to annex the State of Mirapore to the British Crown.

Gavin now had supreme control on behalf of the company and Nawab Mohammed Hassan Khan reluctantly signed the document ceding his State to the British. He was allowed to retain his beautiful palace, where he lived out the remainder of his days on a generous pension awarded by the British.

Gavin told Helen, 'I could not help feeling a deep sadness for the Nawab when he looked at his signature on the document and with tears in his eyes said, "So, Sir Gavin, I have signed away the sovereignty of my State, which my ancestors had won with blood, sweat and tears almost three hundred years ago."

'In that moment of surrender, Mohammed Hassan Khan displayed a dignity and courage equal to any of his warrior ancestors,' said Gavin, and Helen knew that her husband was distressed that after all his work for the Nawab and Mirapore, he was the one to witness the ruler's downfall.

Life returned slowly to normal for both the Indians and the British. The French Consul was closed and Helen and Gavin were guests at a farewell dinner hosted by their dear friends, Comte and Comtesse de Colbert, who returned to Paris with promises not to lose touch with their English friends, 'Especially with you, my dear Helen,' said Blanche, with tears in her eyes.

On the first of September, 1858, almost a year since the Mutiny had come to Mirapore, the rule of India was, by Act of Parliament, transferred from the Honourable East India Company to the British Crown and the administration of that strangest of trading companies came to an end.

Gavin, a Company man to the end, decided to turn down a prestigious administrative appointment in the new Indian Civil Service. He wanted to return to England with his wife and Rosita.

'My father, although he does not say so in his letters, my darling, is feeling his age and I know he would love us all back at Charnwood Hall and for me to take over the running of the estate. What do you think? We will be

337

able to take the horses with us on a ship used by the cavalry, who always ensure their beloved animals are well quartered aboard ship.'

'Oh yes please, Gavin, I am sure Rosita, too, would like to return to our more temperate climate. Besides, I believe I am pregnant again and would love this child to be born in England,' said Helen quietly, watching her husband's dark eyes fill with wonder and joy as he lifted her off her feet, swung her around and shouted loudly, mimicking the Scottish brogue of their friend, John MacGregor.

'My darling, wee lassie, are you sure? Do you ken how much I love you? You have made me the happiest man in the world!' Her laughter and his wild kisses on her mouth, made it impossible for Helen to reply.

* * * * * *

Before they left for India, this time by the shorter sea route of the newly-constructed Suez Canal, Gavin took Helen to Kashmir once more. Rosita had been invited to join them but declined, saying she preferred to remain with her friends in Mirapore. Helen guessed that her Spanish friend's uncanny sixth sense knew that the lovers wanted to be alone on what was for them a sentimental journey.

* * * * * *

As if to celebrate their happiness, Diwali, the Hindu Festival of Light, was being observed by the minority Hindu population of the State of Kashmir, when they arrived.

'This is the happiest festival in the Hindu calendar, devoted to the Goddess Lakshmi,' Gavin told Helen.

She was entranced by the little, clay oil lamps used by the people to decorate niches, windows, trees and gardens and floated on the waters of the lakes; the tiny lights at night resembling myriads of fireflies. At the end of the festival, Helen bought some sugared sweets carved in the form of animals for the servants' children and rockets and fireworks and the cook's wife showed her how to tie the beautiful gold, silk sari Gavin had bought for her in the bazaar.

Perhaps, because she was wearing this elegant Indian garment, Helen felt the need to honour the Goddess and under cover of the noise of the fireworks, she went down the steps of the houseboat and floated four little lamps on its waters, one each for Gavin, herself, Rosita and their unborn child.

When she looked up, she saw Gavin leaning on the verandah balustrade, watching her. He smiled and coming towards her, opened his arms and drew her to him.

So, Lady French, or should I say my beautiful Indian princess, because that is who you resemble in that lovely sari, are you, too, saluting the Goddess Lakshmi?'

'I thought I should make a little offering for all of us - you, Rosita and this little one and because of my own happiness, my darling.'

Gavin held her slightly away from him and lifting her hand to his lips, could not fail to notice that she was wearing the diamond ring cut into the shape of entwining hearts - his wedding gift of love - a love she was now convinced was hers alone. Helen looked into his eyes, dark with deep emotion and knew there was no need for any explanation, especially when he said, 'You know I have always adored you and when I thought I was losing you, I nearly went mad. Now you are mine and I will never let you escape again,' and as if to reinforce his promise, he held her closer in his arms and kissed her tenderly.

No matter what the future held for them, Helen knew that she would never forget their belated honeymoon In Kashmir. They had spent their days leisurely, enjoying the breathtaking scenery of this Oriental Switzerland, visiting all the places of interest and when, at the end of the day the servants had left the houseboat, Gavin carried Helen to their bedroom and showed her again and again how much he loved her.

'I love you, my little sweetheart. How I love you!' he had cried last night when their lovemaking had carried them both to new peaks of ecstasy.

It was dawn when she awoke and saw Gavin standing at the window, his tall, athletic body silhouetted against the morning light. She lay for a while admiring his masculine beauty which, since they now shared a bed, she had ample opportunity to do, because her husband never wore clothes in the privacy of their bedroom. Once again. Helen was reminded of

Michelangelo's 'David'. Gavin turned and saw his lovely wife watching him through half-closed eyes.

'Are you awake, darling? Come and see this beautiful sunrise. Kashmir is putting on such a display, determined we will never forget her.'

Helen climbed out of bed and into Gavin's enveloping arms as he pulled the thick *rezai* off the bed and wrapped it around their naked bodies, because there was a distinct chill in the morning air.

Helen saw the panorama that was entrancing Gavin and which she remembered so well from her first, unhappy visit to Kashmir - Lake Dal set alight by the rising sun until her waters resembled burnished gold, a kingfisher perched on a water lily nearby, looking for his fishy breakfast, little fishing boats in the distance casting their nets, encircled by eager birds and all around the mighty Himalayas, their snow-capped peaks tinted gold by the rising sun.

'I shall miss this fascinating country, Gavin, despite all its recent upheavals,' said Helen, unable to hide a note of nostalgia in her voice.

'I know, little sweetheart, so will I. I told you India will get into your blood. But I promise we will come back one day,' whispered Gavin burying his face in Helen's scented hair, his hand stroking her still flat stomach, 'and we will bring our offspring with us, especially this little one who was conceived in this beautiful land.

'We'll show our children the Tag Mahal by moonlight; our lovely valley of Mirapore where their father was Resident and their mother a famous doctor and last, but not least, this beautiful Vale of Kashmir where a jealous husband first made savage love to his beautiful wife,' said Gavin huskily, turning her in his arms to face him and kissing her hungrily.

'But he brought her back again to this lovely valley to fill her heart with his love, something she has always desired,' whispered Helen and sighed with happiness as Gavin lifted her and carried her back to their bed.

Glossary

Word	Meaning
Afridis	a race of Afghans on the N.W Frontier
Alaikum Alsalām	Peace be with you (Muslim greeting)
Angressi	English
Ayas	nursemaids
Badmash	Scoundrel
Badshah	Emperor, Ruler
Baksheesh	alms, tip
Bunia	merchants/shopkeeper
Beedi	rolled tabacco leaf cigarette
Bharata Natyam	temple dancing in the classical mode.
Bhisti	Water Carrier
Chaatri	Monument
Chappatis	flat round unleavened bread
Chaprassi	Servant

Audrey Blankenhagen

Word	Meaning
Chokra	an Urchin
Chowkidar	Watchman
Dak bungalow	rest house, originally for mail.
Dandy	open palanquins carried on poles on the shoulders of four men.
Dharshan	Blessing
Dhai	Yoghourt
Dhobis	washer men
Diwan	Revenue Collector
Doonga	a pleasure boat in Kashmir
Effendi	Arabic for a man of high social standing.
En verdad	in fact (Spanish)
Feringhi	Derogatory word for white man.- Urdu origin.
Ghat	Wharf – used for religious ceremonies
Hadji	Title for a Muslim who visits Mecca
Huzoor	Lord

Word	Ji
Meaning	Honorific suffix to a name

Word	Kala Pani
Meaning	Literally black water – ocean

Word	Kameez
Meaning	long tunic worn by Muslim women

Word	Karma
Meaning	Destiny

Word	Kukree
Meaning	curved knife used by the Gurkhas

Word	Lassi
Meaning	Yoghurt drink

Word	Lathi
Meaning	stout stick

Word	Machan
Meaning	wooden hunting platforms built in trees

Word	Mahout
Meaning	Elephant master

Word	Mali
Meaning	Gardener

Word	Memsahib
Meaning	Madam

Word	Muezzin
Meaning	Person who calls Muslims to prayer

Word	Namaste
Meaning	Indian greeting with joined palms

Word	Nawab
Meaning	Governor

Word	Nirvana
Meaning	State of absolute peace

Audrey Blankenhagen

Word	Nimbu pani
Meaning	citrus drink
Word	Paan
Meaning	Betel Leaf
Word	Phaeton
Meaning	horse drawn carriage
Word	Pugree
Meaning	Turban
Word	Puja
Meaning	prayers and offerings
Word	Punkah
Meaning	ceiling fan
Word	Querida Mia
Meaning	Spanish for 'My darling"
Word	Queridisima
Meaning	dearest (Spanish)
Word	Ramasi
Meaning	ancient language of the Thugs
Word	rezai
Meaning	quilt
Word	Shalwar Kameez
Meaning	North Indian women's Dress
Word	Sarp
Meaning	Snake
Word	Sepoy
Meaning	Indian private in infantry
Word	Sher
Meaning	Tiger
Word	Sher Saitan
Meaning	Devil Tiger

Word	Shikar
Meaning	Hunt

Word	Shikara
Meaning	small rowing boat in Kashmir

Word	Shikari
Meaning	hunter

Word	Shruti
Meaning	Enlightenment

Word	Subhadar
Meaning	Governor

Word	Sunyassi
Meaning	Wandering holy man

Word	Suttee
Meaning	The act of self immolation by a window on her husband's funeral pyre.

Word	Swaraj
Meaning	Freedom

Word	Syce
Meaning	Groom

Word	Talwar
Meaning	curved sword

Word	Tamasha
Meaning	a Show

Word	Thuggees, Thugs
Meaning	Cult of professional robbers and murderers

Word	Zenana
Meaning	Women's quarters

Audrey Blankenhagen

ABOUT THE AUTHOR

Born in Calcutta, Audrey Blankenhagen's ancestors had a long history of service in British India in the Civil Administration and the British Army. She, herself, was educated at a boarding school in the foothills of the Himalayas and returned with her family to England after India was granted Independence from British Rule in 1947. Audrey now lives in leafy Surrey near Epsom Downs, the home of the famous Derby, the blue riband of the English horseracing season.

Printed in the United States
870900001B